RWBY

BEFORE the DAWN

RWBY

BEFORE the DAWN

By E. C. MYERS

Story by KERRY SHAWCROSS and MILES LUNA

Based on the series created by MONTY OUM

Scholastic Inc.

ROOSTER TEETH®

Library of Congress Cataloging-in-Publication Data available

ISBN 978-1-338-30575-3

10 9 8 7 6 5 4 3 2 1 20 21 22 23 24

Printed in the U.S.A. 23

First printing 2020

Book design by Betsy Peterschmidt

Cover illustration by Breica

PROLOGUE

Sun Wukong had been back in Vacuo for a month already, but it was only now that he felt like he was truly home.

It was nighttime in the city, and Sun was on a dark street facing off against three goons who were up to no good. At least he'd assumed they were up to no good when he spotted them stalking a woman out of some new nightclub downtown. Sun had trailed after them silently, but they somehow noticed him anyway and turned to confront him.

They were a strange trio. The woman on the left had spiky pink hair and a loose black robe over a white tunic. The broad guy in the middle wore a green muscle shirt, cargo shorts, and sandals. The lanky guy on the right had a brown jumpsuit and combat boots, with a brown patterned bandanna covering his hair and ears. The only things they had in common were matching silver armbands around their right biceps and masks on their faces.

At least they weren't the creepy Grimm face masks that some members of the White Fang wore. These were just average gas masks with large eyepieces and big, round filters in the front resembling pig snouts. You didn't see people wearing masks in Vacuo every day, or any day really. Sun bet they got pretty sweaty inside.

"Aren't you out past your bedtime, kid?" said Pink.

"I'm kind of a night owl," Sun said, yawning. A lot of people in Vacuo were, simply because the desert cooled down in the evening and that was when walking and breathing didn't make you want to die. Until it got too cold, like it was now, and you started to question whether it was a good idea to go around with your shirt open all the time.

But this was late, even for Sun. It was almost dawn, in fact, and he had to get back to school. He didn't want to make a bad impression his first week at Shade. Or, rather, he didn't want to make a bad first impression even worse.

Well, this shouldn't take long, he thought. Once they stopped their verbal sparring and started the real fight, things would go pretty smoothly. These clowns didn't even have weapons.

"Night owl? Looks more like a monkey to me," said Green.

"Why were you following us?" That was from Brown.

It was hard to tell because of the jumpsuit and bandanna, but Sun thought Brown might be a Faunus. He carried himself like he was taking in more of his environment and knew how to move within it. That was a trait everyone had to learn in Vacuo at some point if they wanted to last there, but it came more naturally to Faunus, like Sun. Part of it was their enhanced animal senses; part of it was the fact that they had learned to be on guard around humans and aware of their surroundings. If Brown was a Faunus, that would explain how the group had detected Sun pursuing them.

"Why were you following that woman?" Sun countered. He

glanced behind them and was glad to see she'd gotten away while their attention was on him.

Pink cracked her neck. "You're about to find out."

"Okay, go ahead and tell me. That's why I asked." Sun waited a beat. "Oh, was that meant to be a threat? You should have followed it up with something menacing, like shaking your fist angrily." Sun demonstrated. "Are you guys new at this?"

The group advanced toward him.

"Wait!" Sun held out his hands, and they hesitated. "I don't want to hurt you guys."

They looked at one another and laughed.

"It's three against one," Pink said.

"Really? Count again." Sun put his hands together. He closed his eyes. And he focused. As always, he started with an image that centered him so he could use his Semblance: a desert willow, green and flourishing with white, rose, and violet flowers.

He had seen it once, when he was traveling with his clan across the vast Vacuo desert looking for a new place to live for a while, when their previous settlement had become too attractive to Grimm. Sun, only seven at the time, had been frustrated.

"We should stay and fight," he had said. "Why don't we?"

"Not everyone here is as strong as us." His older cousin Starr Sanzang put a hand on his head and ruffled his spiky hair. "Or as hotheaded as you. Ow!" She yanked her hand away and shook it, pretending to blow on it.

Despite himself, Sun grinned, but he wouldn't be so easily distracted. "I'm tired of running. We should pick a place and stay there. Keep the Grimm out."

"We're on our own out here," she said. "Most of our clan doesn't know how to fight, and they aren't interested in learning. It's not how we do things."

"Maybe if they had learned, my—" Sun swallowed. "More of them would be alive." He hated the way his voice trembled. Starr pretended not to notice.

"One day what you want may come to pass. But not today. Try to get some rest."

He took her advice, the way he usually did, but just as he drifted off to sleep he spotted the tree. Its leaves had a golden glow in the evening sun. The sight had filled him with a strange peace, and a sense of purpose, that he hadn't felt in a long time.

That's the perfect place to stop, *he had thought.* I would defend a place like that to my death. Why are we still going?

He drifted off to sleep, and when he woke, he asked Starr about the tree. She didn't know what he was talking about. No one did. It seemed no one else had seen it, either.

"You must have dreamed it," she had said. "It sounds like a nice dream."

"I didn't," Sun insisted. "It was real." But from that time on, the tree had been his alone. He remembered every detail of it vividly, too vividly for it to have come from his imagination. He remembered it better than he did his parents' faces. And whenever he pictured it, he felt that calm again, that purpose. It had led him to discovering his Semblance, Via Sun.

Two glowing clones of Sun flared into existence, one facing Pink and the second squaring off against Green. That left Brown—whom he figured was both the leader of the group and the most dangerous. Why? Because he was hiding the most.

Brown slashed a hand toward Sun. "Take him."

"Which one?" Green asked.

"The real one," Pink said. "These are just flashy illusions."

Sun directed one of his clones to punch Pink in the face.

She blinked and looked more annoyed than hurt.

"That's no illusion!" Green reached for clone Two.

Sun's clones were physical manifestations of his Aura, every bit as capable of inflicting damage as he was. But it could be difficult to control them, especially while he was fighting. They were better suited to giving him the element of surprise, extra pairs of hands, or emergency backup when he needed it.

Unfortunately, he couldn't sustain them long, and they couldn't take much damage, as they drew Aura from Sun himself. If he kept them going too long, or tried to create too many clones, it usually weakened the Aura shield protecting him. But he'd improved a lot with training, and his Semblance was a lot stronger than it used to be.

Sun whipped out his gunchucks, Ruyi Bang and Jingu Bang, spinning them as he and Brown circled each other slowly. At the same time, Sun was fighting Pink and Green through his clones. Pink was some kind of boxer, dancing around and jabbing with her fists, which One was managing to block. Meanwhile, Green was trying to grab Two and wrestle him to the ground.

Brown had some kind of martial arts training similar to Sun's—but he wasn't nearly as good. Sun leaned back as Brown did a high roundhouse kick; he felt a breeze as his opponent's booted foot swept past his nose with a lot of power behind it. Sun flicked his right gunchuck to loop it around Brown's ankle and pulled him out of his stance, hitting him with the closed gunchuck in his left hand. The man took the full blow, but it didn't even faze him.

Sun continued to pull Brown by his leg, using the momentum to spin him around in a circle. But the man quickly regained control and twisted in the opposite direction, yanking Sun toward *him.* Brown grabbed Sun's shoulders and pushed him facedown into his knee. Sun saw a rainbow of colors. Clones One and Two fizzled out.

Oh, that hurts.

Brown kicked Ruyi Bang out of Sun's hand, and his partners closed in on Sun. Sun used Jingu Bang to fire a Dust round at Pink, but the woman went kind of blurry all around the edges and Sun's shots went right through her.

That's a neat trick, Sun thought. He ran toward the wall of a building, and as they turned to face him he flipped over their heads to land behind them. He grabbed his fallen gunchuck and merged the two weapons together into a staff. He twirled it lazily in front of him.

Sun went for Brown again, but this time, no matter what he did, he couldn't quite land a blow on him. His punches and kicks were practically sliding past the guy, just a fraction of a second too late to make contact. It was as if Sun were playing a video game with a busted controller.

The same held true for Brown's attacks. Sun thought he was dodging them, but again, just a moment too late. And the hits were adding up.

Pretty soon, Sun really was moving more slowly. His Aura was creeping into the danger zone, and if he pushed it too hard it would break, leaving him vulnerable to serious injury. He couldn't take much more of this.

Now Green stepped up. Sun used his staff to pole vault toward him, landing his feet against the guy's chest and springing backward. He swept his staff toward Pink, making a solid hit that knocked her into Green. They both went down.

Sun pivoted and swung toward Brown, who took the blow without even trying to block it. But Sun felt the shock of the impact vibrate up the staff and into his bones. Brown grabbed the end of Sun's staff and pushed him backward.

Sun fell but spun around on his back and scrambled to his feet. He planted the staff in the ground, suddenly aware that he needed it to hold himself up. He breathed heavily.

Oh crap, Sun thought. *I'm losing.* How *am I actually losing?*

"Is that all you've got?" Sun gasped. "I've fought stronger guys than you." They were nothing compared to the Atlesian Paladins at Beacon.

Idiot, don't think about that, Sun thought.

Okay, the White Fang on Menagerie. Sun had taken on dozens of those guys at once. Though these three had more impressive Semblances.

"Bigger opponents, too," Sun said. There was that Sea Feilong, on a freaking ocean no less. Yeah, his friend Blake Belladonna had helped him a teeny bit, but he could have handled it on his own if he had to. Just like now.

"I definitely haven't fought anyone uglier than you, though, so you've got me there," Sun taunted. "I mean, I'm just assuming because of the masks."

"You talk too much," Pink said.

"I get that a lot."

"Enough!" Brown, Pink, and Green closed in.

Here we go. Sun dug his feet in and gripped his staff. No way he was going to let these chumps take him down after everything he'd been through. Not on his home turf. Though it could be their home turf, too.

He was starting to wish he'd brought some friends with him.

Suddenly Sun saw a flash of light, and a glowing trident landed in front of Pink, Green, and Silver. They all stared at it for a moment in surprise, then electric energy burst from it and shocked them, holding them immobile.

Neptune? Sun thought, recognizing his friend's weapon. But it was made of hard-light energy, which meant that it was just a *copy* of Tri-Hard, which meant . . .

Great. Team CFVY (coffee) was here.

The charge faded, along with the trident itself. Tendrils of electricity crackled over the thugs. They shook it off.

"Seriously? How much can you take?" Sun said.

"More than you can dish out," Pink said.

"That was just the appetizer," someone called from above. Sun recognized the voice, but he'd rarely heard her sound so confident. Defiant. He glanced up and saw rabbit ears silhouetted against the bright, broken moon.

Velvet Scarlatina leaped down from a low rooftop and landed lightly next to Sun.

"Just wait until dessert!" Yatsuhashi Daichi rushed out of the shadows and sent Brown flying into a wall. A spray of sand settled over the baddies. Of course the big guy was there; wherever Velvet was, Yatsuhashi was close behind.

"Hey, Sun," Velvet said.

Sun smiled. "Nice entrance. Did you two rehearse that?" He couldn't remember the last time he'd heard Yatsuhashi say so many words at once.

"Later," Yatsuhashi grunted.

That was more like it.

Velvet hefted her camera. "Need some backup?"

"Nah, I got it under control," Sun said. "But since you're already here, if you wanna get in on this . . ." He gestured toward the three opponents. "Knock yourself out. Better yet, knock *them* out."

Yatsuhashi drew his greatsword, while Velvet summoned hard-light copies of Scarlet David's gun, Hook, and his cutlass, Darling. She was favoring weapons from Team SSSN (sun) tonight, which Sun doubted was a coincidence.

Velvet nodded toward the enemy, her ears dipping. "Time for a little street cleaning."

"Come on, you've been practicing quips, haven't you?" Sun said.

The three students rushed toward the three bad guys. Sun once again faced off against Brown, while Yatsuhashi took on Green and Velvet sparred with Pink.

Sun had seen Velvet in combat only a few times. She was whipping out a whole set of moves he didn't know she had in her, some of them clearly informed by Scarlet's fighting style. However Pink's Semblance worked, it seemed she could only phase out against attacks briefly—Velvet was managing to hit her over and over again with her hard-light sword. Even so, Pink barely seemed hurt.

Meanwhile, Yatsuhashi had Green pressed below his massive blade, the squat thug holding it inches away from his face with his bare hands. The goon's Aura should have been dropping fast, but he remained on his feet.

And Brown still seemed fresh for the battle, too. Sun had pushed him up against a wall, giving him a beating, but Sun was going to wear himself out before his foe did.

"Screw this," Brown said. "Smoke them!"

"Uh. What's—" Yatsuhashi started to speak but then he began coughing. Sun saw smoke pouring out of Green's skin, which reminded him of the way Grimm disintegrated into black vapor. Then Sun smelled it.

"Ugh! That's gross!" He began coughing, too, and his eyes teared up.

"You got lucky, monkeyboy," Green said as he walked off, his companions following him through the cloud of foul vapor. "This time."

"No, *you* got lucky!" Sun choked.

Lucky more of my friends didn't show up, he thought. Then he coughed some more.

With Green and his awful stench gone, along with Pink and Brown, the air soon cleared and they were able to breathe again.

"So that's why they were wearing gas masks!" Sun gasped.

"Something else was strange about them," Yatsuhashi noted. "As if they were . . . invincible."

"Right?" Sun said. "Glad it wasn't just me."

"But it *was* just you," Velvet said softly. "Where's your team?"

"Oh, you know, back at Shade. Sleeping or studying probably. Doing something responsible."

"Do they know where you are?" Velvet asked.

Sun stalked off, heading back toward Shade. "What is this? A therapy session? A lecture? Where's the rest of Team CFVY?"

Velvet and Yatsuhashi followed him.

"Coco and Fox are doing the same thing we were when we found you. Patrolling the city," Velvet said.

Sun bristled at the implication that Velvet and Yatsuhashi had rescued him. Showing up those hotshots out in the desert had been one of the best moments of his life. CFVY's reputation had apparently preceded them to Shade Academy, where they had relocated after their original school, Beacon Academy, had fallen to Grimm over a year ago. In their first two years at Beacon, they had stood out as the best of the best, but they had a lot more competition in Vacuo, which hardened students into the toughest Huntsmen and Huntresses—unless it broke them.

Arriving at Shade with Team CFVY, having helped them complete their rescue mission, had immediately elevated Sun's team—Team SSSN—to lofty heights.

But now here was Team CFVY—half of it, anyway—bailing him out. At least Velvet wasn't the kind of person to rub it in. If Scarlet, Sage, and Neptune heard about this, they'd never let him live it down. And his teammates already had plenty to hold over his head.

He wondered when they were going to get over it. So what if Sun had gone off to do his own thing for a while? That was just the kind of guy he was; he had to go where he was needed. The gang had been back together for weeks now, but it still hadn't blown over. Scarlet was acting bossier than usual, and Sage had been giving

Sun the silent treatment. At least Neptune always had his back, but something seemed to be off with him, too, no matter how much he insisted that everything was fine.

"Want to tell me what you guys are doing out patrolling so late?" Sun said.

Yatsuhashi looked around. "Not really."

Velvet was a little more forthcoming. "We're looking for the Crown."

"The Crown?" Sun asked. "Is that what you're calling them now?" It was a lot better than *Carmine and Bertilak's mysterious employer*, anyway.

"We've been hearing that name more and more," Velvet said. "We think that whoever they are, they're the ones gathering people with powerful Semblances. We've been digging for more information about them, and keeping an eye out for Carmine and Bertilak."

The rogue Huntsmen team of Carmine Esclados and Bertilak Celadon had escaped from the authorities shortly after CFVY and SSSN had delivered them to Coquina, one of the few settlements in Vacuo with a prison and court.

Velvet was worried the duo would return to kidnap her friend Gus Caspian, whose Semblance made it possible for him to bring down entire settlements single-handedly. Gus could amplify negative emotions, and that negativity summoned creatures of Grimm, the dark manifestations of evil that roamed the world with the sole purpose of destroying humans and Faunus.

"You know, you have a powerful Semblance, too," Velvet pointed out. "You shouldn't be out here alone, Sun."

Sun rubbed the back of his neck. "I'm used to it," he said. "Besides, the guys are still a little annoyed with me for ditching them."

"To chase a girl," Yatsuhashi added.

"It wasn't like that." *Not entirely.* "Blake needed a friend."

"And your team needed *you*," Velvet said firmly. "After everything we saw at Beacon, with everything going on in Mistral—"

"They were fine."

"But you're their leader," Yatsuhashi said.

"They'll come around."

"Maybe you would be able to regain their trust if you didn't keep running off without them," Yatsuhashi added, sheathing his greatsword.

Sun narrowed his eyes. "I liked you better when you didn't say much." He sighed. "You think they don't trust me?"

Velvet looked at the ground. "What were you doing out here, anyway?"

"I saw those three following a woman. I thought she might need help."

Yatsuhashi smirked.

"Really!" Sun said. "Since I've been back, I've been trying to reconnect with some of my old friends. But a lot of them are . . . gone."

"It's Vacuo," Yatsuhashi said. "Fox says people leave every day."

Sun shook his head. "They didn't leave. They just vanished."

"Did they have strong Semblances?" Velvet asked.

"I don't think so. They didn't when I knew them," Sun said. "You know me—I'm not usually one to worry, but it bothers me that so many people are missing and the police aren't even looking for them."

"It sounds like the police haven't been all that reliable," Velvet said. "They probably couldn't hold things together without Headmaster Theodore and Huntsmen helping keep the peace."

"Anyway, aren't you supposed to survive on your own here?" Yatsuhashi asked.

Sun was always explaining how things worked in Vacuo. "A lot of people assume that. Yes, being able to survive on your own isn't just a skill here, it's a necessity. But that doesn't mean you turn away from helping others if you can, or let your own people fend for themselves. Vacuans still watch out for their tribe. At least they're supposed to." That's why he'd stepped in to help that woman.

"Speaking of survival skills, do you know where we're going?" Yatsuhashi asked.

"You don't?" Sun asked.

Velvet and Yatsuhashi glanced at each other. Then they shook their heads.

Sun laughed. "Thanks. That makes me feel better."

"It's dark . . . ," Velvet said.

"You can see just as well as I can," Sun said. Though it wasn't true for all Faunus, Velvet and Sun's Faunus eyes gave them excellent night vision. "And it's a full moon."

"This city seems like it's all alleys. None of the streets make sense," Yatsuhashi said.

"That's because it *is* all alleys." It wasn't like the city was planned out, like Vale, or engineered, like Atlas. When he first came here, Sun had learned that the city just kind of happened.

People settled wherever they stopped moving, and the city sprouted up gradually around Shade Academy wherever houses and buildings fit, typically clustered around the small oases and patches of greenery that were too stubborn to give in to the desert.

The city of Vacuo had *some* order to it, with different districts for residences and businesses, and a wide street down the center for the market. But the outer edges of it were periodically wiped out, because of sandstorms or sinkholes or earthquakes. Occasionally a big enough Grimm burrowed under the wall, churned up the sand, and knocked everything down. Or Ravagers would attack from above. A rare, heavy rainstorm might last for days—a mixed blessing that both brought water and washed shelters away. None of this was bad luck, it was just life—and death—in Vacuo.

Luckily, it wasn't too hard to get oriented right now. "To find Shade, you literally just have to look up, and there it is," Sun said.

Buildings in the city were usually no more than a few stories tall, which gave you a clear view of the terraced fortress in the middle, the site of Shade Academy and the Cross Continental Transmit (CCT) tower. It loomed high over the desert, tall enough to be viewed for miles around. During the day, wide awnings were extended from its walls on all sides, providing broad coverage and relief from the harsh sun.

"Seeing it is one thing," Yatsuhashi said. "Getting there is another."

"You'll be glad for it if the city is ever invaded," Sun said.

"Who would invade the city of Vacuo?" Yatsuhashi asked in disbelief.

Sun snapped, "Who would invade Beacon? Or Haven?"

A dark look crossed Velvet's face.

"Besides, people have attempted it before," Sun said.

"Back when Vacuo had something valuable, like Dust," Yatsuhashi said.

Sun whistled low. "Spoken like a true outsider. If you don't want to turn Vacuans against you, you'll stop making comments like that."

Yatsuhashi looked away.

"Anyway, whoever's behind the attacks on the academies will get around to us eventually, if Blake and her friends can't stop them first." Sun's money was on Team RWBY (ruby), or it would be if he had any money. The last time he'd seen them, a few months ago, they were taking the Argus Limited to Atlas. They were probably there now, living a life of luxury.

"I hope they're okay," Velvet said. "Wherever they are."

"They can take care of themselves, now that they're back together," Sun reassured them.

But Velvet and Yatsuhashi had a point about Team SSSN. Sun had to make sure his own team was okay, now that *they* were back together, too. Since he'd been back with them, and hauled them halfway across Remnant to Vacuo, he felt like he didn't quite fit in anymore. It seemed like the team had been just fine without him, and now he was messing everything up.

Okay, it was true he'd been keeping them at a distance. No wonder he felt out of step with them. *But was it more than that?* he sometimes wondered. Maybe what Team SSSN needed was something to bring them back together.

"We'll help you," Sun said impulsively.

"We?" Yatsuhashi asked.

"Help us with what?" Velvet asked.

"We, Team SSSN, will help you hunt down the Crown. More people looking means you'll cover more ground. And besides, you need us."

"How's that?" Yatsuhashi asked skeptically.

"You don't know this city the way I do. You've had a hard time getting information because people don't trust you. They don't trust outsiders—especially Huntsmen trainees from other schools who are only in Vacuo because they have nowhere else to go."

"Ouch," Yatsuhashi said.

Velvet elbowed him. "We'd be glad for the help."

"We would be," Yatsuhashi began. "But you'll have to convince Coco first. And your teammates."

"I'm their leader, aren't I?" Sun asked.

Velvet and Yatsuhashi looked away.

"That wasn't a rhetorical question. I *am* their leader."

Yatsuhashi's right eyebrow went up.

Sun stood taller and thrust out his chest, striding confidently in the direction of Shade Academy. "I totally am."

CHAPTER ONE

"You can stop laughing, Coco." Sun sighed. "Anytime."

"I'm not laughing," Coco said, innocently sipping her coffee.

It was surprising when Team SSSN joined Team CFVY for breakfast in the lower courtyard before class, but she was glad they had. Velvet told everyone about their misadventures the night before, and Coco would not have missed it for the world.

"Okay, stop *smiling*, then," Sun said.

"I thought boys liked it when girls smiled."

"For some reason when you do it, it isn't friendly. It looks like a threat."

Yatsuhashi nodded solemnly.

"You have to admit," Neptune Vasilias told Sun, "you getting beat up by three random thugs, on your own turf, *is* pretty funny. Wish I'd been there."

From the hard edge in Neptune's voice, Coco wondered if he meant he wished he'd been there to *watch* more than help. But she doubted Sun had the awareness to see that. And from the way Sun's other teammate Sage Ayana was glaring at him, she guessed that he understood where Neptune was coming from. Last night wasn't just about Sun being wacky old Sun—it was another example of him putting himself before his team.

"I'm telling you: There was something really weird about those guys!" Sun protested. "They were unbeatable."

The news that Velvet and Yatsuhashi had saved Sun had pretty much made Coco's morning. It restored some of the balance that had been lost since Team SSSN had come to Shade, gloating that they had rescued CFVY on their mission last month.

"Rescued" was a strong word, Coco thought. They had certainly *assisted*, and she was grateful. But SSSN's bragging had not only taken the shine off CFVY's reputation—it had fed brewing resentment that Coco and the others had been getting from some students at Shade. Despite CFVY's reputation and demonstrated awesomeness, the native Vacuans called them weak for abandoning Beacon Academy. Now it felt like CFVY had to prove themselves with every assignment, every mission, and SSSN didn't make that any easier.

Coco was more than a little hesitant to accept Sun's offer to help them track down the Crown. He had a habit of attaching himself to better teams, like RWBY, to make up for the fact that he and his own team were mediocre at best. They had potential, Coco thought, but they needed a strong leader—and Sun wasn't it. What kind of leader abandoned their team, especially after what they'd been through at Beacon?

Sun was too unstable, too unreliable, for her to want to partner with him and his team. She didn't even like eating with SSSN, usually. Team CFVY worked best on their own, because they trusted one another completely.

"Look, Sun, I'm sorry about your missing friends," Coco said. "And I appreciate your offer to team up. But the only help we need right now is from Headmaster Theodore and Professor Rumpole." She was certain that was the best way to track down the Crown, if the two of them would ever respond.

Unfortunately, Rumpole, Theodore's right hand, had been brushing off Team CFVY lately. After their mission debriefing last month, Coco had requested a meeting with the headmaster to discuss the Crown, but they still hadn't heard anything. Either Rumpole hadn't passed on the message or Theodore didn't think it was worth his time. Coco was trying to be patient, but Team CFVY wasn't waiting around.

Scarlet David lifted his head. He'd been listening, not saying much. Coco got the feeling he wasn't particularly enjoying being at Shade. Vacuo was a bit of an acquired taste and took some getting used to, especially after everything he'd been through—losing both Beacon and Haven to the same people, whoever it was who had been working with the White Fang.

This enemy was a threat, clearly, but so was the Crown. Why couldn't Theodore see the urgency?

"Hold on," Scarlet said. "Are you saying you don't have permission to investigate the Crown?"

"We don't *not* have permission," Fox Alistair said.

"We don't have explicit orders to pursue the Crown, no," Coco said. "But I see this as an extension of our original mission to support the Schist refugees. It's unfinished business." Carmine and Bertilak were still out there, and the Crown—if that's who they were working for—still posed a danger.

Why did the Crown need so many people with powerful Semblances? Coco wondered. She doubted the Crown was collecting them to perform petty crimes. And it was taking away people who could become valuable Huntsmen one day—people who might be needed if there was ever a full-on attack on Shade.

"But it is *our* business," Coco added. "We don't need you. No offense."

Scarlet stood. "Why would I take offense?" he asked. "Just because you think you're too good for us."

Coco glanced at her team. Velvet avoided looking at her, which meant she wasn't on the same page this time. Yatsuhashi looked uncomfortable, but he kind of always did during personal conflicts. And Fox—

"It wouldn't hurt to have some reinforcements," Fox sent, using his telepathic Semblance, presumably just to her.

"I don't disagree," Coco sent back. *"If it was the right team."*

"That's fine. We hadn't even discussed this yet, since Sun only sprang the idea on us this morning," Scarlet said.

Coco blinked. Sometimes it took her a second to process things when she was having a telepathic conversation with Fox in the middle of a regular conversation with other people. Was Scarlet saying Team SSSN *wasn't* offering to help? Did SSSN even have a plan?

"We'll let you know when we need backup," Coco added. "This is a major problem, and I don't understand why Theodore and Rumpole don't see that finding the Crown should be Shade's biggest priority right now."

"Theo has a lot on his mind," Sun announced.

"Theo?" Coco repeated incredulously.

"Headmaster Theodore," Sun said.

"I know who you meant. I *didn't* know that you were on such familiar terms with him. You just got here."

"And you're not exactly the best and brightest student at Shade," she added silently.

"Harsh," Fox sent.

Okay, so she hadn't thought it silently enough.

"But fair," Fox added.

"When we arrived, Theodore wanted an update on everything that went down in Mistral," Sun said. "He asked why we came to Shade instead of waiting for Haven to reopen."

"I've been wondering that myself," Sage said quietly.

"Hey, I agreed to come because you talked up how much fun Vacuo is," Neptune said.

"Has Vacuo been fun so far?" Sage asked.

"Not really." Neptune's eyes widened. "Sun *tricked me*?"

"It wouldn't be the first time," Scarlet said.

"Look, we need to get ready for whatever's coming," Sun said. "This is the best place for that." His tail swished angrily.

It pained Coco to admit it, but she agreed with Sun. Just this once.

"There's a difference between the *best* place and the *only* place," Scarlet grumbled. "Beacon's gone—"

"For now," Velvet said.

Scarlet rolled his eyes—or at least, the one eye that wasn't covered by his red hair. "Sure. And with Atlas's borders closed, Shade Academy is the only place to train. I wouldn't call that a choice."

Sun rose from his seat and faced Scarlet. "You do have a choice. You can stay or you can go."

"I'm not the one who has a problem staying in one place," Scarlet retorted.

"Harsh," Fox sent again. This time to Coco, Velvet, and Yatsuhashi.

"Come on, guys. Can we not do this?" Neptune said.

"At least not in front of other teams," Sage muttered.

Yatsuhashi pushed his plate away, most of his breakfast still uneaten. Velvet's ears wilted, matching her downcast expression.

This was no good, Coco thought. Team SSSN's dysfunction was affecting her team's morale.

"Can we get back to Theodore?" Coco said. "Sun, why do you think he isn't worried about the Crown?"

"He's focused on the bigger picture. Shade could be attacked at any moment."

"Keeping us in the dark isn't going to help anyone," Coco said.

"You keep forgetting," Scarlet scoffed. "We're just students."

"We're already better than a lot of trained Huntsmen," Coco said.

"But we still have a lot to learn. And we've already failed to defend one school."

Coco corrected him. "We were all taken by surprise. Haven fared better."

"Most of us weren't even there, and I still wouldn't call that a win," Scarlet replied.

Coco shook her head and repeated her point. "We need to see the headmaster. He may be too preoccupied to look into the Crown, but he also can't ignore it. He just needs to take us seriously."

"I'll see what I can do," Sun said.

She threw up her hands. "I don't want *you* to do anything!"

"Hey. I'm trying to help," Sun said.

"You say Vacuans won't trust us without you, but you're wrong. When we were out there in the desert—"

"City Vacuans are different from desert Vacuans," Sun said. "Besides, Slate vouched for you. That's probably why people gave you a chance."

"I thought it didn't matter where you're from as long as you can survive in Vacuo," Velvet said quietly.

Sun looked at her and his face softened. "That's true—to an extent. But resentment of the other kingdoms still runs deep here."

Fox nodded. "That's true," he said aloud, for Team SSSN's benefit. "Beacon students may have been accepted, grudgingly, because Vale was the only kingdom to side with Vacuo in the Great War. But Headmaster Theodore's decision to welcome us clearly wasn't popular. Judging by the reactions of some of our fellow students."

"The Great War again." Coco shook her head. "Ancient history. Let it go."

"Easy for you to say," Sun said. "But have you let go of what happened to Beacon?" He sat down and put his hands together. "You. Need. Us."

"I agree with Sun," Neptune said.

"Of course you do." Scarlet crossed his arms.

Neptune's face grew red. "What's that supposed to mean?"

Coco leaned back. *"These guys think they can help us when they can't even help themselves?"* she sent to the group.

"Maybe they need our *help,"* Yatsuhashi sent.

"They definitely do. Besides, you know Sun is going to get involved no matter what you decide," Fox said. *"Just like you would."*

Coco pursed her lips. Her teammates knew how to get what they wanted. But it wasn't manipulation as long as she knew they were manipulating her, right? Really, they were just saying things she already knew, things she needed to hear, to come to a decision that was best for the whole team. And for Shade Academy and Vacuo and anyone who might fall prey to the Crown as well.

"What do you think, Velvet?" Coco sent.

Velvet was quiet for a while before she lifted her eyes and looked directly at Coco. She smiled. *"I like proving people wrong."*

"Me too," Coco sent.

While they were having their private conversation, Sun, Scarlet, Sage, and Neptune had reached a new level of anger.

"Just because Team CFVY wants to do something doesn't make it important," Scarlet shouted.

Coco slowly rose from her seat, and the boys fell silent. She had to admit she liked that. She had seen the kind of respect that leaders like Slate commanded, and okay, this was probably more fear than respect, but still, Coco would take it.

"Stopping the Crown is important because it will help people," Coco said. "That's what we do. That's what we're training to do. And if we can't help others, whenever we can, however we can—then what are we here for?"

"We should focus more on our training—becoming the best Huntsmen we can," Scarlet said. "Anything else is a distraction. And I don't like going behind Rumpole's back."

Sage nodded. "The best way to help Shade when they come

after us is to be prepared to defend it. Better than we were at Beacon."

Coco took off her sunglasses. She looked around the table. She still had to convince them.

"We need one another," she said. "We're among the few who know what we're up against, because we were there at Beacon, and we fought. And we lost. You guys were at Haven. We know what's . . ." She gestured vaguely. "Out there. And how much it can threaten what we have here. We have our history, too—but we also have one another."

She put her sunglasses back on. Team SSSN really needed to get their act together, but CFVY had been there once before, and she knew a little about the challenge of winning back her team's trust.

There was no denying that Sun had access to resources that would help them track down the Crown. It made sense to combine their efforts—if only to make sure Sun didn't get in their way, or to make sure Scarlet didn't rat them out to Rumpole.

"We're stronger together." Coco smiled in what she hoped wasn't a creepy way. This whole "accepting help" thing wasn't exactly her style.

Scarlet opened his mouth, but Coco held up a hand to stop him from speaking. "And I will talk to Professor Rumpole after class to make sure she's on board. To make this an official assignment. Okay?"

Scarlet closed his mouth. He nodded.

Coco glanced at Sun, but he was pointedly looking away from Scarlet.

"Speaking of class," Velvet said. "We're late."

"And those who miss history are doomed to repeat it," Fox said.

Coco stifled a yawn and sat straighter in her seat, trying to make a good impression on Professor Rumpole, even though it might already be too late for that. When Team CFVY had walked in a few minutes late—heads still held high—Rumpole merely shook her head and continued lecturing about the origins of the Dust trade two hundred years ago. Some might have called it grandstanding, which CFVY had been accused of before, but the team had an image to maintain.

Coco had mastered the delicate art of balancing respect for authority with a certain level of disdain for rules. Or, at least, she had at Beacon. She hadn't been Professor Glynda Goodwitch's favorite student—if she even played favorites—but at the same time, Goodwitch and Headmaster Ozpin knew the team had talent. CFVY sometimes got a pass on breaking the rules if things worked out in the end.

She'd had her share of disciplinary meetings, of course, but Coco had actually appreciated the feedback. In retrospect, it had made her a better Huntress and a better leader. If only she could have finished her training at Beacon like she had always planned.

Here she was getting nothing. No one held your hand at Shade Academy if you needed help, but they were quick to slap it if you fell out of line. No one high-fived you for good work, either.

Maybe they expected that if you were doing well, you knew

it, and that was all you needed? Fox had tried explaining that in Vacuo, you didn't do things for praise—you did them to survive. Coco didn't see why it couldn't be both.

"I don't need praise," Coco had retorted. But she did need *something* to gauge her performance. A wink or a thumbs-up or a medal for exceptional service. She wasn't asking for much.

Fox had laughed out loud, startling students in the library who had no idea they were carrying on a silent conversation. Fox's telepathy came in handy for more than coordinating fights with Grimm.

"You do need praise," Fox had sent. *"No one spends as much time in front of a mirror as you do if they don't care what people think of them."*

"You're just jealous that you can't see how awesome I am."

"I don't need eyesight to know you're great, Coco. But maybe those shades of yours have been distorting how you *see things. Try taking them off once in a while. You'd be surprised to learn there are lots of people outside of our team worthy of praise."*

"Bzzt!" Fox's voice jolted Coco awake. She had nodded off in class. Too many late nights patrolling with nothing to show for it.

She glanced to her left, where he was sitting. *"Thanks,"* she sent. Velvet choked back a giggle on her other side.

An 8 a.m. history class seemed unnecessarily cruel, but Rumpole herself had never seemed cruel. Demanding, yes. Harsh, often. Stylish? Definitely. She reminded Coco of herself, which was maybe why Coco liked the professor despite her frustrations. Besides Goodwitch, she was the only other Huntress that Coco wanted approval from, but in that way the two women were similar: Showing approval wasn't really their thing.

Coco considered what Fox had said. She pulled her glasses off and sat forward, wondering if she would really see things differently without them. On the edge of her vision she noticed Velvet casting a questioning look her way.

No one knew where Professor Rumpole was originally from, but like most people who lived in Vacuo—who didn't use the right skin care—Rumpole had a deep tan. It was hard to tell how old she was, but she seemed young, first because she was short—about four feet tall—and also because of her fine features and mischievous expression.

Her sandy brown hair reached her ankles, in a long braid bound by golden cord. She had a wide, squarish frame that exaggerated her shortness, and she wore brown pants with a loose, dark green tunic cinched with a brown leather belt at her waist.

But Coco's favorite part of Rumpole's outfit was a sleeveless long coat, dark brown and coarse on the outside with glittering flecks, like rock infused with pyrite—or perhaps cloth studded with yellow Dust—and a silky, gold lining. Coco had dreams about that coat; it must have cost a fortune. It was both rustic and gaudy, but somehow Rumpole made it all work.

Without her glasses, Coco saw the essence of Rumpole: Despite her showiness, her style was functional, all business.

And she clearly loved history—enough that her enthusiasm for the topic was almost infectious. Almost.

"And so, Vacuo was faced with a choice," Rumpole said. "To sit out the war and take its chances that the other kingdoms would leave it alone, or side with their neighbor to the northeast—Vale." She paused and added, "We all know how that turned out."

"But you're going to tell us, anyway," Fox sent. Coco didn't even crack a smile; she was so intent on looking interested.

"Why did they decide to ally themselves with Vale, who'd done nothing but watch as mining companies from Atlas and Mistral drew resources out of the ground, taking the Dust from Vacuo and leaving behind barren sand?" Rumpole swiveled her head back and forth. She wasn't looking for a volunteer—there were several hands up already. She was looking for a victim.

When she noticed Coco, Rumpole zeroed in on her. "Adel. What do you think?"

Coco's heart beat faster. No matter how many Grimm she fought, nothing was quite so terrifying as being called on in class. (Aside from dark, enclosed spaces—that was still top on her list.)

"Because no matter what their differences, Vale and Vacuo shared the continent of Sanus," Fox sent.

"I knew that," Coco sent back. But she repeated what he had said, word for word. She loved Fox's Semblance. She also added a bit of her own: "Our fates are linked."

"'Our,'" repeated Rumpole. "Are you speaking as someone from Vale or someone living in Vacuo?" she asked.

"It doesn't matter," Coco said firmly. "I'm from Vale, but as long as I call Vacuo home, I'll fight for it."

Seemingly satisfied—and maybe even a little surprised—Rumpole turned away.

Their conversation with SSSN this morning fresh in her mind, Coco suddenly realized something. Since the news from Haven Academy had arrived, Rumpole had switched her history lessons from the establishment of Shade Academy to discussions of the

Great War. That couldn't be a coincidence. Did Rumpole think a second war was coming?

Coco raised her hand, but she didn't even wait for permission to speak. "May I ask *you* a question, Professor?"

Rumpole turned back to her. She studied Coco's face, then nodded.

"I've noticed you've switched to a different time period in your lectures recently. Shouldn't we be going through events chronologically, starting with ancient history?"

Rumpole pressed her lips together. "When you tell a story, do you always tell it in the order that things happened? Or do you start at the end to entice the audience, and then back up to the beginning? Add little details out of sequence as they occur to you?"

Coco waited. Was she supposed to answer? No, Rumpole had more to say.

"Does that diminish the telling? I believe the best way to properly consider the past is to provide the right context for it, and sometimes you need to know how things ended up before you can consider why they turned out that way."

Rumpole hopped up and stood on her desk, which she often used as a stage, or a soapbox. At Beacon, all the classrooms were lecture halls with tiered seats, so the professors were always center stage. Here at Shade, though, student desks were arranged in a circle around each teacher's desk, placing students and professors on the same level, and theoretically facilitating discussion.

"But I'm also not sure what you mean by 'ancient history,'" Rumpole continued, now towering above her class. "That could be subjective. I am sure that, to some of you, things that happened even fifty years ago might feel like ancient history, while something more recent—say the Fall of Beacon—doesn't feel like the past at all."

That was a cheap shot, Coco thought. From the way Velvet and some of their classmates who had fought at the Battle of Beacon—Iris Marilla, Reese Chloris, and Bolin Hori—shifted in their seats, she knew they felt uncomfortable, too.

Vacuans, it seemed, cherished their history but kept their focus on their future. It was one of the many contradictions that made it harder for Coco to adapt to the culture.

"Pay attention to people's reactions," Coco sent to Fox, trusting him to pass it on to Yatsuhashi and Velvet.

"It's just that I'm curious what life was like in Vacuo before the war and the Vytal Peace Accords," Coco continued. "Before the Dust companies destroyed it."

She heard grumbling from some of her classmates, but Coco pressed on. "What was it like when monarchies ruled the four kingdoms, when the *crown* was the center of authority in Vacuo?"

Rumpole couldn't have missed the significance of Coco's question, but she didn't show it. "I see. This happens to be one of my particular areas of interest, but I'm afraid much of that knowledge has been lost in Vacuo thanks to conquest and war. We can only guess at what life was like for those who lived in a paradise filled with verdant life, with a formalized government and royalty. Few documented accounts or records remain from that far back—though some families have claimed otherwise over the years."

After Rumpole dismissed class for the day, with an assignment to write a lengthy essay on the causes of the Great War, Coco, Fox,

Yatsuhashi, and Velvet hung back. When the rest of the students had departed, Rumpole addressed Team CFVY.

"I don't have an answer to your real question, Adel," she said. "I haven't even spoken to the headmaster about your request yet."

Coco couldn't believe it. "Why not?" she demanded. "The Crown is important, and we've also been hearing about widespread disappearances throughout the city."

Rumpole hopped to her feet and hooked her thumbs over her belt. "It's up to me to determine if it's important enough to bring to Theodore. He has been preoccupied lately."

"You mean with the attacks on the other academies? I understand his concern, but does he really think anyone is going to attack Vacuo right now? The kingdoms have already taken everything it has," Coco said in frustration.

Rumpole took a deep breath. "If you think Dust is all Vacuo has to offer, then what are you doing here? After your response this morning, I had hoped you thought better of your new home than that."

Coco wasn't about to back down on this one—it might be the last chance she got to make her case. "I do think highly of Vacuo, and that's why I'm worried about what's going on here. Right now. Instead of what *might* happen tomorrow."

"That's a luxury you have as a Huntress *in training.* Theodore has to be concerned with both today and tomorrow. And all the days that follow. It falls to him to keep our academy and students safe above all else," Rumpole said flatly. "Which is why *I'm* investigating this 'Crown' personally, and will report my findings and recommendations to him—in due time. Not when it's convenient for you."

"You've been investigating the Crown?" Coco said. "We can help!"

Rumpole sighed. "Of course you can. It's only because of your team that we know about them at all, and if your suspicions are true, we will have to deal with the situation sooner or later. But I can't officially assign you to the case without drawing undue attention to it, or running my few leads to ground."

She paused to let that sink in, then added a warning. "And if I ever find out that you've been continuing to investigate the situation on your own, I would have to report that to Theodore immediately. While he doesn't believe in coddling his students—"

Fox snickered.

Coco might have imagined it, but Rumpole's mouth twitched in a half smile. "He does intend to protect you all. Even teams as capable as CFVY."

Wow, is she actually praising us? Coco thought.

"The headmasters of the other schools have been reckless, negligent, or overprotective. Theo's first priority will always be helping you reach your full potential, making you strong enough to survive anything that comes your way. He has your best interest in mind, no matter where you come from or where you started your training. Who else can say that?" Rumpole spread her hands. "Give us some time."

Coco nodded. "Okay, that seems fair," she conceded. "Until we start to run out of time." She put her sunglasses back on.

Rumpole drew her coat closed and looked at the door. "Now get out of here before I give you extra homework for being late to class."

Coco left the professor's classroom knowing two things. One, she not only admired Rumpole but trusted her. She hadn't been sitting around ignoring Team CFVY's warnings—she had been out there taking quiet action.

Which led to the second thing: Coco wanted Rumpole as a mentor. Just think what she could learn before she graduated Shade!

"So I guess that's it," Yatsuhashi said, processing what they had learned. "She's onto us. We have to stop what we're doing or she's going to tell Headmaster Theodore."

"That's not what I heard," Fox sent.

"We can't stop now!" Velvet said.

"We aren't going to, and Rumpole doesn't want us to," Coco said. "She told us she knows we can handle ourselves, but if we get too much attention and she's forced to act, she'll have to report us to Theodore."

"She basically told us to be careful," Fox sent.

"Oh," Yatsuhashi said. "Are you sure she said all that?"

"It's Vacuo," Coco said. "Nothing is ever what it seems."

CHAPTER TWO

Velvet was glad that Sun was helping them now, if only because it was nice to have someone who knew how to get around the city. It kept changing so much, it was difficult to map the streets on Scrolls, and she kept getting lost on their nightly patrols. Like so much in Vacuo, you just had to get used to it . . . or ask people for directions.

Only, nothing advertised you were an outsider more than asking for directions. Sometimes people would point them the wrong way just to mess with them.

Sun moved so quickly through the labyrinth of unpaved streets and shadowed alleys that Velvet and the others had to hurry to keep up. At night, those narrow passages were a nightmare to navigate, even dangerous depending on who was lurking in them. Velvet preferred to travel across the low rooftops whenever possible, which made it less likely that she would get turned around.

But in the daytime, she saw that there was some order and reason to the crowded buildings. Even though the brick and stone structures were usually no more than a few stories tall, they cast shadows that helped cool you as you traveled. It was a walking city, not that large from end to end but with a lot packed in. The only quiet time was midday, when the sun was highest and hottest and all the shops shut down for a couple of hours.

"You know this place so well. Did you grow up here?" Velvet asked Sun as she followed him.

"My family and I moved around a lot," he said. "My dad didn't like the city. I didn't come here till I was older."

Out in the desert, Velvet knew, clans rarely settled in one place for long unless there was some reason to. A rare oasis, say, or a CCT relay—something worth defending. A place to call home, until you were forced to move on.

A lot of the philosophy of Vacuo focused on making the best of what you had for as long as you could hold on to it. Velvet glanced back at Coco, Yatsuhashi, and Fox.

"I don't really like the city, either," Sun said. "At least, not this one. It cramps my style, literally."

"He likes climbing things," Neptune offered. "The city's too small for much climbing." Velvet wondered how he could have forgiven Sun, sticking by him like nothing had happened. Scarlet and Sage were trailing behind the group as if trying to show they weren't really with them.

"Didn't you say your cousin's dojo was around here?" Neptune asked.

Sun's face paled.

"Ooh! Can we see it?" Velvet asked.

It was pretty clear Sun didn't want to talk about it. "I'd rather not," he said. "It's probably not even here anymore. I'm not sure I remember where it used to be . . . the city changes so often."

"You have family here and you haven't told them you're back?" Yatsuhashi asked.

Scarlet laughed. "That's Sun for you."

Velvet puffed out her cheeks and sighed. She was grateful that Team CFVY had worked out their past difficulties. She didn't know what she would do without her friends. They knew one another as well as Sun knew the streets of this city.

Sun lowered his head, and his tail dragged behind him. Velvet decided to rescue him—again.

"So you don't like the city. Is that why you decided not to attend Shade?" Velvet asked. She knew why Fox had left Vacuo for Beacon, but he hadn't lived here the way Sun had. For Velvet, going to her local academy had made the most sense.

"No." Sun cast a sidelong glance at her. "I left because I was tired of looking at it." He turned around and pointed. "Wherever you turn, there it is!"

Velvet looked behind them. Sure enough, she spotted the top of Shade Academy rising above the roofs, even though she could have sworn it was west of them. She really had no sense of direction here.

Shade Academy was the exception to whatever building codes there may once have existed in the city of Vacuo. As the tallest structure for hundreds of miles around, it cast a long shadow, in more ways than one. Right now its awnings were fully extended, shielding the citizens below from the brutal sun.

The campus was surrounded by a low wall, which served mainly to mark boundaries. And perhaps to send a message, just like Scarlet and Sage were doing now: *We're a part of you, but we are separate.*

Like the city itself, the academy packed in a lot—vertically—with classrooms and academic spaces in three tiers, and Headmaster Theodore's office at the apex, which also housed the CCT transmitter. Shade Academy, and Theodore himself, were the center of everything in Vacuo—holding it all together.

"Remnant is a big place," Sun went on. "I wanted to see more of it."

"I spent a summer in Atlas once," Velvet said. "Before I went to Beacon. It was . . . overwhelming." So overwhelming, she had spent most of the time in her room or a community makerspace, though she did get to see her father's lab a few times.

"Atlas is pretty amazing, eh?" Velvet's father said.

"Yeah," Velvet said, not looking up from her Scroll.

"Especially that giant statue of Pumpkin Pete," he said.

"Uh-huh." Velvet swiped at her Scroll, sending the wire schematics on the screen spinning around rapidly. She jabbed a finger to stop it, spread two fingers to expand the diagram, and frowned as she peeled it away layer by layer. Something about the projection system wasn't quite . . .

"Wait, what?" Velvet lifted her head and turned from left to right, peering around. She saw a lot of silver-and-glass skyscrapers, busy streets, flying vehicles streaming through the skies, but no statue of a cartoon rabbit. Because of course there wouldn't be one, especially not here of all places.

"Gotcha," her father said. "I didn't think you were listening."

"So no Pumpkin Pete?" Velvet said.

"No."

"Oh."

He was quiet for a little while as they rode in the back of the Atlesian transport taking them from the train station to his apartment. Had he been hoping to impress her with that, show her what a big shot he was? That would have had exactly the wrong effect on her. Velvet wasn't interested in spending a month with Will Scarlatina, Atlesian engineer—

Sorry, "tinkerer," as he preferred to describe himself. She just wanted to spend time with her father. The man who had helped her build her first computer, and didn't get angry when she stole his power tools, and made the most amazing pancakes she had ever tasted.

On the other hand, could he have turned down the military escort if he'd wanted to? Velvet's mother said that his mind was too important—too important to risk his personal safety on public transit. Too important for him to return to Vale. Too important to be a good husband or father anymore. As long as he was helping design new top secret technologies for Atlas, that meant Velvet wasn't *important enough. She didn't deserve his full attention, so he hardly had room to complain that he didn't have hers.*

"Just another way I've disappointed you, huh?" he said.

"Dad. No!" Velvet paused. She didn't want to hurt his feelings, but she didn't have much to follow that up with, nothing that would convince him, anyway. It was hard to argue with the truth.

He chuckled harshly. "I thought so. I'll talk to General Ironwood and see if we can't commission a rabbit statue before you leave."

"I can't imagine why he wouldn't want that." Velvet smiled. From what she'd heard, the head of Atlas and its military didn't have much of a sense of humor. She was glad they hadn't taken that from her father at least.

"I bet it would do wonders for the tourist business." He laughed. "I'm really glad you came to visit. We're going to have a wonderful time."

"Of course I came. This is the center of technology and innovation in Remnant. I've been wanting to visit Atlas since I first picked up a soldering iron." Atlas was the birthplace of the CCT, Scrolls, artificial Dust types—all the things that captured Velvet's imagination and fueled her creativity. She might have her mother's ears, but she was her father's daughter.

"You aren't here because you miss me?"

"You know how you always told me there are no stupid questions?" Velvet asked.

He nodded.

"You were wrong. Because that *is a stupid question. Of course I miss you."*

He smiled sadly. "I miss you, too. Every day."

"So why don't you come home, Dad?" she asked. A short-term military contract had turned into a year, and whenever she'd asked her mother why, her mother changed the subject—or left the room.

"Velvet." Her father looked out the window. He pressed his fingers to the glass. "Thing is, I don't think I am. Your mother and I don't see things the same way anymore. Maybe we haven't for a while and we just couldn't admit it to ourselves." He looked at her. "Or to you."

His decision to work for Atlas had gone over even less well with Meg Scarlatina than it had with Velvet. Or maybe it was more the fact that he hadn't discussed it with his family first.

"But you can work it out, right? You always say you could fix anything if you put your mind to it."

He turned back and looked down at his hands. Opened and closed them. "Machines are easier than people."

Velvet glanced down at her Scroll. "No argument there."

"Text from your friends?" he asked.

What friends? *Velvet thought.*

She'd never managed to find her place at Pharos Combat School. She couldn't wait until she got to Beacon Academy after the summer. It was going to be a fresh start. She was going to try harder to be more outgoing, meet more people. She just hoped she would end up with a good partner and team. She was good at planning—she could see it all in her head already. And her latest invention was going to help with all that. Which is why it was so important she get it right.

"It's a new weapon I'm working on," Velvet said. "For school."

"May I?" Her father reached out for her Scroll and she passed it over. He put on his reading glasses and studied her designs. Suddenly Velvet felt anxious.

"This captures images of other weapons . . . and then reproduces them in hard light?" He looked up in wonder. "Velvet, this is . . . astonishing."

Velvet blushed.

"Does it work?"

"I've built prototypes, but I don't have enough hard-light Dust to test it extensively."

"That shouldn't be a problem. Once James hears about this, he'll set you up with all the Dust you need. At the military family discount."

"James?" Velvet asked.

"Sorry. James Ironwood." He went back to looking at her Scroll.

"You mean you really know the general?"

His face showed surprise. "Know him? I work with him. Well, technically I work for *him, but it's basically the same thing. You thought I was making that up?"*

"Maybe exaggerating slightly. To impress me?"

"I see. Were you impressed?"

"I am now."

"These projection relays are marvelous." He pointed to one area of the schematic. "I've never seen anything like it."

"That part's been giving me some trouble."

"You'll get it. You know, I miss working on stuff like this with you. We could use you in our lab."

Velvet wasn't sure that would go over so well. "Mom would love that," she said sarcastically, blowing her bangs out of her eyes. "Home isn't the same without you. It doesn't even feel like home."

"I know. I'm sorry. But hey, you'll be leaving soon, anyway. My daughter, a Huntress at Beacon Academy. I'm so proud of you, V."

"Thanks."

Maybe that was all Velvet needed: a new place to call home.

"I've never been to Atlas," Sun said.

"I hope you'll be able to go sometime. When all this trouble dies down," Velvet replied.

Sun grinned. "Nah. I'm good. Too much technology there."

"But also really tall buildings," Neptune pointed out.

"There's plenty to climb in Mistral," Sun said. "More stuff like that." He pointed, and Velvet saw a natural rock formation springing from a plaza on the outskirts of the city.

"That's the Weeping Wall?" Coco asked. "I was expecting, I don't know . . . a *wall*?"

The mass was technically wall-like, Velvet thought, about ten feet long and three feet thick and forty feet high. On the shady side of it, two kids had set up an old wooden crate to sell misshapen clay models of the wall.

"It isn't weeping, either," Neptune said. "Those aren't

tears—they're sweat." He wiped his brow for emphasis. Neptune was referring to a trickle of water seeping out of the rock and running down in a narrow rivulet to disappear into the crevice between the rock and pavement.

"Things aren't named literally in Vacuo," Sun said.

"How is it doing that?" Yatsuhashi asked as he caught up to them, the others close behind him.

"*What* is it doing?" Velvet asked.

"Hard to know without digging it up and ruining it in the process," Sun said. "Which people in Vacuo are generally against, for obvious reasons. But there must be some kind of underwater reservoir beneath the stone. The rock is porous. It draws the water up and then it trickles down. Once in a while after it rains, the stone will 'weep' for weeks afterward."

"I've heard of this," Fox said. "People sell vials of the water, don't they? 'Vacuo's Tears' or some nonsense."

"Why don't they drink it instead?" Sage asked.

"Because then it would dry up and we would just have an ugly rock," Sun said. "Some of the water evaporates, of course, but a lot of it seeps into the ground and makes its way back to the reservoir, and probably some of the local oases. It's as close as we have to a renewable resource around here."

"This is nice and all," Coco said. Her tone suggested she meant the exact opposite. "But why did you want to show it to us?"

"I think it's truly breathtaking," Fox said.

"Wait. Aren't you blind?" Neptune asked.

Fox turned his head toward him and didn't say anything.

"What's he doing?" Neptune said nervously.

"That was the joke," Yatsuhashi explained. "Sorry. Don't be mean, Fox."

"Please stop staring at me," Neptune said in a small voice. "I mean—" He covered his eyes and turned away.

Fox grinned.

"Take a closer look," Sun said. "Come on."

The two teams gathered on the cooler side of the stone formation. Velvet saw the base was cluttered with an assortment of stuffed animals, bunches of desert flowers, shoes. Glasses filled with water and plates of dried meat. After a moment she put it all together: This was a shrine.

Loops of thin wire were wrapped around the wall, with pictures and posters pinned to them. Some of the pages were faded, nearly blank and in tatters, while others had been freshly printed or handwritten. Many of them had the same chilling word in block letters at the top: MISSING.

Velvet whispered a description of what they were seeing to Fox, avoiding teamspeak for SSSN's benefit. No one found out about Fox's Semblance until he trusted them enough to let them in on it.

"What is this?" Coco asked.

"These are the missing and lost of the city of Vacuo," Sun said. "People who have disappeared without a trace. Most of them in the last year."

"Where'd they go?" Sage asked.

"They wouldn't be missing if we knew where they are." Scarlet patted Sage on the arm.

"Oh, right."

Velvet walked along the wall, taking in all the pictures.

There were so many. Children, parents, brothers, sisters, cousins. Husbands and wives, boyfriends and girlfriends. These were people who had left someone behind to miss them, to mourn. To wonder what had happened to them.

"I guess they're a low priority for Headmaster Theodore, too," Velvet said.

"Even though people expect a lot from him, he doesn't have complete authority," Fox said. "And we're still in Vacuo. Resources are limited. The Huntsmen he works with regularly have got to be stretched pretty thin already, if Rumpole has them on the lookout for the Crown."

Velvet tried to imagine what it was like for the people who only had the resources to put pictures of their missing loved ones on a wall and hope they would come home one day.

"These people could be in trouble," Velvet said.

"That's what I'm worried about," Sun said. "I've gotta find them."

"There you go being all noble and selfish again," Scarlet said. "Both at the same time."

Sun didn't rise to Scarlet's bait, which was pretty strange. But it also wasn't his style to devote himself to a cause like this. He usually went wherever his whims took him, whether that was across the sea to help a friend or to get noodles at three in the morning. To pledge to fight a *big* cause with no clear solution or end in sight? That *really* didn't sound like Sun. Maybe his time with Blake in Menagerie had changed him.

"We'll help you," Velvet said with conviction. "We'll find them."

Coco cleared her throat. "After we track down the Crown."

Velvet walked around the wall to the other side, trailing her fingers over the posters. There was a laughing boy balancing a plate on his head. A smiling man holding a baby in his arms. A teenage girl with her head bent over a Scroll.

Velvet froze, staring at a picture of a gawky teenager with short hair. Velvet knew her.

"Guys!" she called. "Look at this!"

Yatsuhashi was the first one to reach her. Velvet pointed. "Look familiar?"

Yatsuhashi squinted.

"What's wrong?" Coco asked.

"I know this girl. We ran into her last night," Yatsuhashi said.

Sun's eyes widened when he saw the spiky pink hair. "Pink!"

"This was one of the three people in masks who we saved Sun from," Yatsuhashi said.

"Hey," Sun muttered. "I had it under control."

Coco leaned closer to the picture and lowered her sunglasses. "So you're saying this missing kid has a Semblance."

"She seemed to be able to phase her body so physical objects could pass through her."

"That's impressive," Coco said. "The kind of person the Crown would be interested in."

"But she didn't act like someone who'd been kidnapped," Sun said. "More like she was a kidnapper herself."

"Like Carmine and Bertilak?" Coco asked.

"Oh, good point," Sun said.

Coco smirked. "I know."

Velvet used her Scroll to take a picture of the picture. The girl with pink hair was named Rosa Schwein and lived in Gust Downs.

"Someone should go talk to her family, find out what they know," Coco said. "Maybe these missing people are connected somehow."

"The boys and I will take care of it." Sun gave her a thumbs-up. Scarlet tossed up his arms in frustration. Sage sighed and Neptune shrugged.

Velvet started snapping pictures of wide sections of the wall with her Scroll. Some of them were already fading, bleached by the sun. Soon they'd be gone forever—a small tragedy that Velvet was all too familiar with. All of them were potential leads, as long as they lasted.

She handed her Scroll to Yatsuhashi. While he got pictures of the ones too high for her to reach, she went to the little souvenir table near the wall.

Velvet slipped the kids a Lien in exchange for one of their handmade sculptures. She handled it carefully since it was still damp. It looked like it had been made right here, from the wet clay at the base of the wall, but it was actually a pretty decent likeness of the Weeping Wall, if you knew what you were supposed to be looking at.

When Team SSSN and Team CFVY were nearly done photographing everything on the wall, a girl about their age approached. Her curly brown hair almost obscured perky mouse ears.

Neptune was friendly. "Hey," he said. "How's it going?"

The girl burst into tears and held up a flyer. "My older sister is missing!"

Neptune froze, not knowing how to react.

"Here, let me help you with that," Sun said. He took the flyer and pinned it to an empty spot on the wire. There weren't many empty spaces left now.

Coco got right down to questioning. "When did she disappear?" she asked brusquely.

"Two nights ago." The girl looked around in confusion, suddenly aware of teams CFVY and SSSN and the fact that they were all paying attention to her. "Um. She went to a club or something to watch a fight."

"Where was it?" Coco asked.

"Downtown. I don't know. She had an address on a poster. She likes to gamble, but only because she's trying to make money so we can eat." The girl broke down crying before she could offer more detail. "I don't know what we're going to do without her."

Velvet snapped a photo of her flyer. The girl's sister was named Lily, and she looked like an older version of the girl.

"We'll keep an eye out for her," Velvet promised.

"Does she have a Semblance?" Coco wanted to know.

"Sure," said the girl. "Nothing too useful, though. She can make things sticky."

"Uh, what?" Neptune asked.

"She can make things stick to each other. Little things, like rocks, or the pages of a book. We used to make houses of cards together." The girl wiped her nose with the back of her hand. "But it doesn't last long. A few minutes, and then—" She splayed her fingers out. "Poof."

"Okay," Coco said. "That's not gonna rock anyone's world."

The girl scowled. "She *is* my world." In a huff, she walked away.

Coco's face flushed. "I didn't mean to upset her."

"She was already upset," Fox said.

Scarlet crossed his arms. "But you just made it worse."

Coco was trying to piece together what they knew. "Well, I don't know if their situation fits," she said. "That girl—"

"Lily," Velvet supplied.

"*Lily* probably got in too deep with gambling debt and got into trouble," Coco suggested. "Or she was too embarrassed to go home to her family."

"She wouldn't have left her little sister alone," Velvet said. "And it sounds like her family would support her no matter what."

Silence fell over the group.

"You're right," Coco finally said. "Because that's what families do. Even in Vacuo."

"Especially in Vacuo," Sun said.

"And speaking of families . . ." Velvet looked around at her teammates. Coco and Yatsuhashi nodded. "Now it's our turn to show you guys something."

CHAPTER THREE

That night, as Sun looked around the dorm common room at the other students gathered there, he felt strangely disconnected from his body. Unsettled.

"Hey, everyone," Velvet began. "As you can see, we have a few new faces here. Since we all voted to invite Team SSSN to these meetings, here they are. Sun, Scarlet, Sage, Neptune—welcome to the Beacon Brigade."

The group applauded softly. Neptune beamed, seemed to think better of it, and his face went flat. Then his mouth stretched into a weird, wide grin that Sun knew meant his friend was about to lock up.

"Um, thanks," Sun said awkwardly. "I'm still not sure if we really belong here, but . . ." He rubbed the back of his neck.

In the last few weeks, he had seen these kids in the classrooms and hallways of Shade Academy—they were his new schoolmates. But they weren't exactly strangers. He had seen a number of them at Beacon. He had fought against some of them in the Vytal Festival Tournament. He had fought beside others at the Battle of Beacon.

And they had lost together, watching Beacon fall.

"Everyone here helped defend our home and school, even though they didn't have to," Velvet said. "We're grateful. As far as we're concerned, you're all honorary Beacon students."

Whatever that means anymore, Sun thought. Then he chided himself. To the others here, it still meant a lot. Sun liked to move around so he didn't get too attached—to a place or the people there—but that's not how other people operated. Most people's identities were built around where they lived and trained. Their friends, their culture. That was the whole point of the team system—to become part of something, to define yourself, to lose yourself in it. A team made you someone new, someone better.

Sun hadn't really been a big fan of that mentality, either, come to think of it.

And now here they were, creating a new group named after a place that didn't even exist anymore. *The Beacon Brigade.* There was Team CFVY, of course, but also Team ABRN (auburn), consisting of Arslan Altan, Bolin Hori, Reese Chloris, and Nadir Shiko. They had gone back to Haven Academy with Neptune, Scarlet, and Sage, where they watched the school nearly fall to the White Fang. And like Team SSSN, they were one of the few groups who had decided to pick up their training in Vacuo rather than lose another semester. ABRN had beaten them to Vacuo by a couple of weeks, though, since Sun had insisted on taking the scenic route—luckily for Team CFVY.

Sun recognized a few other faces from Beacon, even if he only remembered Iris Marilla's name. But he was surprised to see Nolan Porfirio, the only one here who was an original Shade Academy student.

Nolan had lost the rest of his team, BRNZ (bronze): Brawnz Ni, Roy Stallion, and May Zedong. And it showed. He was even thinner than he'd been last year at the Vytal Festival, and his rose-colored glasses couldn't hide the dark shadows under his eyes.

"Who wants to start?" Velvet asked. "What's on your mind?"

Bolin raised his hand tentatively. "Is it just me, or does it seem like we aren't really wanted here?"

"It isn't just you," Nadir said. "Let's just say some of the Vacuan students here are giving a new meaning to 'Shade' Academy." He looked around. "Because they've been throwing a lot of shade at us?"

"We get it," Fox said.

"It's true that they have been giving us a hard time since we arrived," Arslan said. "They like to remind us of the fact that we have abandoned two other academies now, as they put it. While I appreciate that they have their own perspective, it is not a very productive attitude."

After a brief pause, Yatsuhashi spoke up. "It's tough here, but that helps keep me focused. That, and meditation."

Several heads nodded around the room. Sun had seen Yatsuhashi leading meditation groups early in the mornings at Shade. They reminded Sun of the exercises Starr had forced on him at the dojo when he was young. For him, sitting in one place and doing absolutely nothing for long stretches of time was the opposite of relaxing.

"It feels like a punishment," a high voice said.

Sun winced and looked at Iris.

"Is that weird?" she went on. "I'm just being honest. It's like, it's so hard here, I'm not sure I can make it, but the alternative . . ." She swallowed, and her voice softened, but not enough. "I think I deserve it, you know? Because I survived and some of—some people didn't."

"Thank you, Iris," Velvet said. "Does anyone else feel that way?"

Some murmurs of assent.

"Sometimes I feel that way, too," Velvet acknowledged.

"Really?" Sun said. He was surprised to hear that. Velvet had never mentioned it.

"When we first got here, I hated Vacuo," Velvet admitted. "But I also know that this is the best place to get stronger. To learn what I'm really capable of. And to realize that at Beacon I did my best, but my best can still be better."

"Yeah." Iris drew in a shaky breath. "This week has been hard for me. It would have been Castor's birthday yesterday."

"I'm sorry," Velvet said.

"I miss him so much," Iris said, wiping her eyes.

"We all do," Yatsuhashi said, as if he'd been close with Castor, too.

Who's Castor? Sun thought. *One of Iris's teammates? Her boyfriend? Both?*

His thoughts were interrupted by another student. "I should have died there," Nolan said flatly.

At that, a silence fell over the group.

"I thought I was going to. I was afraid . . ." Nolan scanned the room, looking for support, though not everyone met his gaze. "But I didn't." His voice shook, but the set of his jaw was determined. "We didn't die. There's a reason for that."

Yeah. Because you ran away, Sun thought, unable to stop himself, even though this was the exact thing the other Shade students were thinking of the Beacon and Haven survivors. No wonder Nolan was here—he was probably getting criticized worse than anyone, because Shade students were supposed to be stronger than everyone else.

"I'm going to make my life count," Nolan said. "I'm not going to waste this chance."

That's more like it, Sun thought. But he'd believe it when he saw it. It was easy to talk about doing something, and another thing to follow through on it. Maybe that was what he didn't like about this group. So far it was all just sitting around and talking. They should be focused on moving on—channeling their strength toward protecting their new home, their new friends.

"I think we all feel that way," Velvet said. "Thank you for sharing, Nolan."

Sun couldn't contain himself; he rolled his eyes. This therapy thing felt weird, like a shirt that didn't quite fit. It had its own language, and everyone was so careful about how they phrased things. It ran counter to everything he was.

"You have something to contribute, Sun?" Coco asked.

"I don't think so," Sun said. "I'm sorry. I don't think this is for me."

He stood up. Neptune jumped to his feet, too, and then they stood there awkwardly, unsure of what they were doing.

"You don't have to stay, of course," Coco said. "Maybe you're not ready for this."

Sun scowled. There was an implication there he didn't like.

"That's not what I meant. But I don't have anything to say that I think you'd want to hear. So I'm just gonna go."

Velvet stood up and put an arm out to stop him "Don't. This is a safe space, Sun. It's like a family. And whatever you're thinking, I think we've all been there. I think we all need to hear it from each other."

Sun hesitated.

"Go on." Scarlet tapped his foot. "Don't keep us waiting. Again."

Sun narrowed his eyes. "Look, I understand why you've started this little group, but I think it's a mistake. For a lot of reasons." Now everyone was staring at him, their eyes burning as hot as Vacuo's noontime sun.

"You've only been here for ten minutes, and you've figured us all out?" Nolan said, incredulous.

Sun shook his head and started to leave. "Come on, Neptune."

But his teammate didn't move. Neptune glanced at Sun and then at the group and then back. Finally he sat down. "I'd kind of like to hear what you have to say."

Sun was exasperated. "Okay, for one, Theo really wouldn't like this," he burst out. Sun circled his hand in the air, indicating the whole room. "*This* is why Vacuans won't trust you. Because you're holding on to who you were and where you came from instead of focusing on where you are."

He caught his breath and continued. "I get it. Beacon was your home. But it belongs to the Grimm now. We all survived, but it's like you haven't left Beacon at all. And if you don't leave it, that darkness is going to eat you alive."

"That's not what this group is about," Velvet told him. "We've all lived through something that no one else can understand."

Sun laughed. "You don't think Vacuans understand what you've been through? People stay in Vacuo because it's our home, no matter what. We're making up for our failure every day, punishing ourselves with the heat and the hunger and the thirst. Because we deserve it, and because we don't want to forget."

Scarlet stood. "You mean like you didn't *forget* about us? Like you didn't *leave* us the first chance you got to chase after someone you barely knew who didn't want your help? You didn't even stay in Vacuo for school—you chose Haven." Scarlet flipped his bangs away from his face and glared at Sun. "You wouldn't know anything about loss, Sun. You never stay in one place long enough to learn."

The room was quiet. Sun's face was flushed. "You all belong in Vacuo more than you think," he snapped.

"Thank you, Sun." Velvet's voice shook. She looked resolute and genuinely appreciative, but Sun couldn't stay there any longer, not with Scarlet airing Team SSSN's dirty laundry for everyone to see. Sun pushed his way through the common room doors a little more roughly than he needed to. He stalked down the hall and out into the cool night air.

He still couldn't figure out what was going on with Scarlet. Yeah, Sun had left his team to support Blake, because she needed a friend and her mission was way more important than just settling back in at Haven and picking up his studies. And he still didn't regret leaving—without him, who knows what would've happened with the White Fang on Menagerie or Haven. Blake may not have needed or wanted him, but there was no doubt in his mind that he *had helped.*

The doors opened again a moment later, and Velvet emerged. "Sun, you don't have to—"

"I'm sorry about that. This just isn't my thing."

"It doesn't have to be. It's helpful to everyone in there, and that's all that matters. You'll find your own way to work through it."

There's nothing to work through, Sun thought. *We just need to move on.*

But Sun just smiled at Velvet. "I'll see you guys for patrol later."

CHAPTER FOUR

Fox crouched on the low rooftop beside Coco, thinking there were better things he could be doing than staking out a gambling house, thinking there were better people for the job than the blind guy. But Coco had insisted, and Fox trusted her instincts. Coco knew what Fox was capable of and how boring this assignment would be for him, so she must have had a good reason for dragging him along.

Unless he'd done something to get on her bad side.

"Did I do something to annoy you?" Fox sent. *"Lately?"*

"No. Why do you ask?" Coco sent back.

"Team SSSN just joined us, and now they get to do all the fun stuff," Fox sent.

With Team SSSN joining Team CFVY for the first time on one of their nocturnal patrols of the city, Coco had changed up their strategy a bit. There was a little debate from Sun and Scarlet, but as usual Coco got her way.

And so Sun and Neptune were making the rounds of the downtown hot spots, which was a generous description for the clubs and restaurants that entertained the locals at night. That had been

Fox's favorite beat, because it kept him moving. Not sitting around, waiting for something to happen.

"Sun knows this city better than anyone," Coco sent. *"He's the best person for the job."*

"I could have gone with him instead of Neptune."

"You looking for some quality time with Sun?" Coco asked.

"No, but I'd rather be doing something, and someone needs to keep an eye on him. So to speak."

"But then who would watch Neptune?" Coco asked.

"You've got me there. I wouldn't want that job," Fox had to admit.

"So . . . you don't trust Sun?" Coco asked.

Fox wasn't sure where he stood on that question. *"I don't* know *Sun yet. Not really. I guess I don't trust Team SSSN to not mess things up for us. They're sloppy and off-balance right now."*

Coco sighed. *"I agree with you there. They have some stuff to work through. But then again, most teams do. Anyway, we'll see how it goes tonight,"* she sent.

"You didn't split up Scarlet and Sage, either," Fox observed.

The other half of Team SSSN was guarding the wall that separated the rest of the city from Shade's campus. Scarlet had insisted that if the Crown was going after people with powerful Semblances, they would eventually be moving on the academy—which had the highest concentration of people with powerful Semblances for miles around. Though Scarlet didn't venture to guess as to whether it would be little disappearances spread out over time or one big, coordinated attack.

The tension in Coco's voice told Fox she was scowling.

"It's what Scarlet wanted. He's determined to protect Shade Academy—maybe a little too zealous about it. But that doesn't mean he's wrong. If we

don't want them to get in our way, or worse, raise a big enough stink that we can't continue our investigation, it's better to keep them involved in a limited capacity. Plus, I don't think it's a good idea to put Scarlet anywhere near Sun right now . . . not after that scene they made earlier."

"Fair. And conveniently enough, this way you don't have to break up our team, or mix them and us."

"If you already know all the answers, why do you bother asking?"

"To pass the time. So why are Velvet and Yatsuhashi on Grimm watch?" Fox sent. *"Did* they *do something to annoy you?"*

Grimm watch was the duty of the low-rent Huntsmen who worked loosely with local law enforcement to help keep the peace.

"There's been a rise in incidents of Grimm wandering into the city lately," Coco sent. *"Nothing that isn't handled quickly before the attacks escalate, but more than usual."*

"How do you know that?" Fox asked. He hadn't heard a word about it.

"Professor Rumpole requested reports from the sheriff on recent police and Huntsmen activity."

"So how do you *know that?"* Fox asked.

Coco laughed. *"I snuck into her office."*

"Coco!" Fox said.

"Don't lecture me, Fox."

Fox smiled. *"How dare you do that without inviting me,"* he sent. *"What were you looking for?"*

"Anything she had dug up on the Crown," Coco explained. *"I didn't find anything, but she had left the report on Grimm activity out on her desk, plus a list of missing person cases linked to a club in the Pits."*

It was kind of odd for a nightclub to pop up in the old district locals referred to as the Pits—because of all the sandpits and traps that could grab someone who didn't watch where they were going.

"That girl at the wall mentioned a club," Fox said. *"I don't get why you're worried about Grimm, though."*

"Because either there have been too many for the regular Huntsmen to handle or the Huntsmen aren't doing their jobs. Something's changed in the last few months. And—hold on. Someone's coming out."

The door of the gambling house opened and the raucous sounds of laughter invaded the quiet night.

"Two people are leaving, a Faunus male and a woman wearing a truly horrific ensemble," Coco sent.

"—not your night," Fox overheard the woman say. "Better luck next time."

"But how'm I gonna eat?" the man responded as they moved out of earshot. Nothing about them seemed suspicious.

"You were saying?" Fox asked. *"About why Velvet and Yatsuhashi are watching for Grimm."*

"Right. They aren't only watching for Grimm. I've been thinking—"

"Always dangerous," Fox interrupted.

"Ha ha. I've been thinking that the Crown may not be operating in the city itself. It would make sense to set up their base of operations nearby, but not directly under the nose of Headmaster Theodore."

"That's not an idea. It's a guess," Fox noted.

"When you don't have enough information, a guess is the best you've got, and I'm rarely wrong."

"Which brings me back to why we're here and why me in particular—" Fox began. If the others were watching for the Crown, why was he stuck here?

"Because you're a great conversationalist, when you don't want to make any noise," Coco sent. *"This would be way more boring for me if I didn't have someone to talk to. And we're here because if the Huntsmen aren't watching for Grimm, then what* are *they doing?"*

"Gambling." Fox nodded to the club.

Nothing much happened in Vacuo, and when there was an argument or a crime, people tended to sort things out on their own—with their fists. But when it came to Grimm, Vacuans depended on Huntsmen to fight their battles for them.

Any large gathering of people—whether a temporary settlement like most of the ones in Vacuo, or a village, or a major city—naturally drew Grimm on a regular basis. But between Shade's students on training missions and the hired Huntsmen on guard duty, it was rare for a Grimm to cross into the city—almost as rare as Coco's instincts being wrong.

"So that's why Theodore's been sending more students out lately, clearing the immediate area of Grimm," Fox sent. *"Maybe the Huntsmen are getting lazy."*

The door below them opened again. Coco and Fox stilled, listening.

"Don't you worry. We'll get you home," a man said in a deep voice.

"We're trained Huntsmen. The best in the city," came a second man.

"I don't know," a third man said. "I think I can manage on my own. I always have before."

"I'd be careful if I were you," the first speaker noted. "A number of people watched you leave with your winnings, and sometimes bad things happen on the way home."

"I'd sure feel better seeing you there safely. And you can certainly afford our reasonable rates tonight," the second male said.

"Well . . . okay." The third man gave up and went with them.

"Three males. One short with a green tank top and cargo shorts. His partner is taller, a Faunus with pig ears," she sent.

Fox was glad they were using teamspeak. With ears like that, a Faunus would definitely have heard them whispering.

"So there are our Huntsmen," she went on. *"The person they're protecting is average height, definitely not a fighter. Vacuan head covering and loose clothes, no weapon I can see. A merchant, maybe."*

"This doesn't feel right," Fox sent.

"Agreed. These Huntsmen are already paid to protect the city from Grimm, not escort private citizens home with their winnings. So . . . let's follow them."

Coco and Fox waited until there was some distance between them and the group, then dropped down silently to the sand. They crept after the trio.

"Should I update the others?" Fox sent.

"Not until we have a situation."

They followed quietly, Coco in the lead. Fox concentrated on the group they were following and drew in a sharp breath.

Coco elbowed him. *"Shhh. What?"*

"Two of these guys have a lot of Aura," Fox sent. *"Basically off the charts."*

"The Huntsmen, I bet," Coco said. *"Flanking the guy in the middle?"*

"Right. Their Auras are weird, so vivid I can see *them. And they're the same color."*

"Is that unusual?" Coco asked.

"Auras are usually more unique, but these seem identical."

Fox and Coco continued to tail the two Huntsmen and their charge.

"Wait, this isn't the way to my house," the merchant said. "We should have turned left back there."

"This is a shortcut," the tall Huntsman said.

"No, it isn't," the merchant said nervously. "Thank you, but no thank you. Here's some Lien for your trouble, but I can take things from here."

"Not so fast," the tall Huntsman said. "We don't want your money."

"What do you think you're—" Fox heard them struggling. "Get off me! Let me go!" The merchant was fighting them off.

"You're coming with us," the short Huntsman said after a scuffle.

"I'll pay you more if you want. Here, take everything!" the merchant insisted.

"We don't want your money. We want you," the tall man said.

"Now we have a situation," Coco sent, rushing ahead of Fox. *"Alert the others. Call in Sun and Neptune."*

Fox wasn't sure Velvet, Yatsuhashi, Scarlet, and Sage were in range of his teamspeak, but he broadcast wide to everyone, anyway.

"We have a situation," Fox sent.

"What was that?" Sun sent back. *"Uh, hello?"*

"It sounded like Fox," Neptune returned loudly. *"What are you doing in my head?"*

"Calm down, it's just teamspeak," Fox sent.

"Since when can you do that?" Sun asked.

Velvet jumped in. *"It's Fox's Semblance. He's telepathic. And he likes surprising people with it."*

"We don't have time for this," Fox sent. *"A couple of Huntsmen are abducting someone. Sun, Neptune, get to the Pits district. Scarlet and Sage, you, too, if you can hear me. Velvet, Yatsuhashi, hold your position in case they get away and try to flee the city."*

"On our way," Sun sent.

Fox ran toward Coco's location. She was trying to intervene, and the tall Huntsman wasn't taking her seriously.

"Go on home, sweetheart," he sneered. "This doesn't involve you."

Oh, that was definitely going to annoy her.

"*I'm* involving me," Coco retorted. "What are you doing? You're a Huntsman; you're supposed to be fighting Grimm, not kidnapping helpless people."

"I'm not helpless!" the merchant said.

Fox could only imagine the expression on Coco's face. "Oh, all right, then, tough guy," she said. "If you think you can handle this, I'll just go—"

"No! Please!" the man begged.

Coco had a real sadistic streak sometimes. Just one of the reasons she and Fox made great partners.

His head was full of Team SSSN now.

"Man, I used to think that guy never talked. Has he been using telepathy all along?" Sun sent.

"I bet he's been talking about us, right in front of our faces," Neptune sent.

"It's kind of cool, though, right?" Sun said.

"I can still hear you," Fox sent. He drew his tonfas and took up a defensive position beside Coco.

"Great, another one," the short guy said darkly.

Sun and Neptune were quiet for a while.

"How does this work?" Sun asked.

"I'll explain it later. Just get over here," Fox sent.

"We're here!" Sun shouted, and Fox heard his actual voice, then a soft thud as Sun landed in front of him and Coco. Neptune rushed over just behind him.

"Oh, come on!" the tall guy said.

At the exact same time, Sun said, "You again!" sounding surprised.

"You know these guys?" Coco asked him.

"Yeah, we fought a few nights ago, only they were all covered up," Sun said. "Two against four this time."

"We can still take you," the tall guy said.

"How about two against six?" Scarlet called from above before landing softly next to Fox.

The short guy sighed. "These kids are becoming a real problem. Let's get out of here."

"Not with that guy, you don't," Coco warned.

"She won't be happy if we come back empty-handed again," the short guy said to his partner.

"Shut up," the tall guy shouted.

"Drop him, or else!" Sun demanded.

Something crashed into the ground and the two Huntsmen took off.

"Drop him?" groaned the merchant.

"Fox, if you can track those Huntsmen by their Auras, go after them," Coco sent. *"Find out where they came from."*

"On it," Fox sent. He sped off after the two bright Auras, plugging his earbuds in and tapping the Scroll in his belt to turn on ADA, his Accessibility Dialog Assistant. She immediately started feeding him information on his surroundings so he didn't run into a wall or fall into a hole while pursuing the would-be kidnappers.

They seemed to be heading out of town.

"Velvet, Yatsuhashi, I think these guys are heading your way. You'll recognize them from the other night—you fought them with Sun."

"You mean the ones we rescued *Sun from?"* Velvet asked.

"Come on!" Sun sent.

"We'll be ready," Yatsuhashi confirmed.

Fox let the Huntsmen get farther ahead of him so they wouldn't realize they were being followed. He had a good lock on their Auras now, so he wouldn't have had any trouble finding them again. Just before they hit the northern border of the city, they stopped. Fox crept to their coordinates and listened. It was quiet.

"ADA, what's in front of me?" Fox whispered.

"One kilometer north there is a five-story building constructed of steel and concrete, rectangular in shape."

"That's pretty tall for Vacuo, and it's made of concrete?" Fox said. "What building is it?"

"It is currently abandoned."

"It isn't abandoned now. Someone just went inside."

"It has no designated purpose on public record at this time."

"What used to be there?" Fox asked.

"The Mistral Trading Company owned and operated it as a Dust refinery."

"That would have been before the war."

"Correct."

Fox relayed the info to Velvet and Yatsuhashi.

"They're inside now," Fox sent, concentrating his Semblance. *"I can't pick them out because there are a lot of people inside and a lot of their Auras seem the same."*

Velvet and Yatsuhashi soon joined Fox. "We happened to be nearby," Velvet said, relieved. "Glad we could get here."

"So . . . how do you want to play this?" Yatsuhashi asked.

"I want to know what's in there. *Who's* in there," Fox said. He had a bad feeling about this.

"So let's open it up," Yatsuhashi said. He stepped forward and Fox heard him grunt with exertion. "I can't . . . budge this door." Yatsuhashi drew his sword, and a moment later Fox heard a massive clang of metal on metal.

"Ow," Yatsuhashi said.

On the other side of the door, Fox heard shouting and clapping, then banging. Yatsuhashi hadn't broken the door down, but it was okay. Now someone was opening it to them.

A metal bolt slid on the other side of the door and a woman's voice asked, "What do we fight for?" Was she looking for a password?

"Um. Fortune and glory?" Fox said.

The door slammed shut. "I guess that was the wrong answer," he said.

Fox knocked on the door and tried to get her attention again. "How many guesses do I get?"

"Maybe we should go," Velvet said.

"ADA, mark this loc—" Fox faltered. He was scanning everyone in the building with his Semblance, noting the variations in Aura and trying to pick their Huntsmen out of the crowd. There had to be around fifty people in there, but at least one of their Auras was familiar.

"Fox?" Velvet asked. "Are you okay?"

"I'm fine," Fox said. He could hardly believe what he was about to say. "But I'm pretty sure Professor Rumpole is inside."

"In *there*?"

Fox nodded.

"Then we're gonna bust in." Yatsuhashi reached for his greatsword.

"Hold on, Yatsu," Velvet said. "Fox, is she in trouble?"

"There's no way to know from out here," Fox said. But he was worried.

Just then his Scroll vibrated. "Coco Adel," ADA announced.

Quickly, Fox answered and put Coco on speaker. "Status," Coco asked.

"Confused." Fox hung up and switched them all to teamspeak, updating Coco on how they'd come to the supposedly abandoned Dust refinery and the fact that Professor Rumpole seemed to be inside.

"If the professor is in there, I'm almost certain it's because she wants to be. Her own investigation must have brought her there. We shouldn't interfere," Coco sent.

"Are you sure?" Scarlet asked suspiciously. *"Or are you saying that because you don't want us to get caught? Because if something happens—"*

Coco shut the idea down quickly. *"If we interfere in her investigation and blow whatever she's doing, we'll get worse than detention. She'll probably kick us out of Shade. And we'll have ruined the usefulness of the information she's gathering. I say we give her time to do her thing."*

"What about the guy they were trying to abduct?" Fox asked. *"What have you found out about him? Does he have a Semblance?"*

"He says he doesn't," Coco returned. *"He was kind of rude about it, too."*

"He threatened to report us to the headmaster, once he found out we're only students, not licensed Huntsmen," Scarlet said.

"Students from Beacon and Haven," Sage pointed out. *"He cared more about where we came from, I think."*

Coco sounded smug, like a decision had been validated. *"He refused to talk to anyone but Sun once the danger was over."*

Sun laughed nervously. *"For what good it did us. He didn't tell us much, just that he'd never figured out his Semblance—"*

"Were those two who were following him really Huntsmen?" Fox asked.

"The owner of the club said they are. He likes that they hang around his club, in fact, because they make him feel safer. Plus, their presence discourages people from cheating. Usually," Coco sent.

"They didn't want his money," Velvet sent. *"But if they were working for the Crown, why would the Crown be interested in people without Semblances, like this guy and that woman the other night?"*

"Well, this has been a good night so far. We have two new leads," Coco sent.

"What's that?" Velvet asked.

"That Dust refinery, for one. We know it was harboring at least two criminals."

"And the other lead?" Neptune asked.

"Professor Rumpole," Coco sent. *"Tomorrow, I'll go to her office—"*

"And snoop around some more?" Fox asked.

"No," Coco said. *"I'm going to ask her some questions."*

CHAPTER FIVE

Yatsuhashi shifted his weight from one foot to the other as he waited with all the other Shade Academy students in the Meeting Grounds, the wide-open area on the highest level of Shade Academy where school assemblies were usually held. Yatsuhashi loved it up here.

It was early morning, so the temperature was as pleasant as it ever got in Vacuo, as the sun began to warm the night-chilled desert. Among the green spaces scattered throughout the city, this was the most lush: an artificial oasis meant to evoke Vacuo's former splendor, dense with trees and flowering plants. It was as much a statement for those who gazed up at the academy as a pleasure for the students and their headmaster. The Meeting Grounds reminded Yatsuhashi of his mother's healing gardens in Mistral, his favorite place to go for meditation.

Of course there wasn't much but flat desert for miles around, yet having some extra distance from the harsh, deadly terrain allowed Yatsuhashi to appreciate its beauty. Clear blue skies, sand tinted with gold in the early sun. It was hard to believe that there were deadly things lurking just out of sight—Grimm like Dromedons, with their venomous spit and bone armor protecting their swollen humps. Not to mention the natural wildlife, like the horrifying mole crabs that slept just below the sand and could cut a person in two with their massive claws. All that besides the more insidious threats, people like the Crown.

Yatsuhashi rubbed his right shoulder, still sore from when he had tried to break down the steel door with Fulcrum last night.

"You okay?" Velvet asked. From his right, she placed a delicate hand on his injured arm.

"Fine," Yatsuhashi said, more gruffly than he'd intended. "Thanks to you. Just wish we'd gotten more sleep." They had snuck back into Shade just before dawn, right when a notification had been broadcast to all student Scrolls: "Report to the Meeting Grounds at eight a.m. for an important announcement." It came directly from Professor Rumpole.

The crowd around them murmured hushed speculations about what they were gathered for.

Velvet stifled a yawn. "Sleep would have been good. Especially before whatever this is." Her rabbit ears drooped and her boundless energy seemed to have bounds after all. Yatsu and Velvet hadn't been this tired since they had tried to clear Beacon Academy of invading Grimm a year ago. At least last night's mission had brought them some new information and a renewed commitment to finding and stopping the Crown.

"Do you think it's about us?" Yatsuhashi asked fearfully.

"It's not *always* about us." Velvet smiled. "As I'm often reminding Coco."

From Yatsuhashi's left, Coco approached and leaned forward to peer at Velvet from over the rim of her sunglasses. "I heard that."

"Good. I hope it'll sink in one day," Velvet said cheerfully.

"It does seem like an odd coincidence, though. If Fox is right, Professor Rumpole was out last night, too," Coco said, settling in beside them. "So this *could* be about us."

Velvet rolled her eyes.

"I was hoping to talk to her before class, but I guess our chat will have to wait." Coco pushed up her glasses and rubbed her eyes. Yatsuhashi saw dark bags under them as she lowered the glasses back into place.

"Looks like she's in a hurry to talk to us," Yatsuhashi said. "Sometimes it's better to slow down a little, let things come at their own pace."

"I'll pass on your unsolicited advice when I talk to her," Coco said dryly.

Yatsuhashi crossed his arms, then grimaced as a fresh pain shot through his shoulder. *Come on, Aura,* he thought. *Do your thing.*

His advice may have been unsolicited, but it was good nonetheless. Aura regenerated over time, and resting helped the process. Pushing on without sleep, day after day, not to mention exhausting your Aura in battle, took its toll. Right now CFVY was operating at much lower reserves than they should, and in Vacuo not being at your best could be fatal. Yatsuhashi made a note to talk to Coco about easing up on the team. If this was hard on them, what would it do to SSSN?

Finally the double doors to the headmaster's office opened and

Theodore strode out, his glittering red-gloved fists raised above his head like he had just won a fight. Or was raring for one.

“Good morning, Shade Academy!” Headmaster Theodore's voice boomed over the crowd. “How are you doing?”

The students erupted into applause and cheering. It was what Headmaster Theodore expected. It was what he inspired whenever he appeared.

Yatsuhashi had only spoken to the headmaster once directly: when Team CFVY had first arrived from Vale following the Fall of Beacon, bearing a letter of recommendation from Glynda Goodwitch that Theodore handed unread to Professor Rumpole. “I know who you are,” he said. “You're in. You're all in.”

“Sir?” Coco asked.

“I try to keep informed about students at the other schools.” Headmaster Theodore sniffed. “And I did extensive research before the Vytal Tournament.”

“You *did?” Professor Rumpole spoke up from beside the headmaster's desk, watching the proceedings with a kind of bemusement.* She's seen this show before, *Yatsuhashi thought.*

“Well, Rumpole *did. She does all that . . .” Theodore waved his hand. “Stuff, and much more. Regardless, I always thought you kids would do better in the Tournament than the other academies.”*

“So did we.” Coco scowled. Yatsuhashi felt his face warm with embarrassment. He was uncomfortable under Theodore's intense scrutiny, those blue eyes peering at him like he was a specimen in a collection.

“It still bothers you, doesn't it?” Theodore walked around his desk. He hardly ever sat, hardly ever stopped moving. His dark hair was close cut, almost

shaved off—practical for the desert climate. His checkered vest showed off his wiry frame—thin but with sharp lines of muscle, like he had been chiseled from stone.

That was Headmaster Theodore: He put everything out there. He had clearly worked hard to get his body into peak physical condition, and he wanted to show it off. A flowing gray-blue cape, the color of a stormy sky, was clasped around his shoulders with a silver chain. He had a silver belt with a round buckle, matching boots, and bright white slacks with deep side pockets, all carefully orchestrated to draw even more attention to himself. Headmaster Theodore's whole style should have been ridiculous for a man likely in his forties, maybe older, but the hardened Huntsman made it work. Yatsuhashi got the impression he could make anything work.

Yatsuhashi looked over at Coco then, and as tired as she was from their long journey across half a continent and the burning sands of Vacuo, he saw a faint smile tugged at her lips.

Coco could be judgmental, and she didn't take long to form an opinion. But she usually wasn't wrong. That smile made Yatsuhashi feel better about their choice to come to Vacuo.

Though if Coco ended up being wrong, she was usually the last to admit it.

"It does bother me," Coco said. "I hate to lose. Fortunately, it doesn't happen often."

Headmaster Theodore clapped—just once, like a crash of thunder between his gloved hands. "Excellent. Welcome to Shade Academy. Rumpole will arrange everything."

Headmaster Theodore strode away without another word.

"That's it?" Coco asked.

"You expected some kind of trial?" Theodore spun back around, cape flaring dramatically around his ankles. "Wasn't the Battle of Beacon enough?"

"But we failed," Velvet said. Her voice was a moment away from breaking. Though her stoic expression held.

"Ah, she speaks!" Theodore strode toward Velvet. His voice softened. "You didn't fail, my dear. You fought. You stayed, far longer than anyone would have asked or expected of a student. And now you're here. Do you want *to be here? Will you fight for Shade the way you did for Beacon, Velvet Scarlatina?"*

Velvet hesitated, but she nodded. "I will."

Theodore stood in front of Fox. "Will you, Fox Alistair of Kenyte?"

"I will," *Fox sent. Headmaster Theodore didn't even blink at hearing the boy's voice in his head.*

Headmaster Theodore turned to Yatsuhashi. "And you, Yatsuhashi Daichi?"

"Yes, sir," Yatsuhashi said. "You can count on me."

Theodore nodded. "Coco Adel, will—"

*"No," Coco interrupted. She hesitated just long enough to make Yatsuhashi feel shocked and then nervous. "I'll fight for Shade even harder. I won't fail again." She looked at her team. "*We *won't fail again."*

Theodore grinned.

"You will make Shade stronger, and Shade will make you stronger," he intoned.

Theodore struck a fighting pose, fists raised. "But if you ever doubt that you belong here, you're welcome to take me on for the right to stay."

"Perhaps another time," Professor Rumpole intervened. "I'm sure they're tired from their journey."

"Of course. That wouldn't be a fair fight. Another time. I look forward to it."

Yatsuhashi shook his head at the memory. Headmaster Theodore was so different from the more reserved Headmaster Ozpin, who had been younger but seemed much older. They were almost like opposite sides of the same coin. Ozpin had believed in you before you did, almost like he knew your true potential, despite what your transcripts or fighting abilities looked like. Theodore believed you had potential, but you had to earn it and prove yourself to him first.

It wasn't unkind; it was just very practical and demanding. It was very *Vacuo*—or so Fox had described it.

Now Headmaster Theodore was dancing around the circle of students, jabbing fists at them, feinting left and right, beckoning them to come fight him. His youthful energy was palpable and infectious.

Theodore finally goaded someone into stepping forward for a match, a girl named Umber Gorgoneion. They faced each other and bowed as the noise died down. Then a voice cut through the air.

"Headmaster, that isn't why we're here." Professor Rumpole strode forward.

"But—" Theodore began.

"Please save it for later," Rumpole said briskly.

"You're no fun," Theodore sighed. "But you're right." Theodore rubbed his hands together, the crystals on his gloves catching the light. "Let's get started, then." He gave Umber a high five and she returned to her spot beside her friends, cheeks blazing red.

Headmaster Theodore hopped up onto the short stage and joined Rumpole at the microphone.

"We have received some reports—" Theodore began.

Rumpole cleared her throat.

"Some *complaints* from local security forces about Shade Academy students operating in the city at night, and interfering with official Huntsmen business."

"I told you it was about us," Coco muttered.

Yatsuhashi clenched his jaw. This wasn't right, though. If they hadn't interfered, those Huntsmen would have kidnapped an innocent person. They had to be compromised by the Crown.

He felt Velvet put a hand on his arm. He glanced over at her, and she shook her head slightly. She knew his anger had been boiling up, but she wanted him to watch and wait.

"We need to maintain a good relationship with the police and Huntsmen, now more than ever. You know we don't have many rules here, because all Shade students have to be responsible for their own actions—and willing to accept the consequences." Theodore glanced at Rumpole. "However, effective immediately, students must remain on campus after sundown unless otherwise assigned to a mission and approved by Professor Rumpole or myself."

"Damn," Coco muttered.

Students murmured in confusion and anger. Yatsuhashi saw Sun raise his hand, but Theodore ignored him. He held up one hand to silence the group, and it worked because it was Headmaster Theodore.

He grabbed the microphone and moved around the front of the room. "As you know, the safety of our students is my top priority. Some of you recently came from academies that were run a little differently, but Vacuo is a more dangerous place than Mistral and Vale."

Theodore looked out at the crowd as he strolled. Was it Yatsuhashi's imagination, or did his gaze linger on Team CFVY for a moment? He had to know that these reports were about them, but then why hadn't he spoken to them directly?

He continued, "I have also heard the rumors that people have been disappearing in Vacuo. I understand that this is a matter of concern for all of you. You probably want to help. Good—that's why you're here. But we already have the best people working to get to the bottom of it, and we want to avoid distractions. When it's time, when we know more, we will seek help if necessary."

Professor Rumpole cleared her throat.

"In short, don't you worry. We know what's been going on out there, and we have another solution," Theodore said. "Don't we, Professor?"

"We do." Rumpole took the microphone and fixed it back into the stand. "Shade Academy has been through a lot of change lately. Last year we took in students from Beacon, and more recently we welcomed eight new arrivals from Haven as well."

There were scattered boos from the audience, but they died down at one fierce glance from Headmaster Theodore. Velvet's face flushed, and this time Yatsuhashi put a comforting hand on her shoulder.

Rumpole looked around. "This has clearly been a challenge for everyone—the strain on the dormitory space and the overcrowded classrooms . . . and we haven't yet addressed the issue of team assignments for some of you. It is understandably difficult to adjust to a new school, an entirely new group of classmates, and most of all to life in Vacuo. Yet some of you have been separated from your original training teams."

That's one way to put it, Yatsuhashi thought. *Separated by battle, or death.*

"And so," Professor Rumpole added with a flourish, "Shade Academy is holding its first Reinitiation Ceremony." She placed her hands behind her back and smiled.

Yatsuhashi's blood ran cold.

"What?" Velvet whispered.

"What!" Coco yelled.

The raucous reaction to the previous announcement was nothing compared to the furor that now electrified the crowd. Everyone started talking at once, or shouting questions to Professor Rumpole. Theodore held up a hand, but even that wasn't enough this time.

He slammed a fist into his hand and the resulting *boom* finally settled down the crowd.

"When is this happening?" Coco called out.

"It's already begun," Rumpole said. "Everything you do from this moment forward will factor into your evaluations for new teams."

"What about our existing teams?" Scarlet asked.

"Your old teams no longer exist. New teams will be formed," Rumpole said crisply.

Coco tore off her glasses. "For how long?"

Rumpole didn't blink. "For the time being," she said.

Headmaster Theodore strode forward. His voice projected

easily without the aid of a microphone. "This is going to be fun! I wish I'd thought of it sooner. It's the perfect way to get everyone back on equal footing and improve our teamwork. New teams will be formed without regard for what year you are, or where you came from. Vacuo, Vale, or Mistral—it doesn't matter anymore." He clapped enthusiastically.

What year *we are?* Yatsu thought. *This can't be right. How could a first-year keep up with fourth-years?*

"Our longtime Shade students are already familiar with our initiation ceremony. Luckily, Professor Rumpole has cooked up something new so that no academy's students will have an advantage."

Yatsuhashi turned as he heard the whirring motors of an airbus. Then four buses lifted up into view beyond the edge of the terrace.

"When you reach your destination, your goal will be to locate a gold figurine and bring it back to the school," Rumpole said.

"Great," Fox sent. *"Glad this is fair for everyone. Who can* see.*"*

"All aboard!" Headmaster Theodore called out. The doors of the hovering airbuses lowered. Students began filing uncertainly into the vehicles.

"We haven't even had breakfast yet," Sun protested.

Meanwhile, Yatsuhashi felt like he was having an out-of-body experience. He needed to keep his team close to him. Especially Velvet. If they weren't separated, they couldn't be assigned to different teams.

But when he looked up, the first airbus was already pulling away, loaded with students. It reminded Yatsuhashi uncomfortably of the evacuation of Beacon Academy, of that horrible day they'd left their home behind forever. He felt the breath catch in his throat.

"Stay together," Coco called, bringing him back to the moment. She and Fox stepped aboard an airbus, but another line of students cut in front of Yatsuhashi. He stopped himself from shoving them aside and watched as the airbus filled and carried away his friends.

"Stick close to me," Yatsuhashi said to Velvet. "We'll find them." When she didn't respond, he looked for her. She wasn't at his side.

He caught sight of the tips of her ears among the rush of students. She was being propelled backward. Her eyes locked on Yatsuhashi's.

"Yatsu!" she called.

"Velvet!"

This time, Yatsuhashi pushed forcefully through a pack of his schoolmates. "Sorry! Sorry! Sorry, that's my ride," he shouted as people fell or scrambled out of his way. He had to get to Velvet.

She waited for him by the door, arm outstretched. But the airbus hatch started to close. She reached out one last time in an attempt to hold the door, but someone pulled her inside.

"Yatsu!" she called.

"Don't worry! I'll find you!" Yatsuhashi bellowed. After all, they were going to the same place.

Weren't they?

Yatsuhashi clambered onto the last airbus. As it floated away from Shade Academy, he looked back at the roof. All the tranquility Yatsuhashi had felt there only moments before was gone. The turbulence from the ships' rotors churned the water in the pool and shook tree leaves as though they were in a windstorm, mirroring his internal anxiety. Headmaster Theodore was waving and whooping, like it was all some terrific game, while Professor Rumpole watched silently, her hair whipping around in the wind and an unsettling grin on her face.

CHAPTER SIX

Velvet stared at the closed door of the airbus, feeling the same shock and dismay she had seen on Yatsu's face as the vehicle pulled away from the roof terrace. She wrapped her arms around herself and stumbled over to a seat, head low.

This can't be happening, she thought. No matter what terrible things Team CFVY had been through, it had always been bearable because Yatsuhashi, Coco, and Fox were at her side. They could survive anything together, and even if she sometimes wished they weren't so protective of her, she was mostly grateful that they had her back. They were more than just teammates—they were her family. Even more so than her own parents, who never talked to each other anymore.

As much as Velvet disliked the thought of being on her own again, she was most nervous about who she might be paired with in this reinitiation.

"Why's everyone so down?" a familiar voice called from up ahead. Velvet caught sight of Sun at the front of the airbus, hanging upside down with his tail wrapped around a handrail. He wasn't with the rest of his team, but knowing Sun, that might have been his decision. Sun saw her, smiled, and waved. Velvet looked away.

A moment later, he sat down next to her.

"Hey, you okay?" Sun asked.

"No," Velvet said. "Yatsu and I were separated." She swallowed hard, trying not to cry.

Sun stared ahead, like he couldn't quite manage to feel bad. "I'm sorry," he said. "Seems like most students aren't too thrilled with this."

The airbus shook, and Velvet took hold of the railing. "I just wonder what the point is of this whole reinitiation," she said, steadying herself.

"It isn't a bad idea," Sun said. "It's been hard for some students to settle in at Shade, like those who lost members of their teams. Maybe this is a chance to really commit to our new school and our training, and learn from one another in a new way."

Right, Velvet thought. "Or maybe some of us burned bridges with our team and might be looking for an easy way to avoid fixing those relationships," she said.

Sun's face went red. "I don't remember you being this harsh."

Velvet raised her eyebrows. "Call it tough love."

"I still think this might be the best way to move forward at Shade."

"Maybe, but the timing makes no sense," Velvet said. "If they want us prepared for an attack, breaking up teams seems counterproductive."

"Professor Rumpole is all about preparing us for the unexpected,"

Sun said. "She likes shaking things up. Sometimes I think maybe we get too comfortable in the roles we're used to, you know?"

"That's true," Velvet said. She could see that.

Sun smiled. "See? Everything's going to work out."

"Well, I still want to try to find Yatsu," Velvet said. "Sun, you do whatever you want. That's what you're good at."

"We all have our talents." Sun crossed his arms and leaned back in his seat. "I bet it's not going to be as easy as you think."

"I think you're right," Scarlet said, making his way through the crowd. "For a change."

"Have you been listening the whole time?" Sun asked.

"Yes." Scarlet put his hands on his hips. "I've been standing five feet away. Maybe I'm ready for a new team, too," he said pointedly.

"Great," Sun said, avoiding his gaze.

Velvet did her best to change the subject. "What's the usual initiation like at Shade?" she asked.

"From what I hear, they usually transport students in windowless airbuses to random spots in the desert and wait for them to come back," Scarlet said. "They're assigned to teams in the order they appear in, and the manner in which they survived."

Velvet groaned. She had disliked the whole initiation thing at Beacon, but she had been comforted that she only had to do it once—and it had worked out pretty well in the end. Now she had to start all over again from scratch, only this time it was going to be worse. And what if she ended up with someone from Team NDGO (indigo), who were among the Shade students most vocal in harassing recruits from Beacon and Haven?

"You've been in the desert before. You can handle that," Sun said.

"Assuming that they do the same thing they always do," Scarlet said. "But if Shade students have already done it once—"

A screen came to life at the front of the airbus, displaying Professor Rumpole's face.

"I'm sure you're wondering what your goal is in this exercise. The first order of business, as always, is survival. The second is to find your way to the airbus, which will take you back to Shade Academy. The third, and this is very important, is to locate and retrieve a golden trinket."

"A golden trinket?" Sun wondered out loud. "What's that supposed to mean?"

"I imagine you'll know it when you see it," Scarlet deadpanned. "Because it will be gold. And a trinket."

Professor Rumpole went on. "Hopefully, you all remembered to bring your weapons with you this morning."

Unlike at Beacon, Shade students didn't have weapon lockers. You were expected to have your weapons with you at all times. To be ready for anything.

Rumpole had more information for them. "For this exercise, all communications via Scroll will be blocked, not that communicating with one another would be much help to you, anyway. However, your Scroll will display coordinates for your airbus home once you retrieve the trinket."

At least this time we aren't being thrown into the air, like we were at Beacon, Velvet thought.

"Prepare for drop-off," Rumpole said. "And good luck. See you back home soon."

Machinery whirred and clicked in the airbus. The floor trembled, and Velvet looked down to see a line appearing in the center of the floor.

"Oh no," Velvet said.

Air whooshed through the cabin as the gap widened. The floor was retracting.

"You've got to be kidding," Sun said.

Panic ensued in the airbus. Some students edged away from the sliding floor, crowding on the sides of the ship. Others simply jumped out with either a grin or a shrug of resignation.

Scarlet saluted Sun and Velvet. "Good luck." Then he drew his sword and hopped through the crack in the floor, into the open air.

"He'll be fine," Sun said.

"I'm not worried about *him*." Velvet stood on the edge of the diminishing platform. The only thing directly below was sand, sand, and more sand. It looked soft, but the desert wasn't going to soften a fall from a few thousand feet. She'd have to figure out a way to slow her descent with one of the weapons in her camera.

"Here we go again," Velvet said. Sun stood across from her, ready to jump.

"On three?" Sun said. Velvet nodded.

"One . . . two . . . th—"

"Wait!" Velvet shouted. Sun leaned forward too far, windmilled his arms, and grabbed a handrail with his tail to stop himself from falling.

"What?" Sun asked.

Velvet turned to look for a locker on the airbus. It was in the back, close to where she had boarded. She hurried over as more of the floor disappeared and students either jumped or fell from the bottom of the vehicle.

The small chest was locked, but she broke the hinge with the edge of her camera box. She lifted the lid and grinned.

"Parachutes?" Sun asked, looking over Velvet's shoulder. "Isn't that cheating?"

Velvet pulled out two parachutes, leaving a couple behind. "The first and only rule is survival," she said. "But if you don't want one—"

Sun snatched the second backpack from her. "Good thinking, Velvet."

He and Velvet strapped on their backpacks.

"Stay close if you can," Sun said.

"You too," Velvet said. Being with Sun would be better than being alone.

They jumped.

The sky was filled with students, and Velvet couldn't help feeling a flash of anticipation. Then that flash reminded Velvet of Beacon Academy, and Ozpin, and Professor Goodwitch, and she felt a fresh pang of guilt and sadness for all they'd left behind. Then she kicked into action, because she was falling.

Velvet glanced at the ground to estimate the distance before she needed to pull the cord on her parachute. She quickly looked away—that was coming up fast. Way too fast.

The other two airbuses were miles apart from one another, so the three groups of students were clearly not going to the same place. Would this test just be a matter of surviving in the desert after all?

Around her and below, students were deploying their weapons or Semblances to arrest their falls in various ways, but there wasn't much else to work with in the open desert. Nearby, Sun's chute opened and he dropped away from her.

Velvet looked down. The ground was so close! She hastily pulled the cord and felt the backpack open, the chute unfurling behind her. Then a moment of fear just before the cloth caught the wind and she was yanked backward.

Velvet grabbed the cords dangling down to her shoulders from the chute's canopy. She tugged on the left one and the chute dipped and turned to the left slightly.

Now that she was falling more slowly—but still falling!—Velvet took better stock of her situation. On the horizon, she saw a massive cloud, likely a sandstorm. It was moving in their general direction, so it could become a problem if they weren't done with their mission quickly.

But that was a problem for later.

The desert wasn't quite as featureless as it had seemed from the airbus. To the northeast, students were falling toward what looked like an abandoned city, its buildings half covered with sand. Velvet was pretty sure that hadn't been there the last time she looked, or if it was it had been hidden completely under the sand. Vacuo's shifting sands often changed the landscape of the desert moment by moment.

Another group of students was heading down toward a rocky area less obscured by the sand but pockmarked with holes.

Velvet remembered a little from Rumpole's history class. These were all that was left of the underground mines, the Drylands, the site of the old Paradise Oasis, long since dried up following Dust mining and the Great War.

Velvet hoped Coco wasn't headed in that direction. Coco wasn't exactly good with dark, cramped spaces. No one was, really, Velvet supposed, but Coco had an intense phobia. Some people would consider that a sign of weakness, but Velvet always appreciated the reminder that CFVY's fearless leader wasn't quite as fearless as she let on. What made her a good leader was how she didn't let it get in her way—she led, anyway, and she had learned to rely on her team as much as they relied on her.

But Velvet soared past the Drylands, drifting toward a great chasm, what looked like a giant, angry scar in the earth. This, too, she remembered from her history notes. *It had to be one of the old Dust quarries*, she thought. The Dust companies had carved up the ground where they could, literally digging out Vacuo's riches, and then they used the areas to prep Dust for the refineries before hauling it off to their own kingdoms. The quarries were so deep, even the sands hadn't been able to fill them.

The quarries were physical manifestations of the wounds that still ran deep in the people of Vacuo, Velvet thought. And maybe that was why Rumpole was sending students there.

As she dropped closer and closer to the ground, Velvet steered toward the gash. She knew she was just imagining it, but she seemed to be falling faster as the surface approached, racing to meet her. She began kicking her feet and hit the sand at a run when she landed.

The chute pulled her to the left, toward the pit in the ground. She tried to unclip the chute from the pack, but the clasp was stuck, and there was too much tension to shrug out of the shoulder straps.

Not for the first time, she wished she carried a bladed weapon like Fox or Yatsuhashi. She had a solution for that, if she could call it up in her camera in time. She fumbled with Anesidora, the chute dragging her closer and closer to the quarry every second. What if she tumbled in?

And then the chute jerked up and away, and the sudden slack dumped Velvet on her backside. She blinked sand out of her eyes and sputtered, spitting the bitter grit from her mouth. A redheaded girl in a blue waistcoat, silver pauldrons, and an orange-and-cream skirt stood over her, whirling a wicked long dagger.

Great, Velvet thought. Octavia Ember, formerly of Team NDGO. One of the people she least wanted to run into.

"Thanks?" Velvet said.

"Whatever." Octavia sheathed her blade and started walking away.

That was more like it.

Velvet pulled herself up and trailed after her. "I'm lucky you happened to be nearby. With something sharp."

Octavia agreed. "Yes, you are."

"How did you get to me so fast?" Velvet asked.

"I'm good with sand."

Now Velvet remembered seeing Octavia's Semblance in action back in the Vytal Tournament, when Team NDGO had fought Team SSSN: She could skate over sand. With that kind of an advantage in a desert, it was no wonder she had decided to study at Shade Academy. She would also make a pretty good ally.

"So you're following me now?" Octavia said.

"I'm not following you. We're just heading to the same place." Velvet pointed to the chasm ahead. "That's the only thing around for miles, and I imagine we were dropped here to check it out. It would make more sense to hide the trinkets down there than in the open sands, if they're trying to be fair about it, anyway."

Octavia shrugged. "You can stick with me if you're afraid to be on your own out here. Just don't get in my way."

Velvet bristled. "I'm not *afraid.* But it's foolish for anyone to wander around alone in the desert if they don't have to. And don't forget—we're being graded on everything we do. Including how we treat each other." Octavia had to know something about being on a team, right?

Octavia paused. She looked back at Velvet and scrunched her nose. "Fine. Just try not to run when things get too tough."

Velvet closed her eyes and took several deep breaths, like Yatsu had taught her. She opened her eyes and smiled. "I'll try."

Together, they looked down into the rocky crevasse. Octavia sighed. "It's going to take forever to climb down there."

"Then we'd better get started." Velvet dropped over the edge and worked her way downward. She took a small measure of satisfaction in the fact that she was better at climbing than Octavia.

When they neared the bottom, there were smaller outcroppings that they used to jump down more quickly.

The floor of the chasm was covered in sand, with more sand drifting down the sides as the desert shifted hundreds of feet above, and wind blew it down over them like snow.

Snow was another thing Velvet missed from back home. One welcoming feature of the quarry, this artificial valley in the desert, was that the long shadows cast by the high walls kept the temperature cool. Velvet even saw green plants scattered amid the usual desert scrub. She was constantly in awe that anything could grow and flourish in Vacuo, whether wildlife or people.

She and Octavia moved along as quickly and carefully as they could, Octavia setting their pace.

“My clan sheltered in one of these quarries once during a sandstorm. That was a mistake.” Octavia paused for a long moment before she went on, her voice softer. “We stumbled across a nest of Blind Worms. There was nowhere to escape; the walls were too high. We lost a third of our family.”

“I’m sorry,” Velvet said. Team CFVY had tangled with just one Blind Worm recently, and they were all lucky to be alive.

Octavia drew in a breath and swiped at her face, though her eyes were dry. Velvet had learned that people rarely cried in Vacuo. Part of it was their stoic nature and broad acceptance of the hardships they had all faced, but part of it was the practicality of not wasting any precious water in the desert. They simply did not have the luxury of showing emotion.

“So I don’t want to spend any more time in here than we have to. And I'm sure some of the others are ahead of us," Octavia went on. Velvet took that to mean that she was slowing down her reluctant partner, but it was a good sign that Octavia wasn't choosing to leave her behind.

Octavia climbed onto a large piece of ancient machinery. The quarry was littered with broken rocks, fragments of abandoned equipment, and other detritus from the old Dust refining industry here. The other kingdoms had come into Vacuo, taken what they wanted, destroyed the land, and then left their trash behind on the way out. Velvet was ashamed of Vale for its role in all this—though it played a smaller role than Atlas and Mistral.

Right now she had a better understanding of the resentment that Octavia and the other Shade students were harboring against refugees from Beacon and Haven. Once again, people from other kingdoms were only coming to Vacuo because they wanted something from it. And many of the refugees hadn't stopped complaining about the hardships they faced here, or pining for their old schools. Even Velvet had been guilty of that, she realized. It had to be hard to believe they were fully committed to Shade when they had one foot in Vacuo and the other back home.

Octavia poked around the rusted and sand-pitted metal machine. It might have been a transport of some kind, once upon a time.

"Nothing here." She jumped down to rejoin Velvet. "The others probably grabbed all the trinkets already," Octavia said resentfully.

"They missed one," Velvet said, peering up at the branch of a scraggly acacia tree.

"Not too likely," Octavia said. She pushed forward and cut through long, dry grass with her dagger.

"No, I can see it: They missed one," Velvet insisted. She pointed to the top of the tree, where something glinted in the crook of a branch.

Octavia shielded her eyes and squinted. "Wow. How did you see that?" She almost sounded admiring.

Velvet blushed. "I have good eyesight."

She pushed away the memory of a childhood bully asking her if she had better eyes because she ate so many carrots. Comments like that had always hurt, although she did have sharper vision because she was Faunus. Even knowing that the skills others mocked made her more powerful couldn't take the sting off those hateful interactions. A Vacuan would just let it go and move on, but Velvet had to work to do that.

Oh. That gave her some perspective on the constant bullying from the Shade students, too. What if it was just another thing people were supposed to survive out here? Vacuo didn't care about your feelings, and most Vacuans didn't, either. They just said whatever came to mind, even if it was rude. Exhibit A: Fox.

That didn't excuse Vacuans' behavior, but it did take away some of the bite. If Velvet and the others from Vale and Mistral could weather it like any desert sun or storm, maybe they would be accepted here.

Octavia surveyed the trinket. "I'll get it," she said. "Be right back."

She quickly scrambled up the acacia tree. At the top, she grabbed the trinket and called out triumphantly, "Got it!"

Then she screamed and fell.

Velvet leaped into action, reaching the base of the tree just in time to catch Octavia.

"Thanks. Looks like we're even," Octavia said, a bit shaken.

"What happened?" Velvet asked.

Octavia pointed up. "Ravager."

Velvet looked up and saw a dark shape swooping down at them. Octavia dropped onto her feet and coasted away on the sand, Velvet running right behind her.

"I'm sorry I didn't see that," Velvet said.

"Not your fault," Octavia said. "I almost didn't see it myself until it tried to bite my head off."

"Watch out!" The bat-shaped shadow hovering over them loomed larger as the flying Grimm dove. Velvet and Octavia separated as it raked the ground between them with its long talons. Octavia swiped at it with her dagger and the Ravager screamed. It beat its massive, leathery wings and took off, kicking up a cloud of sand that momentarily blinded Velvet.

The Ravager's scream reverberated through the chasm. And as it faded, more shapes began peeling from the walls and hidden crevices—a whole swarm of Ravagers.

Octavia held up her Scroll. A light was blinking on it, just ahead. The airbus.

"You held on to the trinket?" Velvet asked.

Octavia held out her other hand and opened it. A small golden palm tree rested in it, shining in the light. "Let's get out of here."

"But I still need one!" Velvet said in a panic.

Octavia's voice was steady. "I would have missed this without you. Technically it's yours."

"Maybe we can share?" Velvet checked her Scroll. She was

relieved to see the airbus coordinates blinking on her display as well. Then the chasm suddenly grew dark.

Now the sky was blotted out by dozens of Ravagers above them. Velvet shrank away from them in fear, and even Octavia seemed a little less Vacuan for a second.

"Remember how I told you not to run when things get tough?" Octavia asked. "Forget it."

They ran. The Ravagers screeched. One dove and hovered in front of them, its wings beating the air, blocking their way to the airbus. Octavia drew her long dagger and Velvet pulled out her camera.

Octavia raised an eyebrow. "Really?"

Velvet smiled. Few at Shade had seen Velvet use Anesidora, both because hard-light Dust was extremely scarce these days with the Atlas embargo, and because Coco always liked to preserve the element of surprise. She called Velvet Team CFVY's secret weapon, which was actually true since everyone just thought Velvet liked taking pictures.

Some students in the know were also a little uncomfortable with the idea that she was copying their weapons and mimicking their moves with her photographic memory.

But right now Velvet had a better idea. She held up her camera and pressed the shutter button. The camera clicked and the bulb on top flashed, flooding the canyon ahead of them with stark white light.

The Ravager screeched and flapped away, lurching to the right, disoriented. It crashed into the side of the quarry and tumbled to the ground.

"Nice!" Octavia cheered.

The ground rumbled, and Velvet's heart raced at the sound as she remembered Octavia's clan and the Blind Worms. If she never had to face another one of those creatures again, it would be too soon.

Then a rock rolled down the side of the quarry wall, landing near a Ravager's head. Other stones followed, along with a cascade of sand. In spite of the avalanche, Velvet and Octavia kept moving, dodging Ravagers who'd recovered from the flash. Other Ravagers circled overhead, and the sound of crashing rocks and angry Grimm was deafening. It became difficult to see with the dust filling the narrow canyon, but Velvet squinted and took the lead.

A dark shape loomed ahead. Another Grimm? That was the last thing they needed.

Then bright floodlights turned on. It was the airbus!

"Thank the Brothers," Octavia muttered. "We don't have to climb out of here." Soon they clambered aboard and the ship started to lift off.

This part of the initiation had been brief but terrifying. Velvet wondered how the rest of her team—her old team—had fared. Then she stiffened with a new fear. "Wait!" Velvet said to the airbus pilot. "Did we get everyone?"

"You two are the last," the pilot said. "That guy made us wait."

Sun hurried over. "Are you hurt?" he asked Velvet.

She nodded, rubbing at her eyes, which were irritated from the sand and also brimming with tears.

"She's fine," Octavia told Sun. Velvet was grateful to her for doing the talking.

"You woke up the Ravagers." Sun shook his head. "And you lived to tell the tale." *Was that respect in his eyes?* Velvet wondered. She couldn't wait to tell Coco about it. What if Sun had passed by the trinket in the tree, knowing it would be too dangerous to retrieve it? She and Octavia had not had that luxury.

The airbus tilted to the right as a Ravager dove by it. Machine guns fired on the Grimm, keeping them at bay until the airbus got a safe distance away. Velvet watched as the shape of the quarry changed and expanded; the ground around it was collapsing, the sand swirling in fury.

Velvet sighed. The initiation ritual had been hard and almost deadly, and even worse was yet to come: the assignment of the new teams.

CHAPTER SEVEN

Scarlet was disappointed that there'd been no big celebration following reinitiation. Unlike Haven Academy, Shade wasn't much for parties.

Scarlet especially felt like celebrating his new team assignment: Team ROSC (rosy), joined by Reese Chloris, Olive Gashley, and Coco Adel. Of course he knew Reese from Haven—though the athletic, green-haired girl didn't strike him as a born leader. On the other hand, she wasn't Sun, so she was definitely an upgrade. He didn't know Olive, either, but having a wolf Faunus on your side couldn't be a bad thing. And then there was Coco. Scarlet used to think Team CFVY was overrated, but after seeing them in action, he had wondered what it would be like to be on Coco's team. And now he would get to find out.

Alas, it looked like the best Scarlet was going to get was a *pity* party: another meeting of the Beacon Brigade. He felt like he had to hide how happy he was about his new team because everyone else was depressed and angry. Worst of all, Velvet had dragged Sun back here for some reason, just when Scarlet was ready to get a little distance from him at last.

Scarlet was careful around Neptune and Sage. He didn't want them to think he was *too* thrilled about the reinitiation, because he genuinely liked them. He just wanted a fresh start, and they were never going to get that with Sun in charge.

Things had turned out well for Neptune, anyway. He had landed on Team BYRN (burn), with Bolin Hori, Yatsuhashi, and a Shade student named Rae Noire. He looked uncomfortable, though, sitting stiffly between Bolin and Yatsuhashi on the other side of the room. *Relax, guy*, Scarlet thought.

But poor Sage was still stuck with Sun, on Team SSEA, along with Electra Fury and Ariadne Guimet. And Sage had been designated team leader, too, which was proof of the utter randomness of the exercise. *Good luck with that*, Scarlet thought.

As far as Scarlet could tell, Sun didn't seem bothered in the slightest by not being the boss. He probably didn't care who was in charge because he wasn't going to listen, anyway. Which gave Scarlet hope that if Team SSSN were ever reinstated, Sun might just step aside. That hadn't been an option at Haven, but here at Shade, surely Headmaster Theodore wouldn't want anyone leading who didn't want to—or hadn't proven themselves to be the strongest choice for the team. Perhaps that was one reason for the shake-up. Now Theodore had rearranged things to make the teams, and the whole academy, stronger.

"Hi, everyone. I know today was a shock for all of us, but regardless of our assigned teams, we'll always have the Beacon Brigade," Velvet said to start off the meeting. Scarlet had never seen her so down before. She always at least tried to put on a bright face, but now it was like her light had gone out. Probably because she was on Team NOVA, with two of Shade's loudest critics of Beacon students: Nebula Violette and Octavia Ember. At least the group was rounded out with Arslan Altan, recently of Team ABRN. Arslan had always been a better leader than her team deserved, Scarlet thought, so maybe this would be a good change for her, too.

"Here we go again with the Beacon Brigade stuff," Sun muttered.

"Excuse me?" Velvet frowned. "I thought you came back here to apologize."

Scarlet laughed. How could she even believe that? "Sun's pretty bad at apologies."

"I can apologize!" Sun's tail swept back and forth.

"Go on, then," Scarlet said, prompting him.

Sun put his hands into his pockets and looked down. "I'm sorry I said all those mean things and stormed out of here last time," he said quickly.

"Thank you—" Velvet began.

Sun lifted his head. "But I was only trying to help you understand how elitist this group looks to everyone else."

Scarlet rolled his eyes. He leaned back to watch the show.

"I'm just saying," Sun said. "*Beacon* Brigade. It's right there in the name. You're telling everyone that you don't belong at Shade. That your heart's always gonna be back there."

Velvet shook her head.

"That's why this whole reinitiation thing is a good idea," Sun continued. "Theo wants to integrate us into Shade, and to do that, you have to start over. I say give it a chance. You have to leave the past behind in order to move on."

The gall of it. It was so obvious what Sun was doing—he was practically gleeful to be rid of his teammates. Scarlet had promised himself he wouldn't rise to the occasion, but he suddenly found that he couldn't just sit there, silent. "I guess it's not hard to move on when you're always moving, huh?" He sat up straight and looked at Sun. "Just how ecstatic are you to be moving on from us? Be honest. While we're at it, maybe you can explain why."

Sun was taken aback. "What?"

"Well, you were always leaving *us* and going solo. We were never sure why," Scarlet said. They might not be on the same team now, but his questions hadn't gone away.

Sage still had questions, too. "Were we not good enough for you?" he asked.

Sun looked back and forth between them, suddenly deflated. "No! I never wanted you to think that." He glanced at Neptune. "I didn't know you thought that."

How could he not *know?* Scarlet wondered. "Our team is—was—Team SSSN. *Sun.* It's practically named after you! But most of the time, you weren't part of it," he said.

"It's just a name—" Sun began.

"Names are important," Velvet jumped in. "They're part of our identity. That's why it's upsetting when our names—when pieces of our identities—are taken away from us. Without asking us, without warning. Think about what happens when you lose *a part of yourself.*"

Scarlet's glance fell on Nolan. One of the undeniable benefits of the reinitiation was that Nolan had a team again: Team FNDU (fondue), with Fox, Dew Gayle, and Umber Gorgoneion. Already the pretty boy looked a little perkier than the last time Scarlet had seen him.

"Sun, *Beacon* is like our clan name," Fox said. Sun turned to look at him. When Fox spoke, you couldn't help but pay attention, even if half the time his rare pronouncements were just sarcasm.

"It was Fox's idea. We're part of Vacuo now, and to belong, we decided to take a name," Yatsuhashi explained further. "Beacon was the obvious choice."

"We know we might not ever retake our old school. I know I'd like to . . ." Velvet looked around. "Of course we'd like to go back there one day. But that's not what the 'Beacon Brigade' is about."

"It's not?" Sun asked.

"Beacon is a symbol," Coco said. "It represents our common bond—because it's the thing that brought us here. All of us, whether you're from Vale, Mistral, or Vacuo."

"Oh," Sun said again.

"Remembering Beacon motivates us," Reese said. "To prepare ourselves for next time."

Nolan nodded. "I'm not going to run away ever again. I'm running *toward* the fight—wherever and whatever it is. It's the least I can do for my team. That's what Beacon is to me. It's the light that's leading me to where I'm supposed to be, where I'm needed most."

Now Scarlet could see Nolan's silence as determination. Confidence looked good on him. Nolan wasn't struggling to mourn for his fallen friends after all—he was holding on to that grief. He was using it to drive him. Scarlet had been underestimating Nolan all this time. Just like Sun had been underestimating the rest of them. But would Sun ever see that?

"Well, you've been sending a mixed message with this group, at least to Vacuans," Sun said stubbornly. "It seems like you're just using Shade Academy to get strong enough to go back and save your real home. But when you put it that way . . . I guess it makes sense."

Sun's tail wrapped around his waist as he considered this. Scarlet hoped he wouldn't hurt himself thinking too hard.

"Whether we go back to recover Beacon Academy one day or need to defend Shade from the same enemy, we're training together to be ready—for anyone and anything that poses a threat," Coco said.

"*Maybe* I was wrong," Sun said. Scarlet was almost as stunned to hear him admit that as Sun sounded saying it. "But it just goes to show, your average Vacuan is going to assume the worst about outsiders. I thought you were setting yourselves apart from us instead of seeing that you were trying to be *more* Vacuan." He pursed his lips. "The trick is getting everyone else to see it that way, too."

"Sometimes talking helps," Velvet said softly. "To help everyone understand other people's perspectives. That's why we're here."

Sun shrugged, but he sat down next to Scarlet. It looked like he was planning to stay after all—for now. Maybe they were finally getting through to him.

"Talking does help," Scarlet said. "If you're ready to listen."

"I'm more a man of action," Sun said. "Actions speak louder than words."

Scarlet shook his head. "There's a time and a place for everything."

"Actions speak louder than words," Headmaster Theodore said as he addressed Team SSSN for the first time.

"I completely agree, sir," Sun said. Professor Rumpole put a finger over her lips, but Sun didn't seem to notice. He was as cocky as ever.

"What brings you to Shade Academy?" Theodore asked.

"I grew up here," Sun said.

This couldn't have been news to the headmaster, but he looked surprised. "Oh? But you decided to attend Mistral Academy?" He exchanged a look with Professor Rumpole. Then he looked sternly at Scarlet, Sage, and Neptune.

This is going well, *Scarlet thought.* Maybe we can still catch the same train on the way back to Argus.

"I wanted to see more of the world before settling down," Sun said. He hadn't even noticed anything was wrong.

Sage snickered. Rumpole's eyes flashed gold.

"So you think of Vacuo as 'settling'?" Theodore asked.

Sun scratched the back of his head with the tip of his tail. "Yes?"

Scarlet shook his head.

"I mean, no!" Sun jumped up. Then he sat down again. "I mean, I didn't know what I wanted. But absence makes the heart grow fonder, right? I missed this place."

Theodore tapped his gloved hands together thoughtfully. "Now, obviously, I don't have a copy of your transcript, given Professor Lionheart's tragic but heroic death." Theodore glanced at the pictures on his wall, and Scarlet saw his old headmaster smiling up there. "But I've done some digging, and I heard that you were not actually at Haven Academy last semester, Sun Wukong."

That's that, *Scarlet thought.* Even if he doesn't want Sun, maybe he'll still take the rest of us.

"Yes, Theo. Can I call you Theo?"

"No!" barked Theodore and Rumpole at the same time.

"Right. Sorry. Professor—"

"Headmaster."

"Headmaster Theo . . . dore. I was on special assignment in Menagerie."

"Special assignment? Given by whom?" Rumpole asked.

"By himself," Scarlet muttered.

Theodore looked them over. "Hmmm," he said. "And which of you is the leader again? I know it's not Neptune, but you can tell that just by looking at him."

Neptune's jaw dropped.

"It's Sun, Scarlet, Sage . . . One of you, yes?"

"I am," Sun said, raising his hand. "It's me."

Theodore regarded Sun thoughtfully, as though he'd already known that too. "Really?"

Sun nodded.

Rumpole was momentarily speechless.

I knew that it wasn't just us, *Scarlet thought.* If actions matter to Theodore, maybe someone will finally tell Sun that his behavior isn't acceptable for a leader.

"Well, see—" Sun began.

Theodore held up a hand. "No explanation requested or needed."

Rumpole leaned over and whispered something to the headmaster. He listened attentively while continuing to look the boys over. He didn't seem impressed by what he saw.

Finally he spoke to them again. "Well, frankly, I think Team SSSN would have done better waiting for Haven to reopen," Theodore said. "However, since you've already come all this way, and in consideration of your timely assistance to Team CFVY and the Schist refugees, we can offer you provisional enrollment at Shade Academy."

"Provisional?" Neptune asked.

"Until you wash out, or he changes his mind," Rumpole explained. "Frankly, that happens a lot."

"Which?" Neptune asked timidly.

"Rumpole," said Theodore, indicating she should explain.

She smiled. "The headmaster has a quick mind, accustomed to adapting to new information as it presents itself. And there is information he currently needs from you . . . which brings me to one of our provisions: You will provide us at your earliest convenience with a detailed written report of everything that happened on Menagerie and Haven Academy when the White Fang attacked. Leave nothing out: who was there, what happened, when."

"Written?" Sun said, swallowing hard.

Theodore raised his eyebrows. "You do *know how to write?"*

"I'm more a man of action," Sun said.

Rumpole rolled her eyes.

"Don't worry, sir," Scarlet said. "We'll help him with the big words. That's what teammates are for."

Professor Rowena Sunnybrook's Weapons Training class was definitely a time and a place for action. This morning was the first time all the new teams were gathered together, and there was a fair bit of uncertainty about where everyone should stand and apprehension about how they were going to work together. For his part, Scarlet was excited to stand with Team ROSC and eager to see what they could do.

"Good morning, students," said Professor Sunnybrook. She

walked around a small arena, which was basically a big sandpit. That had always seemed odd to Scarlet. If you wanted to fight in sand, why not just go outside? There was plenty of sand in this place. And why would anyone want to fight in sand if they didn't have to?

The usually cheerful and energetic teacher had an inscrutable expression today. She looked uncomfortable, clutching her long, dark braid in both hands. "I'm sure you can use a break after yesterday's initiation, but you won't often get one in real combat conditions."

Scarlet definitely could have used some rest. Spending hours in an underground Dust mine fighting a herd of Jackalopes wasn't exactly a fun time, nor was staying up so late to clean his clothes and shine his shoes.

"One of the greatest survival skills you can acquire is the ability to push through any difficulty or disadvantage," Sunnybrook went on. She tied that in to their location in Vacuo, which presented plenty of difficulties and disadvantages, which they should consider personal challenges . . .

Scarlet was surprised she was talking so much. Usually by now they'd be sparring with their classmates and running drills.

Then Professor Rumpole stomped into the classroom. "You started without me," she said.

Sunnybrook's eyebrows shot up. "You're late, and this is my class."

Ooh, Scarlet thought. *Sunnybrook just went from chatty to catty.*

Rumpole crossed the arena and said, "I'll take it from here, Rowena."

Sunnybrook shook her head, but she stepped aside and swept a hand out to cede the floor.

"You all performed very well in yesterday's reinitiation." Professor Rumpole slowly turned in place to address the ring of students. "I know it was an unsettling exercise, but our responsibility as your teachers is to prepare you for anything that might come your way. Before you got here, some of you were trained to rely on your teams. But what do you do when your team is gone and you're on your own?"

Scarlet glimpsed a shadow passing over Nolan's face; her remark had landed a little too close to home. Nolan took a deep breath and seemed to steady himself.

"Similarly, many of you are quite skilled fighters, adept with your weapons and your Semblances," Rumpole went on. "But you can't always rely on *them*, either. What are you without your weapon? Today we're going to find out."

The room filled with whispers. Fight without weapons? In *Weapons* Training? Is she kidding?

"Great. What next?" Coco muttered to Scarlet.

Rumpole's announcement took some of the wind out of Scarlet's sails, too. Like most students, his weapons complemented his Semblance and fighting style. Huntsmen trained with their weapons until they were practically extensions of their own bodies, wielding them as effortlessly as breathing.

But Rumpole insisted, "Each of you must become adept at handling yourself with any weapon you can get, or even without a weapon. Without Dust, for that matter. Real combat usually doesn't go according to plan, and it's essential that you push outside of your comfort zone." She waited till everyone had settled down, then said, "So . . . let's begin. When I call your name, put down your weapon and enter the arena. A random weapon will be provided for each of you."

She looked around the room expectantly. Several students looked away as her gaze passed over them. But some students—mostly the native Vacuan students—raised their hands. Scarlet raised his hand, too. Hey, he was always up for a challenge.

Professor Rumpole called out, "Nebula Violette!"

Nebula lowered her hand and stepped forward. The short-haired girl dropped her crossbow at Rumpole's feet. Scarlet had tangled with Nebula in the Vytal Tournament. She was a decent shot with her bow, and skilled at close combat when she converted her weapon into a sword. No match for him and Darling, of course, but he'd be interested in seeing what she could do unarmed.

Professor Rumpole looked around once more, really drawing out the moment. She smiled, then said, "Velvet Scarlatina."

Velvet's face paled.

"Oh, come on!" Coco said, intervening for her former teammate.

Professor Rumpole swiveled to glare at Coco, her eyes flashing. Scarlet heard Coco gasp and realized something: Maybe his new teammate wasn't as unshakable as she usually let on.

Yatsuhashi tried to step in front of Velvet, but she pushed him back firmly. "It's okay," she said. She removed her camera and handed it to him. "Hold on to this for me."

Nebula laughed. "Hardly much of a disadvantage. What good's a camera in a fight, anyway?"

A few students clapped—Shade students, of course—and only stopped when Rumpole spoke, a hard edge in her voice. "Save it for the arena."

Yatsuhashi put a hand on Velvet's shoulder, and she nodded. Then she walked out to meet Nebula in the arena.

"This is so not cool," Scarlet whispered to Coco. Velvet and Nebula were both on the same team. They shouldn't be forced to fight each other. Sure, Coco sparred with her teammates on occasion, but never with the intent of beating them, especially in front of an audience.

"No, it isn't," Coco said. "Nebula is supposed to be Velvet's new team leader! Rumpole can't think this is going to help them build trust. I can't guess what she's up to here."

"Can Velvet take her?" Scarlet asked. Coco would know, better than anyone, what Velvet was capable of.

Coco lowered her glasses and studied the two girls as they approached each other in the arena. "They're about the same size, evenly matched in strength. Nebula's better at hand-to-hand combat, but Velvet is faster and more versatile. She's got a fair shot at this, I think."

Just then, Velvet reached the center of the arena and smiled at her opponent. Scarlet had to hand it to her—she looked strong.

"I must object," Arslan called to Rumpole, who was watching on the sidelines next to Professor Sunnybrook. "They should not fight each other. We're teammates, and we have to learn to work together. This just undermines that goal."

"Good for you, Arslan," Coco whispered.

Now there's *a leader for you*, Scarlet thought.

"That doesn't matter," Professor Rumpole said haughtily. "In the heat of battle, a weak teammate can be worse than the most powerful enemy."

"That's *really* not helpful," Arslan said.

"Rumpole." Professor Sunnybrook put a hand on Rumpole's arm and was surprised to be shaken off.

"Have some faith," Rumpole said.

Arslan looked at Velvet and Nebula and shook her head. She stepped back to stand next to Octavia.

A pedestal rose out of the center of the arena between Velvet and Nebula. Sand cascaded off it, revealing a spear and a heavy club.

"You can pick first," Nebula said.

"Thank you." Velvet carefully considered each weapon before finally selecting the spear. The club looked too heavy for her to carry for long, and the spear was better suited to her speed. Nebula lifted the club and grinned.

"Fight!" Professor Rumpole commanded.

Nebula tossed the club back and forth from one hand to the other, while Velvet tested the weight of her spear and the flex in its shaft.

"Fight!" Rumpole barked.

Nebula lifted the club and rushed toward Velvet. Velvet stepped out of the way easily as Nebula smashed the club down where she'd been standing, sending out a geyser of sand. Velvet planted the tip of the spear into the ground and held on tight, staying on her feet as the force from the blow blasted sand around her.

Then she vaulted up and kicked out, until Nebula knocked her back with the club.

"Is that the best you've got?" Nebula said.

"You'll see!" Velvet ducked as the club swung past her head, clipping the tops of her ears. She winced and tossed her spear into the air, then tucked into a roll toward Nebula. She sprang off her hands and leaped backward, feetfirst, toward the armored girl. Nebula held up her club, and Velvet landed on it, then catapulted from it into the air.

She caught her spear on its way down and aimed the tip at Nebula. Nebula tossed aside her club and planted her right foot behind her. She reached up and grabbed the point of the spear, then pulled it to her right, spinning it and Velvet around 180 degrees before letting go. Velvet was hurled backward.

She twisted in the air and jammed the spear into the ground, dragging a long line in the sand and slowing her momentum—until the tension in the weapon snapped it in half, and she tumbled backward.

Velvet righted herself and looked up to see Nebula running toward her at high speed. Velvet raced toward her, too, scooping up the halves of the spear and holding each section in a fist. Nebula came at her with fists flying, and Velvet parried her blows with the broken weapon.

"I've been wanting to do this for a while," Nebula said between hits. "This is fun."

"Velvet's pretty good," Scarlet commented under his breath. He'd seen her fight at the Battle of Beacon, so he knew she could copy the fighting styles of the owner for each hard-light weapon she used. But he didn't know that her Semblance allowed her to call on those combat techniques at any time. Right now, she was drawing on moves he recognized from other students, like Pyrrha Nikos,

Yang Xiao Long, and even Sun. The moves may not have been original, but Nebula was disoriented by the way Velvet seamlessly moved from one fighting style to the next.

"She's been practicing," Coco replied. "Most Huntsmen reveal their training in the way they handle themselves in battle, but she can fuse multiple disciplines into a brand-new technique—different each time. Velvet may fight like a lot of different people, but no one else fights like Velvet."

Velvet and Nebula continued to trade rapid-fire blows.

"Feel free to quit anytime," Nebula taunted.

"I'm tired of you all thinking you're better than us," Velvet said between gritted teeth. "While I was defending Beacon, where were you? Oh, that's right. On the first transport to Vacuo." She swept the broken staff toward Nebula's head, then jabbed at her with the tip. Nebula spun away gracefully and turned the dodge into a roundhouse kick to Velvet's back, knocking her forward.

"Velvet still gets a point on that one for her snappy comeback," Scarlet whispered to Coco, and his new teammate nodded.

Nebula wasn't letting Velvet off the hook. "But I *am* better than you," she said. "We left Beacon because we knew it was a lost cause. Just like you."

Velvet knelt, gasping to catch her breath. Nebula brought her right leg high and then kicked downward. Velvet thrust the two pieces of her spear upward and crossed them, catching Nebula's leg. The force of the blow pushed her into the sand.

Nebula launched herself upward with her pinned leg to free herself. Velvet dropped the broken staff and tried to pull herself out of the sand, but she was stuck.

Nebula landed behind Velvet. She walked calmly around her and picked up the pieces of her spear.

"We're done here," Nebula said. "You should go back to Vale."

Velvet kept scrambling in the sand, but she couldn't dig herself out. Finally her shoulders slumped and she stopped moving.

But Rumpole said, "Keep fighting."

"What?" Coco called out.

"I beat her!" Nebula reached a hand down to help Velvet up.

Rumpole stalked out to the arena. "No, she beat herself," she said. "You don't stop fighting until you can't fight anymore."

"Look at her," said Coco, hurrying out to the arena. "Velvet can't even get up. And you expect her to keep fighting?"

Rumpole consulted her Scroll. "She has Aura enough to continue."

A moment later Yatsuhashi, Fox, and Arslan followed Coco. Yatsuhashi reached down, grabbed Velvet's shoulders gently, and slowly lifted her from the sand. As soon as she was back on her feet, she pushed his hands away.

"What do you think you're doing?" Rumpole asked Coco.

"I could ask you the same thing," Coco said.

"Velvet isn't your teammate anymore. You aren't responsible for her."

"Everyone, stop. I'm not hurt." Velvet brushed sand off her clothes.

"Ms. Adel," Rumpole said. "Please remember that you are now a part of Team ROSC. Ms. Scarlatina is on Team NOVA."

Arslan folded her arms and looked at Rumpole. "I am here to stand with my new teammate."

"Hey, me too." Octavia stepped up beside her. "Velvet did great, but the fight's over."

"Regardless of what team we're on," Coco said, "we'll always have each other's backs."

"And how did that serve you at Beacon when the worst happened—a situation Professor Ozpin never prepared you for?" Rumpole asked.

Scarlet winced. *Cheap shot.*

The comment sucked the air out of the room. Everyone fell quiet.

"No one could have predicted that," Velvet said.

"Exactly, Ms. Scarlatina. But we no longer have that excuse. We know a threat is out there. We know it's coming to Vacuo. To not prepare for that eventuality would be irresponsible, dangerous, and naïve."

Rumpole began walking toward the exit. "Please also remember your place at Shade Academy. Regardless of your accomplishments and the fame of 'Team CFVY,' you are the students, and we are the teachers. As far as I'm concerned, that's as good a reason as any to wipe the slate clean. Put everyone back on the same footing."

Rumpole glanced over her shoulder. "Perhaps Ms. Scarlatina will learn something with the fresh perspective of her new teammates."

When she reached the doorway, she turned and paused. "Your new teams will receive their first missions tomorrow morning. Class dismissed."

Professor Sunnybrook shrugged as if to admit she'd lost control today. "Class dismissed."

Velvet followed Nebula out of the ring, pausing as she passed Coco. "Thanks for that. But you shouldn't have."

"We'll get through this," Coco said.

"I know we will." Velvet gave her a sad smile and left with her new team.

Scarlet exchanged looks with Neptune and Sage before they left with Teams BYRN and SSEA. They didn't need Fox's team-speak to know they shared the same thought: *What is going on?*

Soon Scarlet's new team—himself and Coco, plus Reese and Olive—was the only one left in the classroom with Professor Sunnybrook, and even the teacher looked a bit shell-shocked.

"Does Professor Rumpole seem all right to you?" Coco dared to ask.

Professor Sunnybrook shook her head. "She's always been hard on the students. Maybe too hard sometimes . . ."

"That's fine. But she's never been *mean* before, right?" Coco pressed.

"She has the best of intentions. I don't think anyone cares more about the students and this academy than Rumpole and Headmaster Theodore."

Scarlet had to argue with that. "Maybe I imagined it, but it looked like she was picking on Velvet," he said.

Coco nodded. "I always thought she liked Team CFVY."

Sunnybrook was full of excuses. "She's on edge. We all are. We all have bad days."

But Scarlet knew the real answer. As long as they were here, every day was going to be a bad day in Vacuo.

CHAPTER EIGHT

Velvet crouched in front of the disabled CCT relay tower, blinking stinging sweat out of her eyes. A drop of sweat splashed on the Scroll in her hand, which showed the tower's schematics, and she wiped it away with the cuff of her sleeve. Then she picked up a spanner and ran it across the complex circuitry, patching together the wires that spilled from the open panel in front of her.

This wasn't her Scroll and these weren't her tools. They belonged to the communications technician whom Team NOVA had been escorting through the Grimm-infested mountains just outside of Oscuro Combat School.

It should have been a simple job, but nothing was ever truly easy in Vacuo. The technician had been knocked unconscious in a skirmish with a band of Dromedons. One of the vicious Grimm had spat acid on his leg, so he needed some serious medical attention, which Velvet's friend Gus Caspian was administering the best he could.

Gus was a student at Oscuro, which had sent along some of their trainees to "help" the Shade Academy Huntsmen—a chance to see them in action and get some hands-on experience. Velvet thought it was a little too soon to be sending Gus into the field, even on what was supposed to be a straightforward escort mission, but apparently Oscuro teachers didn't coddle students any more than Theodore did.

Then again, Gus already looked older than he had only a few months ago. Or maybe it was his Oscuro uniform—Velvet had to admit the thin, light vest over an athletic shirt and spandex leggings did complement his features.

In fact, the more she saw of the kids' uniforms—designed to keep students cool and dry on the hottest, sweatiest days—the more she disliked her own outfit, which tended to collect sweat in all the most uncomfortable places. The Beacon students had been slow to adopt more practical clothes now that they were in Vacuo, but Coco had been messing around with new outfit designs for Team CFVY. Of course now there were more important things to worry about. And there was no more Team CFVY.

Velvet's ears swiveled around, listening for danger, making sure Gus and the technician were safe. And listening to the sounds of the fight raging nearby. For her second mission since the new teams were assigned, Velvet was on the sidelines. She wondered briefly if her humiliating fight with Nebula had permanently ruined any chance she had of fighting alongside her new team. Though it wasn't like she didn't have an important task of her own, one that none of her teammates had the expertise to perform. The sooner she repaired the relay, the sooner she could rejoin Team NOVA. Her team.

"Why don't we just retreat, come back later?" Gus finished washing the technician's wound and reached for an analgesic gel.

Velvet prodded at a capacitor with a multimeter and checked the readout. It was dead. Though she could have guessed that considering the scorch marks around the small component.

"Retreating from Grimm isn't an option when you're fighting this close to a settlement," Velvet said. "If we leave without destroying them, the Grimm will just look for another target."

"My school," Gus realized.

"And when a group shows up with wounded and mentions Grimm are nearby, that tends to get people panicked. Which draws the Grimm to them more quickly. You know how it is."

"All too well," Gus said. Velvet and her team—Team CFVY, that is—had met Gus and his grandfather Edward on a mission for Shade Academy three months ago. That's when they had learned about the Crown. Two of their cronies, Carmine and Bertilak, had tried to kidnap Gus for their boss because of his Semblance: the power to enhance people's emotions. Only Gus thought of his ability as more of a curse, since his own internal fear of his Semblance caused him to augment negative emotions more than positive ones.

He'd been learning to control his ability at Oscuro, but he still didn't know if he wanted to be a Huntsman—which was why he was hanging out with Velvet, tending to the technician's injuries, while she tended to the broken CCT relay.

She clipped out the bad capacitor and soldered in a replacement. Then she began vacuuming out all the sand that had accumulated inside the console, since the number-one cause of machine failure in Vacuo was sand. It had a tendency to work its way into almost anything, even through the most expensive Scroll protective cases. Fortunately, Velvet was handy with electronics—Anesidora was incredibly complicated, and she'd designed it herself. In retrospect, they probably should have left the technician at Oscuro—she could have done this on her own.

"I'm glad you're here," Gus told her. "I was actually going to call you myself, but then the relay went down." He started wrapping a bandage around the technician's calf.

"You were? What's going on?" Velvet asked. "Is it Edward?" Her eyes fell on the disc-blade hanging from Gus's belt—his grandfather's weapon from his Huntsman days.

The boy shook his head. "No, no—he's fine. The meditation exercises Yatsuhashi taught him seem to be helping his memory."

Velvet nodded. She had a suspicion it was more than just the mediation exercises that were helping Edward. No one knew for sure what Yatsuhashi had done with his Semblance when he'd tried to heal Edward's mind . . . even Yatsuhashi wasn't sure. His ability was to *erase* memories, but it was possible that there was more to Yatsu's Semblance than that. It was something Glynda had emphasized in their second-year classes at Beacon: Semblances can grow as people do. It was reasonable to assume that he might have been able to nudge Edward's mind enough to give him better recall and help reverse his degenerative mental disease. But Yatsu had always focused more on controlling his power than testing its limits and seeing what else he could do. He hated messing with people's minds.

"I wanted to tell you that two of my classmates disappeared a few days ago," Gus said.

"You think they were kidnapped?" Velvet said.

"They had strong Semblances, and I don't think they would drop out. They're really committed to becoming Huntsmen."

"Were they reported missing?" Velvet asked.

"The teachers told the authorities, and the headmistress called Shade. But when we didn't hear anything, I figured I should call you. I knew you would want to know."

"Do you have any idea where they disappeared from?" Velvet asked.

Gus nodded. "The last place they were seen was some new club called the Mirage." He held up his Scroll, which displayed an ad promising one-on-one arena fights for a championship title, in the style of the Vytal Tournament. A three-pointed silver crown was tilted on the "C" of "Championship." Velvet fixated on that image as Gus kept talking.

"Supposedly they fought in a couple of matches." Gus shook his head. "It wasn't until the next morning that anyone noticed they hadn't come back."

"Where did that ad come from?" Velvet asked.

Gus shrugged. "It only went out to select students. The top of our class. But of course it got around." Gus took a deep breath. "A group of my classmates went, but I've been too afraid to leave campus since Carmine and Bertilak got away."

"I know it's hard," Velvet said. "But you're at Oscuro to get stronger. Someday soon, people like them will be afraid of *you*." She gave him a light punch on the shoulder. "Besides, we've got this. We know who they're working for, and I think that club has something to do with it. Send that ad to me?"

"Sure." Gus looked at his phone. "Still no signal, though."

"One second." Velvet went back to the open panel and checked the connections against the readout on her Scroll. Everything looked good. She plugged in the Scroll and activated the startup sequence.

Lights started blinking inside the panel and machinery hummed to life. But the screen of the Scroll flashed between green and red.

Velvet double-checked everything. She didn't know what was wrong. She glanced back at the technician, Gus still at his side. The guy was out cold. He'd taken a pretty hard knock to the head.

Well, she had tried. Velvet unplugged the Scroll and closed the panel. She noticed now that it had taken a beating itself. The metal was shiny from being sandblasted regularly, but the center of the panel was also dented in places. What could have done that? Had something tried to break into the relay?

Velvet stood and stared at the panel for a long moment. Finally, she shrugged and kicked it with her boot.

The screen of the technician's Scroll turned green and began connecting to the CCT network. Finally it broke through, but Velvet knew the signal was only strong enough to cover local communications in Vacuo. Ever since Beacon Tower had been damaged, global CCT operations had been interrupted.

Velvet's phone rang: a call from Octavia.

Octavia was a wreck. Her hair was plastered to her face and neck with sweat and her clothes were caked in sand. She had dirty smudges under her eyes.

"Velvet! Did the tech wake up?" Octavia said.

"No, I fixed the issue myself," Velvet said. She didn't want to brag, but she wanted someone to know what she'd done.

"Oh. Really?" Octavia said, impressed. "We took care of the Grimm and we're on our way back."

"How are the kids?" Velvet asked.

"They're fine." Octavia lowered her voice. "A little freaked, but they got a good lesson in how to take down Grimm."

Arslan's face joined the call. "Yeah, because Octavia used them as *bait* for the Grimm."

"What?!" Velvet said.

"That's right. And it worked. It's called *strategy*," Octavia retorted.

Velvet could think of some other words for it.

"And they're all safe and sound," Octavia went on.

"Mostly," Arslan said.

"Octavia, you can't do that sort of thing," Velvet said. Someone had to tell her.

Octavia huffed. "They'll be *fine*. Just invite them to your Baby Brigade and you can all cry about it!" With that, she signed off.

Velvet sighed.

"Just ignore her. She'll come around," said Arslan, who was still on-screen.

"I should have been there," Velvet said. If only to try to talk some sense into Octavia. They wouldn't have had to put innocent kids at risk if Velvet had been fighting alongside them.

Of course, the problem was that Octavia wouldn't have listened to her. She didn't want Velvet on the battlefield with her. Velvet had largely held her own against Nebula in their fight, but that didn't matter. All everyone remembered was that she had lost. That Coco and the others had tried to protect her—again.

"We could have used you out here, but you're the only one who could have gotten that relay back up. We all have to play to our strengths—and you happen to have one in technology." Arslan turned away from the screen. "I must go. Truly, great work today. See you soon."

Velvet smiled. She felt at least a little better. "See you. And thanks."

She was frustrated with Octavia, but she knew Octavia had another side—she'd seen it in the reinitiation. And everyone was safe after the mission, which was no small thing. Maybe Velvet had been underestimating her team as much as she'd thought they were underestimating her. Maybe, with time, this could work out after all.

If they had time.

CHAPTER NINE

Sun's mind wandered while Neptune talked to their tenth person of the day. After four hours of visiting people who had posted missing posters on the Weeping Wall, Sun was looking forward to a nice dinner at Bug Burger before continuing their nightly rounds.

Neptune elbowed him and Sun's attention snapped back to the middle-aged man who was speaking. It took Sun a moment to remember his name: Finn Asturias.

"You boys are from Shade?" Finn asked.

"Yeah," Neptune began, "but originally we're—"

"That's right." Sun cut off Neptune. The only reason this man had let them into his home was because Sun was from Vacuo. Telling him they were recently from Haven—implying that Shade was their last choice for training—would end this conversation quickly. *Which might not be so bad, come to think of it,* Sun thought.

Sometimes he wanted to shake these people and ask them why they weren't out there looking for their loved ones instead of just putting their pictures on the Weeping Wall. Vacuans generally weren't the type to wait around and hope for the best—except, it seemed, where their missing kids were concerned. That was a luxury you would only find in the city of Vacuo, where people felt safe due to the presence of Huntsmen and Shade Academy. Clans in the desert were used to fending for themselves more aggressively.

"Did you know there used to be a magnificent palace where Shade is now?" Finn said.

Sun shook his head, eyes wide with feigned interest.

"My children used to be students at Shade, like you." Finn frowned. "But Shade wasn't right for them. They disappeared shortly after they left the academy."

"They went to Shade?" Neptune leaned forward and lowered his voice. "I bet they have powerful Semblances."

"Not Jax. He's never had much Aura. But his sister . . ." Finn shrugged. "Gillian's the one who wanted to become a Huntress. He just followed her. He went wherever she did."

"So they're close," Neptune said.

"I'll say. They're twins."

"Are you getting all this?" Neptune asked Sun.

Sun pulled out his Scroll and attached a note to the photo of the missing poster that had led them here:

Finn Asturias—boring, lonely

Missing twins, Jax + ?

Shade students, left the school (wow)

Semblances???

I want a double bug burger like right now

"I'm sorry, would you mind taking that thing outside?" Finn asked.

"Huh?" Sun held up his Scroll. "This?"

"I don't allow Atlesian tech in my house."

Sun looked around and realized that there was nothing electronic in the house at all. No TV, no phone, no Dust-powered lighting. Just a whole lot of old, thick books. That was so weird he was surprised he'd missed it before now.

"Sorry." Sun started to slip his Scroll back into its pouch. Then he realized that getting some fresh air sounded great right now. He stood up. "I will take this outside." He held up his Scroll and hurried out of the house, ignoring Neptune's look of dismay.

Sun closed the door behind him and leaned against it, glad to be out of there. It was dusk, and the evening crowds were coming out, heading to the downtown clubs and restaurants. More than anything, he wanted to join them.

His stomach grumbled and he pressed a hand against it. He hoped Neptune wouldn't take too much longer to wrap things up and follow him out.

Sun forgot about all that for a moment when Velvet walked past, head down as she studied her Scroll. He ran after her and tapped her shoulder. "Hey—"

The next thing he knew, he was on his back, looking up at

Velvet while she looked down at him. She covered her mouth with a hand. "Sun?"

Sun groaned. "What just happened?"

She helped him back to his feet. "You shouldn't sneak up and grab people. Where did you come from?"

"Over there." Sun pointed back toward Finn's house. "Neptune and I have been talking to people who posted signs on the Weeping Wall. You were supposed to help . . ."

Velvet pressed a hand to her forehead. "I knew I was forgetting something."

Sun shrugged. "It's okay. Neptune and I are good at this stuff, and we've almost gotten everyone."

"It's just that everything's been so confusing and busy lately with the new teams and one assignment after another and the curfew . . . ," Velvet stammered.

He had to agree there. "Yeah, I noticed. Since the teams were reshuffled, no one has time for anything anymore." Not that it was stopping *him*. Sun scratched the back of his neck. "Speaking of curfew, aren't you kind of breaking it right now?"

"You aren't the only one allowed to break rules."

Sun grinned. "The headmaster said no one can leave campus after sunset. So we leave during daylight and we just don't go back." He shoved his hands into his pockets. "So . . . what's so important that you're sneaking out on your own?"

Velvet's face lit up. "You know that fight club we've been looking for in the Pits?" She flashed her Scroll at him. "I just got a name and address."

"No way!" Sun read the advertisement on her phone: VISIT

THE MIRAGE TONIGHT! IT'S SO MUCH FUN, YOU WON'T BELIEVE YOUR EYES.

Down at the bottom, in small print, were the words COME FIGHT FOR YOUR CROWN AND KINGDOM.

Maybe it was a coincidence, maybe not. But he was on it. "Yeah! Let's go," he said.

"You aren't invited," said Velvet flatly.

"Does anyone else know where you are?" Sun asked.

Velvet bit her lip. "No."

"Is it going to be dangerous?"

"Probably," Velvet admitted.

"Then I'm coming," Sun said. "Besides, that guy in there is *so* boring. Neptune has it under control."

"If I refuse, you're just going to follow me, aren't you?"

"That sounds like something I'd do," Sun said.

He thought she was about to give in. And sure enough, she said, "Okay, then. If you promise not to interfere, you can come with me."

"I know better than to make a promise I can't keep. But I *can* promise I'll have your back." He winked. "We Faunus have to stick together."

Velvet laughed and held up her hands. "Fine! I'm actually glad I ran into you."

"You have no idea where this address is, do you?" Sun raised an eyebrow.

"I . . . don't."

"I got you." Sun pointed the way, and he and Velvet started walking side by side. "I've gotta tell Neptune where I'm going."

He texted Neptune: Going with Velvet to a supersecret fight club called the Mirage. TELL NO ONE.

As an afterthought, he sent one more message. No, really. Don't tell anyone where we're going!

"Maybe I shouldn't have told him." Sun slipped his Scroll back into its pouch.

"It's a good step," Velvet said. "Showing your teammates that you trust them. Keeping them in the loop."

"Yeah, but Neptune's not good with secrets." Sun tilted his head back. "And I guess he's not my teammate anymore."

"Right." Velvet looked away.

"You miss Team CFVY, huh?" Sun asked.

"More than I can even say."

"Then why didn't you tell *them* where you're going?" Sun asked.

"They're busy . . . with their new teams," she faltered. "And Team ROSC is still out on some mission in the desert."

Sun considered that for a moment. "That still leaves Fox and Yatsuhashi. And I know the big guy would drop everything to be there for you."

Velvet sighed. "He would."

Sun smiled. "I get it. And you're talking to the right guy. I can give you some pointers on how to set some boundaries with your teammates."

"Is that what you call it? Setting boundaries?" Velvet stopped and put a hand on her hip. "And what makes you think that's what I want?"

"Because you're going off on a mission without them, and that's not something you do when everything's fine." Sun's eyes widened. He slapped a palm against his forehead. "Oh. Is *that* why the guys are so annoyed with me?"

"There are probably a lot of reasons." It looked like she was trying to stop it, but she couldn't help it—Velvet smiled.

"Thanks."

They kept walking, and Sun gave Velvet a sidelong glance. "How come your team works so well together? I see groups like CFVY and RWBY and I wonder why SSSN is different. I mean, I know it isn't all *my* fault. Something's missing."

Velvet pursed her lips, as if to prevent a secret from coming out. "We weren't always a good team," she told Sun. "We made mistakes. Some pretty bad ones, to be honest. But they brought us closer together. I think the main thing is that we stuck together and worked through things together. Now, when it's important, we know we can depend on one another."

Sun stopped suddenly and looked around.

"Don't tell me *you're* lost," Velvet said.

"No, I know exactly where I am." He stared across the street. So it *was* still there after all. And the lights were on inside.

Velvet followed his gaze. "Sanzang Dojo," she read. "Is that your cousin's dojo?"

"Yeah."

"Do you want to stop in? I'll go with you, if you want."

"Nah. Now's not a good time."

"How do you know?"

"Because we have more important things to deal with right now."

"Family is pretty important," Velvet said.

Sun swept his hand toward the dojo, as if pushing it away. "This isn't the right time," he repeated, hurrying off before he could change his mind.

Velvet caught up to him. "When *will* it be the right time?" She just wouldn't let it go.

Sun sighed. "You know I'm not the most dependable person. I like to go where I'm needed, but I always seem to be needed . . . somewhere else, for someone else." He shook his head. "I guess . . . the right time is when I know I'm not going to leave again. And with all of this—" He waved his hands. "Who knows?"

"Well, when you're ready, I'll be there for you." Velvet winked. "After all, 'we Faunus have to stick together.' "

He rolled his eyes. "I hate it when people use my own words against me!"

"Why?"

"Because most of the time they make me sound dumber than I am."

Velvet raised her eyebrows and took the lead.

"Velvet? Velvet!" Sun hurried after her.

"This is the Mirage? I should have known," Sun said.

This was where he and the others had tracked those rogue Huntsmen, Green and Brown, last week. Where Fox had sensed Professor Rumpole the night before she announced the reinitiation at Shade.

"But we still don't have the passphrase," Velvet said. "There's got to be another way inside."

The Mirage was unassuming, like most buildings in Vacuo—except for Shade Academy, which was kind of the point. The school was trying to make a statement and give the people something to look to for strength, but in the rest of Vacuo, function was more important than form.

Simple buildings were more practical, cost-effective, easier to build, and easier to *re*build when a storm took them out or you were forced to move on. Bricks and portable homes were the predominant architectural features—along with industrial decay, the old refineries and factories and warehouses abandoned by Dust companies from other kingdoms. The Mirage was a sturdy warehouse built of steel, the kind of place you'd seek shelter in if you didn't want to be buried by a sandstorm. Its walls were shiny, almost like glass, built to reflect the sun's heat and keep the inside cool. From a distance, you could hardly see the place.

Velvet and Sun approached the solid metal door at the entrance. Sun shrugged and rapped on it with one of his gunchucks.

A narrow panel slid open at the top and eyes peered out at them.

"What do we fight for?" a gruff voice asked.

Velvet glanced at Sun. She started to lift her Scroll to the window. "I have this ad—"

That was it! Sun blurted out: "For crown and kingdom!"

The panel slid shut. Sun gripped his gunchucks more tightly. Then the door creaked open. A large man in a black chestplate stared down at them. A silver armband glinted on his right arm.

Sun stepped back, planting one foot behind him and preparing to fight.

"Check your weapons, Scrolls, and Dust," the man said.

"I thought this was a fight club," Sun said.

"We fight without weapons," the man said.

The two students exchanged a look.

The man held his hands out. Sun reluctantly gave him Ruyi Bang and Jingu Bang. Or he *tried* to, but as the man tried to take the gunchucks, Sun kept hanging on. They played out a brief tug-of-war before the man picked them up—along with Sun, who dangled comically before letting go and pouting.

Sun glanced at Velvet as she started to walk past the guard. The man held out a beefy arm.

"Where's your weapon, girlie?"

Velvet smiled sweetly. "I don't have one."

"What's in the box?" The guard reached down and grabbed the box fastened to Velvet's back.

"Hey!" she protested.

The guard opened the box and looked inside. His eyebrows bunched together. "What's this?"

"A camera," Velvet said. At his blank expression, she explained: "It takes pictures."

"Like Scrolls?" the man said.

"Yup."

He handed it back to her. "No pictures in the club."

"But doesn't it use—" Sun began.

Velvet jabbed him in the side with her elbow. "Ow!" Sun whined.

Velvet said, "Thanks, sir. I won't record anything." Then she reclaimed her camera and grabbed Sun by the shirt collar, dragging him inside the club.

"Sorry," Sun said. "I didn't expect you to lie like that."

"No one does," Velvet said. "That's why it worked. Let's hope I don't need to use Anesidora in here."

They went down a dark, narrow hallway toward the sound of pounding techno music, cheers, and grunts. The temperature was much cooler in here than outside, but it also smelled like sweat and food and old machine oil.

Then they reached a vast room, packed with standing tables, booths along the walls, and people everywhere, all surrounding a large gold cage in the center. Two people were fighting inside, but Sun could barely see them through the throng.

Inside the cage, a tall, gold-skinned woman with bandages wrapped around her muscular body was facing off against a younger girl with mirrored glasses and dreads. Sun recognized her from Shade.

"Isn't that Umber?" Sun asked Velvet.

"Yeah," she said. "She's on Fox's new team, Team FNDU. I wonder why she's here."

"Looks like she's here to fight," Sun said. "Should we hide? Or talk to her?"

"Depends on what she's doing here," Velvet muttered.

Umber looked spent, but still she fought, though her opponent had the advantage of size and strength. Sun also thought her skin might *actually* be gold, considering how little damage Umber's strikes were having against her.

"The newcomer is almost finished!" an announcer called. "She's going to need some of Tayet Aldhahab's bandages soon."

"Let's look around, but try not to draw too much attention," Velvet whispered. Sun hadn't seen her so confident before. Being on her own and in charge suited her. Plus, Sun liked being bossed around by strong women.

Sun and Velvet circled the arena, studying the crowd. He kept an eye on the cage, watching Umber fight. The gold woman, Tayet, was charging at her. Umber's shoulders slumped, and then she looked straight at her opponent and lowered her glasses. The move reminded Sun of Coco when she was trying to look nonchalant, but suddenly Tayet froze in the cage.

The crowd went wild. "A surprising move from Umber!" the announcer shouted. "She has revealed her Semblance at last, some sort of paralyzing stare."

Sun's jaw dropped as Umber now rushed toward Tayet, eyes locked on her. Then she dropped and slid between Tayet's legs, grabbing them with her hands while kicking up and back. Tayet toppled forward like a fallen toy. She shook off the paralysis and climbed to her feet, blinking and looking confused. By the time she turned around, Umber was ready for her. She punched her in the gut, and as Tayet recovered and reached for her, Umber lowered her glasses again. Tayet froze.

"Looks like Umber might just pull this off after all," the announcer crowed.

"Interesting decor," Velvet said to Sun. Apparently she wasn't watching this amazing battle featuring one of their schoolmates. Instead she was staring at the walls.

Sun followed her gaze and saw that weapons were mounted along the perimeter of the club: swords and scythes, shields and guns. Then Velvet gasped and grabbed Sun's arm.

"What?" Sun asked.

She pulled him toward her and turned them around so their backs were to the wall.

"Let's take a picture together!" she said brightly.

She held up her Scroll and took a moment to frame the shot. Sun smiled. The camera bulb flashed as she took the picture. The crowd around them stilled; then someone grabbed her Scroll—the guard from the door.

"'No photos,' I said!" He glanced at the image on the camera and then at Velvet.

She acted shocked. "I'm so sorry! I was so excited, I forgot. It won't happen again," she promised.

"She really loves taking pictures." Sun leaned in close to the guard to explain. "It's a sickness."

The guard frowned, but he deleted the picture and handed her camera back. "Do that again, and you're banned."

"Thank you!" Velvet put her Scroll away, and the man moved back to his station.

"What was that all about?" Sun asked in a low voice.

Velvet tapped at her camera screen. "Good thing a backup of every photo I take is automatically uploaded." She showed the picture to Sun.

He and Velvet were out of focus and the image was badly framed, showing more of the wall behind them than their faces.

"I thought you were a good photographer," Sun said.

Velvet blushed. "I am. Because I got exactly what I wanted." She pointed to something in the background: a golden sai mounted on the wall among the other weapons.

"So?" Sun said.

"I know this one. It belongs to Carmine Esclados."

Sun was stunned. "That rotten Huntress we brought back to Coquina?" He took another look. "You're right. But I don't remember it being gold."

"That makes it even more weird," Velvet said. "Why is it here, and how did it get that way?"

"Maybe it's a replica," Sun said.

Velvet scoffed. "Why would someone make a gold copy of her weapon? The metal is too soft to fight with. And if this place is run by the Crown, I doubt it's a coincidence. I'm gonna send this to Coco, Yatsu, and Fox."

As Velvet texted her former teammates, Sun watched Umber fight. She was winning.

"Umber has an awesome Semblance," he said. She was kicking butt.

Velvet frowned and packed her camera away for now. "That's not a good thing if you-know-who is running this place. Let's try to get a little closer."

They pushed their way toward the cage to catch the end of the fight. Umber was beating Tayet, their Aura meters about evenly matched. Umber's glasses were pushed up on her head now and she was fighting with her eyes closed, opening them only to temporarily freeze her opponent, then move into position to kick or punch her. And then it was over.

"Nice work, sweetheart," the announcer said. "The winner gets a kiss from me. I might have forgotten to mention that before. Come on—"

Umber glared up at him and of course the man froze. Then people started laughing and clapping until a bunch of guys with silver armbands—and guns—started to move on the cage.

"Guess some weapons *are* allowed," Sun noted. He looked around and saw that about half the people in the crowd wore silver armbands like those he'd seen on the bouncer and the guards. How had he missed that before?

Onstage, Umber lowered her glasses and crossed her arms.

"—up!" the man finished. The audience roared with laughter again. "What?" Anger flashed across his face, but then he joined in, his laughter a bit forced. "Ha ha! Good one! Do we have a new challenger?"

The cage door opened and Tayet limped out, favoring her right leg, while Umber looked around. There weren't many takers now that her Semblance had been revealed.

"Who will step up for a chance to be crowned champion?"

"Crowned?" Sun said.

Then, before he knew what was happening, Velvet raised her hand. "I'll go!"

Sun grabbed her hand and yanked it down. "Velvet, no!"

"What did I say about grabbing people?" Velvet pulled her hand away and stalked toward the cage.

"Velvet?" Umber called in surprise. "Did you follow me here?"

"Another girl fight!" The announcer rubbed his hands together, and the crowd responded heartily. "Excellent. Enter the cage, doll."

"No. No! Pick me instead!" Sun said. He summoned a clone to stand in front of Velvet, blocking her way as it waved one hand in the air wildly.

"Impressive," the announcer said. "But wait your turn, Sparky. I wanna see what *she's* got."

Velvet stuck out her tongue at Sun and pushed past his clone. With no other choice, Sun let his avatar fade.

Then a young man stepped out of the shadows and whispered something to the announcer on his platform. That guy looked familiar, but Sun couldn't place him.

"Wait!" the announcer called down to Velvet. "Change in plans. Sparky takes the cage first. Sorry, doll."

Velvet looked surprised and then annoyed as Sun walked past her to enter the cage. She tugged his arm.

"*No*, Sun," she said in a low voice, like she was disciplining a naughty pet. "We have to go. Right now."

Sun grinned, but his smile disappeared at the dark, fearful expression on her face.

"I wanted to fight Umber so I could warn her. You show a powerful Semblance here, and maybe you don't get to leave," Velvet said.

"And what did I just do?" Sun asked.

"Exactly."

Sun looked up at the announcer. "Uh, you know what? I'm good. We've gotta get going actually. It's a school night, you know?"

"You can't back out now," the announcer said. "Get in the cage. Both of you." It was clearly an order, and a bunch of the club's goons started to close in on Sun and Velvet. Sun reached for his staff but came up empty.

"Nuts," he said.

CHAPTER TEN

Staying up late to scour the city for information on the Crown was one thing, but staying up late to keep watch over a barren stretch of desert was another. Searching for the person or persons kidnapping innocent people for some unknown but dark purpose was way more useful than fighting Grimm far from the city—but that's what Professor Rumpole had assigned Team ROSC to do . . . for the last *week*.

This area was called the Wastelands for a reason. It was wasting Coco's time, her talent, and her patience.

She hadn't changed her clothes or taken a shower since leaving Shade, but the worst thing was the boredom. Back in her combat school days, she hadn't thought she'd ever grow tired of fighting Grimm, but here she was. It was routine. And not in the way it had been back at Beacon, after the school had fallen. That had been for a noble cause, but this just felt like . . . busywork.

The thing she missed most was her team, though. Her friends.

And, surprisingly, Coco missed being in charge.

By the campfire, Scarlet rolled over and mumbled something too low for Coco to hear. She shivered and pulled the blanket closer around her shoulders. She watched Reese Chloris and Olive Gashley sleep.

Reese just wasn't a good leader. She liked to lead by group vote, which wasn't leading at all—it was passing the responsibility off to your team. Coco listened to Velvet, Yatsuhashi, and Fox all the time—except when she didn't. Knowing when to trust her instincts and when to listen to their suggestions was one of the hardest things she'd had to learn. Sometimes she still got it wrong. But whether she was making the tough call or not, she trusted them to do what she demanded of them. To do *better* than she expected. And to trust her. That dynamic didn't exist on Team ROSC, and she wasn't sure if it ever would.

After a week of forced togetherness, things should have been clicking, but the four of them still weren't getting along. It was a miracle that they had survived so far, and it was only by virtue of the fact that each was, individually, a strong fighter. At first, when she was a new student questioning Professor Ozpin, Coco had thought the system at Beacon was broken. But she was *certain* it was broken at Shade. Why had Rumpole messed with something that already worked so well?

And it's all my fault, Coco thought.

She couldn't shake the feeling that she had failed Team CFVY and was *still* failing them. Maybe she should have protested when Professor Rumpole announced the reinitiation. Maybe she should have continued to defend Velvet. Now her real teammates were divided, their investigation had stalled, and they were all back to square one. Velvet was with a team that didn't recognize her awesome capabilities. Fox was withdrawing, having lost his family for the second time. Yatsuhashi was going mad with worry about Velvet and his teammates, knowing that he couldn't be there to protect them, and worrying he would accidentally hurt someone on his new team.

And Coco . . . Coco had to take orders from *Reese Chloris*, who dressed like she was a twelve-year-old hanging out at the mall, and acted like it, too.

Coco's Scroll buzzed—one of their perimeter alarms was going off. It could just be another lizard, but it might be something else.

Then several more alarms went off at once. It was definitely something else.

Coco glanced back at the dying campfire. It was just about time to wake Scarlet for his watch, but if something was finally happening, she damn well wasn't going to miss it. She'd just go check it out, and if it was a rare case of something she couldn't handle alone, she would call the rest of them. They'd probably appreciate the extra sleep.

Coco picked up her sunglasses from the rock beside her and slipped them on. Then she pushed the small button on the right temple to activate the night vision filters.

She smiled as the desert lit up in reddish hues for her. She loved these glasses, a surprise birthday present from Velvet last month. Knowing Coco was afraid of dark, enclosed spaces, Velvet had been working on them for more than a year, but parts and free time were hard to come by in Vacuo.

Coco headed toward the perimeter alarms, keeping eyes and ears peeled for Grimm. And then she found them.

Six Jackalopes—big guys—surrounding someone.

"Oh, *come on*," a chillingly familiar voice said. "I don't have time for this. He's going to kill me if I'm not back to the Mirage in thirty."

Coco pressed a button on the left band of her glasses and zoomed in. Seriously, she loved BunnyVision.

In the magnified view, Coco glimpsed the person who had captured the Grimm's interest. This person had flowing red hair capped with a pair of goggles, a short cape, and an even shorter skirt showing off long legs.

"Carmine," Coco said under her breath.

Coco couldn't help but feel some sense of cosmic justice: Not too long ago, Carmine had kidnapped Gus Caspian and held off the combined might of Team CFVY in the desert.

Coco debated whether she should walk away, but this was the first she'd seen of Carmine since she and Bertilak had escaped from police custody. It wasn't likely the Grimm would be able to defeat her; Coco suspected they were more of a nuisance than a real threat for the seasoned fighter. But if Carmine was weakened in the battle, Coco might be able to get an advantage over her.

She watched while Carmine tangled with the antlered Grimm, admiring her strength and skill. The Huntress vaulted over a Jackalope's head to land on its back, then grabbed the horns and twisted them, jerking the monster's head sharply until its neck was broken. As it faded away, she leaped onto another Jackalope. She stabbed down into its back with one of her sai, then threw the weapon into another creature's eye. The weapon electrified, destroying the Grimm. The sai flew back toward Carmine as the

Grimm reared back, sending the Huntress tumbling. She landed hard and her weapon dropped into the sand.

Uh-oh, Coco thought.

Carmine stumbled to her feet. She looked for her sai, but it was lost in the sand. She lowered her goggles and raised her hands. The sand around her started drifting upward. Carmine had a weak telekinetic ability that allowed her to manipulate small objects, like swords and grains of sand. It didn't compare to the ability to lift large chunks of buildings like Glynda Goodwitch could, but being able to manipulate lots of small objects at once still made Carmine quite powerful.

The effort must have distracted her, though, because Carmine didn't notice the Jackalope's powerful back legs kicking out until they knocked into her. Carmine went down.

Coco switched her glasses back to normal magnification. Even as she was thinking about the course of action, she was rushing toward the fray. Sometimes decisions were like that—your body already knew what to do while your brain was still processing the situation. Only in this case, Coco's body wasn't necessarily the clearest judge of character. Her brain would have said that Carmine didn't deserve her help.

Coco ran right up to one of the large Grimm and swung her purse in a wide, upward arc, smacking the creature from behind and sending it flying over the heads of its dark brothers. Carmine stirred and climbed to her feet—holding her sai.

She didn't miss a beat. "Fancy meeting you here," Carmine said to Coco. She turned to the remaining two Jackalopes. "Oh, you boys are in trouble now."

Coco stood back-to-back with Carmine and flicked her bag, turning it into a machine gun.

"You talk to Grimm, too?" Coco fired her gun, and the Jackalope in front of her was shredded into smoke by her Dust bullets, their force augmented by her Semblance.

"A girl has to amuse herself," said Carmine, tossing her sai into the air. It spun in place for a moment, zipping toward and through a Jackalope, then whipped back around and did it again. And again, and again, and again, as though it were a needle threading fabric, until the Grimm collapsed on itself. The sai flew past Coco's face, passing less than an inch from her cheek and into Carmine's waiting hand.

"Where's your other sword?" Coco asked.

"Lost it in a fight," Carmine said.

"Wish I'd seen that," Coco said.

"I didn't lose the fight, though," Carmine said.

"Sorry to hear that."

The first Jackalope Coco had hit came bounding back. Carmine used her Semblance to open a sandpit in front of it while Coco mowed another Jackalope down with her gun. Maybe they were both showing off a little, or maybe they were trying to intimidate each other.

"What about your partner, Bertilak?" Coco asked. "Lose him in a fight, too?"

"*Former* partner," Carmine said.

"He's dead?" Coco asked.

"No, he just needs to . . . recharge a little." Carmine laughed. "Why? You interested in the job?"

"No, thanks. I've seen how you work with others."

The Jackalope in the pit roared as it struggled in the sand and slowly sank into the ground. When it opened its mouth, sand flew inside. The Grimm began to expand until it exploded, sending out more sand and tacky black Grimm matter that coated Coco. Though Carmine easily diverted it away from herself. Coco wiped a hand across her cheek and examined the tarlike substance before it dispersed into smoke.

"I don't know; we make a pretty good team," Carmine said. "But we're far better enemies."

Coco sighed and collapsed her gun into its compact form. She turned to face Carmine.

"I've been dreaming of a rematch with you," Coco said.

"You've been dreaming about me? I'm flattered." Carmine winked. "But as I was telling our dearly departed friends, I don't have time for this."

"Hot date with the Crown?" Coco asked.

Carmine briefly looked surprised, but she covered for it by twirling her sai on one finger. "Don't be jealous, darling."

That wasn't exactly a *no*. Either Carmine didn't realize she'd confirmed that her employer and the Crown were one and the same—or she didn't care.

The sai flew toward Coco's face. Coco smacked it out of the way with her bag and bolted for Carmine. She put all her strength into a blow across Carmine's face, but it barely seemed to faze her. A blast of sand slammed into Coco from her left and she went down.

Carmine should have been at least a little bit worn down from fighting Grimm. Coco struggled to her feet, but more sand piled on top of her, pushing her down onto her back like an overturned tortoise. The Huntress had been challenging before, but she seemed nearly unstoppable now.

Coco's brother Van used to like burying her in the sand on long-ago beach trips, when she was trying to sunbathe. After a year in Vacuo, Coco couldn't believe she'd ever associated sun and sand with fun. The sand just kept on coming.

"Where are Yatsuhashi and Fox?" Carmine asked. "Why aren't they rushing to your aid?"

Coco spat sand and ignored the question. "Where did you say you were—" Coco coughed. "Going?"

"Nice try," Carmine said. Sand continued to pour over Coco. She would never plan a beach vacation again. If she survived this.

The Mirage, she'd said. Why did that sound so familiar? Like she'd heard it before. Or read it somewhere.

Coco nudged up her scarf to cover her nose and mouth. She squeezed her eyes shut as she was plunged into darkness and sand clogged her ears. She held her breath. On those beach trips, she'd been able to hold it for three minutes, forty-two seconds. But this time she hadn't been able to take a deep breath first, and her heart was already pounding. Her lungs burned. If she opened her mouth, it would be all over.

"Oh, right, you brought the B-team out here." Carmine's voice was muffled by the sand covering Coco's head.

How did Carmine know about the reassigned teams and their missions? Did she have a mole at Shade Academy?

"Coco?" Reese called.

I'm right here! Coco thought. One of her worst nightmares was being buried alive, but she'd never thought it would happen in the wide-open desert like this.

I should have woken the team up earlier, she thought.

Suddenly the sand stopped moving. Carmine was probably occupied now, fighting the rest of Team ROSC. But Coco was still under what felt like three hundred pounds of sand and she was almost out of air.

Desperate times called for desperate measures. Coco had one terrible idea, but if it worked, it was going to hurt. A lot.

Coco focused her Semblance on one of the Gravity Dust bullets on her weapon's bandolier/purse strap, hyping up the explosive mineral until it—well, *exploded*.

The shock wave of the gravity-manipulating ordnance blasted the sand off of Coco, but it also exploded the rest of her bullets. The impact knocked her Aura down to a dangerously low level. She wheezed as the air in her lungs was pushed out and then she was gasping to replace it.

Her ears rang and her eyes were bleary, but she was happy to see she had stunned Carmine, who had been standing right on top of her. No, she'd only surprised her. Carmine still seemed as fresh as she had at the beginning of the fight. How was she even doing that?

Reese hurled her hoverboard at Carmine while Olive tossed her pike at her—accidentally knocking Reese's weapon out of the way.

Idiots, Coco thought. They really needed to coordinate their attacks better.

Carmine noticed right away. "They aren't exactly Team CFVY, are they?" she asked Coco.

That was when Scarlet swung his sword at Carmine and hit her from behind. He got sand in his eyes for the trouble.

"Good thing the cavalry is here," Carmine said.

Coco looked up to see a Death Stalker scurrying toward them.

"Uh-oh," Reese said, whipping around. Coco turned. Another Death Stalker was coming at them from the other direction.

"Nice seeing you again, Coco." Carmine twirled her fingers in a good-bye. "Thanks for 'saving' me." Her laughter grew distorted and distant as sand whirled around her like a personal storm that slowly drifted away from the Shade students and the Grimm that their fighting—and Coco's fear and anger—had summoned.

"Thanks," Coco said to her team as they formed up. "We're in real trouble."

"No kidding," Scarlet said. "Death Stalkers are no fun."

"Oh no, we can handle those. Reese and I will take the one on the left, you two take the one on the right."

"Hey, I'm—" Reese said.

Coco cut her off. "No offense, but listen to me," she said.

"You're the one who got ambushed in the middle of the night," Reese grumbled.

"It wasn't a fair fight," Coco spat. "But we can't waste any more time out here. We're needed back home. I think Shade has been compromised, and our friends and the school are in danger."

Reese glared at Coco as the Death Stalkers moved in.

"I need you guys," Coco said. "I'm out of bullets, and I can't take another hit. But you also need me, because let's face it, I'm the best strategist around for miles."

"You aren't wrong," Scarlet said. "We'll back you up. Right, guys?"

Olive nodded and drew her awl pike silently.

"Fine, but if you get us killed, I'm requesting a new team," Reese announced.

"Deal. I haven't lost a team yet," Coco said.

And I hope that doesn't change tonight. She was suddenly struck by a thought. What was it Carmine had said . . .

Where are Yatsuhashi and Fox?

Coco felt the blood drain from her face. Why hadn't Carmine mentioned Velvet?

Maybe because she already knew where Velvet was. Because Velvet was in some kind of trouble.

In spite of everything that had just gone down in the desert, Coco was consumed by one thought now: *I've got to find Velvet before Carmine does.*

CHAPTER ELEVEN

Neptune had just snuck back onto campus and settled into his room for an exciting evening of writing up interview notes when someone pounded on his door. He froze and listened.

Had he been busted for being out late? Even if someone had seen him coming back long after sunset, it wasn't technically against the rules. Headmaster Theodore had said no one was allowed to *leave* campus at night. Neptune's mom was a lawyer, and he was pretty sure it would hold up in court.

The banging resumed. Maybe it was Sun, playing a prank on him. Neptune was kind of annoyed Sun had ditched him, *again*, to go off with a girl he thought needed his help. But mostly Neptune hadn't wanted to hang out alone with that weird Asturias guy. It would serve Sun right if Neptune just ignored—

"We know you're in there, Neptune," Fox sent.

Neptune jumped at the voice in his head.

"Open the door before Yatsuhashi breaks it down."

Neptune slowly opened the door to see half of Team CFVY. He tried to act casual. "Hey, guys. What's up?"

"You tell us," Fox sent. *"Do you know where Velvet and Sun are?"*

Neptune could hear his concern even in the silence.

"You're standing right in front of me. Why are you using telepathy?" Neptune asked.

"Just answer," Yatsuhashi said aloud.

"What was the question again?"

"Do you know where Velvet and Sun are?" Yatsuhashi repeated. "They aren't answering their Scrolls."

"I—I can't say," Neptune said.

Fox stepped into the room and cracked his knuckles. *"That's oddly specific phrasing."*

Neptune stepped back. He glanced at Yatsuhashi, wondering why he wasn't trying to be the intimidating one. Not that either of them had to *try* to be intimidating.

Why was Team CFVY so freaking scary? Since the fall of Beacon, it seemed like even Velvet had a dark side. She was so friendly and cute, but wasn't that what people always said when they found out someone they knew was a criminal or a serial killer?

She was always so sweet; everyone liked her. When I saw the news, I could hardly believe she was responsible for that grisly murdering spree . . .

"I mean, I don't know where they went. How do you know she's with Sun?" Neptune asked.

Yatsuhashi held up his Scroll to show Neptune a selfie of Velvet and Sun in front of a wall with a bunch of weapons on it.

"So you're . . . jealous?" Neptune ventured.

"I'm *concerned*. Sun is a bad influence, and that doesn't seem like a friendly place." Yatsuhashi ducked his head under the doorway and walked into the room. With him inside, the one-hundred-square-foot room seemed suddenly much smaller. The dorms at

Shade were a far cry from the luxury suite at Haven Academy that Neptune had shared with Sun, Scarlet, and Sage. They'd had so much space that they turned Sun's room into a game room while he was off gallivanting with Blake last year.

In Vacuo, luxury was the enemy. Sun had told him that was one of the reasons the kingdom had been so easy to exploit—because the people had gotten lazy and soft. That attitude was in the distant past now, along with the king who had let it happen.

"Hey, Sun's a great guy," Neptune reassured him. "She's as safe with him as she is with you."

"Velvet can handle herself," Yatsuhashi said. "I'm more worried about what stupidity Sun may have gotten her into. Where are they?"

"Maybe you're being just a little overprotective?" Neptune squinted and pinched his thumb and index finger together.

"We're Huntsmen," Fox sent. *"Overprotective is what we do."*

"Huntsmen in *training*," Neptune said.

"We're fast learners," Fox sent.

"Fox is also very impatient," Yatsuhashi said. "He doesn't like to be kept waiting."

Neptune grinned. "You're doing the good cop, bad cop thing. I learned all about this in—"

"We aren't cops," Fox sent. *"And we're both in a bad mood."*

Neptune's smile faded.

"Right now, our business is finding the Crown and keeping our friends safe," Yatsuhashi said.

"What does this have to do with the Crown?" Neptune asked.

"Team ROSC is missing—which means Coco and Scarlet are

missing. They were on a mission out in the desert and they haven't checked in since."

"Scarlet's in trouble?" Neptune asked. He'd be more worried about Scarlet than Sun.

"Umber's also missing," Fox sent. *"And now Velvet and Sun."*

"Sun and Velvet aren't *missing*," Neptune said. "But I'm not allowed to tell you where they are."

"But you can tell us. *Surely we're an exception,"* Fox sent.

"Sorry. Sun said not to tell anyone. If I break his trust, he'll be really upset."

"Sun isn't here," Yatsuhashi said.

"Sure, but when he gets back, he'll be really upset."

Fox stepped toward Neptune again, crowding him in the corner between his desk and his overstuffed bookcase.

"He meant Sun isn't here to stop *us,"* Fox sent. *"And we're upset now."*

"S-stop you from what?" Neptune reached for his weapon, but the room was too small to use it effectively, and Yatsuhashi and Fox didn't need weapons to fight him.

"We have ways of making you talk," Fox said.

"Whoa, you said that bit out loud." Neptune tilted his head. "Somehow that made it creepier."

"Good." Fox smiled.

"You think you can take me?" Neptune said. "Bring it." He assumed his battle stance and accidentally knocked an action figure off his bookshelf.

When you grew up in a port city like Argus, you had to know how to swim, especially if you lived along the coast like the Vasilias family did. By the time little Neptune was four years old, his parents and siblings had had it with his aversion to water: He literally could not get wet.

Baths had always been a difficult time. No sooner would they drop him into the tub than all of the water would be displaced out of it—sometimes explosively. It seemed that at a young age Neptune already had a strong water-related Semblance, like the rest of his family, but he didn't know how to use it. And because he was afraid to get into water, even to touch *it, he never learned to control his power over it. Which gave the water power over him.*

Neptune's older brother, Jupiter, thought he had the solution. He had learned to swim by being pushed into the ocean and figuring it out fast. Swimming was a matter of instinct, after all, especially for a Vasilias. If it had worked for him and their other siblings, it would work for Neptune, he figured. They had to stop coddling him. So Jupiter dragged Neptune to the beach, kicking and screaming all the way, and he threw him off a pier.

That's when they discovered that Neptune's Semblance had another aspect. Not only could he push water away from his body, he could also pull it to him. And he could manipulate the water's cohesion with other things. But four-year-old Neptune knew none of this. All he knew was his brother had tossed him into the ocean, and when he came bursting out of it and scrambled back onto shore, he had brought some of the ocean with him.

Neptune was caught in a bubble of water, which was growing by the second. He couldn't see because it was stuck to his eyes, he couldn't hear because it filled his ears—and he couldn't scream because he couldn't breathe. And then, in his panic, he sent the water away from him, so it gathered around the closest thing nearby: his brother.

Jupiter had been startled to find himself enclosed in water that seemed stuck to his skin. Fortunately, he was comfortable in water and had mastered his own Semblance, so he turned the water into vapor instantly. Then he had comforted his brother, who thought he had nearly killed him, but the damage was already done. Neptune wanted nothing to do with water, and he lived in constant fear that he would accidentally touch it, becoming unable to shake it off. He certainly did not want to swim.

Neptune's parents bought him goggles just to get him to go outside, but eventually the Vasilias family was forced to move farther inland. As a student at Haven Academy, under close supervision from his professors, Neptune gradually came to terms with his Semblance, which he called Water Attraction. Once he made contact with water, he could force it to adhere to other people or objects—it was a useful talent for a Huntsman, as long as enough water was around. But before he could manipulate water in this fashion, he had to touch it and draw it to himself to charge the molecules. Only then could he propel it and control it over a short distance, or propel himself at great speeds in the water.

As far as Neptune was concerned, it was not worth the trouble.

It turned out that Yatsuhashi and Fox *could* take Neptune all right—out to the courtyard in the plaza. Where Yatsuhashi proceeded to dangle him over the water fountain. Slowly, he started to lower Neptune into it.

Neptune's face inched closer and closer to the burbling water. He squeezed his eyes shut against the spray from the fountain. He screamed.

"Great, now I'm deaf, too," Fox sent.

"This isn't cool, guys!" Neptune talked fast. "You're better than this!"

"Just tell us where Sun took Velvet and this can all end," Fox sent.

Neptune twisted around, trying to get away from the water.

"Easy, I'm going to drop you if you keep that up," Yatsuhashi said. "Fox, this is really bothering him."

"That means it's working," Fox sent.

"Maybe this is too mean." Yatsuhashi lifted Neptune up about a foot.

"Yes! Yes, it's way too mean!" Neptune said.

"Come on, Yatsuhashi. You're too soft," Fox sent.

"Better too soft than a bully." Yatsuhashi swung Neptune away from the fountain.

Fox sighed.

"Thank you! You are great. You are merciful," Neptune blabbered.

Yatsuhashi dropped him onto the hard cobblestones.

"Ow." Neptune scrambled into a sitting position. He was trembling all over, and he didn't trust himself to stand.

Yatsuhashi crouched next to him. "I'm sorry," he said. "We went too far on that one. We shouldn't have been so insensitive about your fear of water and used it against you."

Fox snorted.

"It's okay," Neptune said. "But I'm not afraid of water."

"You're . . . not?" Yatsuhashi asked. "Then what's your deal?"

Fox splashed water out of the fountain, and Neptune shrank away from it.

"Fox," Yatsuhashi warned.

"You're really not doing good cop, bad cop?" Neptune sniffed.

"Fox was right. We were both being bad," Yatsuhashi said. "You want to talk about it?"

"Really?" Fox sent.

Neptune sighed. "I just don't like getting water in my eyes. That's why I have these cool goggles." He lowered his goggles over his eyes. "That's the best thing about Vacuo. No water."

"Yeah, thirst and desolation are terrific," Fox said dryly.

"That's it? You don't like getting water in your eyes?" Yatsuhashi asked.

"It stings!" Neptune covered his ears. "And I hate how it clogs my ears."

"I don't enjoy that, either," Fox sent.

"Okay, then. Tell us what you know or prepare to get water in your eyes and your ears!" Yatsuhashi grabbed Neptune's jacket.

"I can't tell you!" But he couldn't handle this interrogation anymore, either. Neptune thought fast, pulling out his Scroll and dropping it on the ground between Fox and Yatsuhashi as if it were an accident. "Oops."

Yatsuhashi let go of Neptune's jacket and scooped up the Scroll. He tried to hand it back to Neptune.

Didn't he understand? "Oh no," Neptune said, pretending to be scared. "Please don't look at my private text messages."

Yatsuhashi knitted his brow together in confusion.

"From my dear friend *Sun*," Neptune hissed.

Yatsuhashi glanced up for a moment at the night sky. Then

he said, "Oh!" He yanked the Scroll back and started thumbing through the apps.

Soon Yatsuhashi tossed the Scroll into Neptune's lap and turned to Fox. "I *knew* Sun was a bad influence," he said. "They went to a club called the Mirage."

"Let's go," Fox said.

"For the record, I didn't tell you that," Neptune said. "And you searched my Scroll without a warrant."

"You aren't going anywhere." Just then Professor Rumpole strode into the courtyard.

"Crap," Fox sent.

"What's going on here?" she demanded to know. "What was all that screaming about?"

Yatsuhashi glanced at Neptune.

"Your fault," Neptune said.

Yatsuhashi took a deep breath and seemed to make a decision. "Professor," he said, "we think the Crown is holding some Shade students at a club called the Mirage. We're going there now to rescue them."

Rumpole scowled, as if she had no concern for Velvet or Sun at all. Her voice was eerily quiet and cold. "You are doing no such thing. And anyone who has defied the headmaster's orders is no longer a student at this academy."

"They didn't technically sneak out," Neptune said. "If they simply didn't return before curfew."

Professor Rumpole glared at him.

"But hey, you make the rules," Neptune said.

Yatsuhashi stepped forward to try again. "Professor Rumpole, Velvet's in trouble. With the Grimm problems on the edge of the city, you need every Huntsman on deck. I'm sure you can't afford to divert resources to this, and you don't have to."

"You've shown enormous trust in our abilities to handle ourselves on missions—and none of our abilities have changed," Fox jumped in. "You can't both train us to fight for what's right and then prevent us from doing so just because the stakes are higher. We need to find our friends."

Professor Rumpole raised an eyebrow, considering. "You make some good points."

"We've fought the worst the world can throw at us, and survived," Fox said.

But that point didn't strengthen the argument. "You haven't fought the worst. You haven't seen anything yet," Rumpole said, grimacing. "Ozpin and Goodwitch placed too much trust in their students. They put everything on the line, and you weren't up to the task. What makes you think you can defeat the Crown? Or what comes next?"

Yatsuhashi was undeterred. "We still have to try," he said.

"We can't just hide here and wait for them to come to us," Neptune added.

"I admire your attitude, but I simply cannot allow you to continue pursuing the Crown."

"That's oddly specific phrasing," Fox said. "Can't or won't?"

Rumpole flashed him a withering glare. "What I mean is: Stay out of it."

"With all due respect—"

"Fox," Yatsuhashi warned.

Fox smiled. "Then please expel us from Shade, Professor. We're not going to sit here and do nothing—it's not what Huntsmen would do. And I don't want to be here if that's all you have to teach me. So I think it's time for us to go now."

Rumpole moved fast. With her left hand she reached beneath the hair at the back of her head and pulled out a large spoked wheel with rimmed edges.

"Where were you hiding that?" Neptune asked in disbelief.

With her right hand, she pulled on the golden cord that bound her hair. The hair fell loose, fanning out behind her, and the cord wrapped itself around the edge of the wheel, which spun in her hand and drew it in. Then she drew her left hand back and tossed the wheel like a discus toward them while holding on to the cord.

The spinning wheel zoomed toward Neptune, Yatsuhashi, and Fox. Then it wrapped the cord around the trio, binding them together, arms pressed tightly to their sides.

"You were saying?" Rumpole said.

Yatsuhashi grunted and strained at their bindings, tightening them even more.

Neptune gasped. "Yatsuhashi! Stop! Can't breathe."

"What just happened?" Fox sent.

"She's been carrying some kind of wheel on her back," Neptune returned. *"And she wrapped a cord around it, then spun it toward us, tying us up."*

"I can't believe she's been carrying that thing around all this time," Yatsuhashi sent.

Rumpole's wheel returned to her. "I'm disappointed. If this is the best you can do, then maybe we *should* expel you. You certainly don't belong here."

Fox was cheerful, since he knew the way out. He flicked his wrists and the binding came loose at once. "Arm blades for the win," he said. "Nice try, Professor!" He ran toward her, and she fled.

"Are we really doing this?" Neptune asked.

Yatsuhashi followed Fox. *"Something's not right. Why is Rumpole fighting us?"*

Fox nodded. *"You know the rule at Shade—the strong survive. Normally, she would never fight to keep us here. She'd just let us leave. We need to figure out what's going on and get to Theodore. There has to be a reason she's holding us back."*

"I guess we're doing this." Neptune joined the chase, all too conscious of the water fountain nearby. *Only as a last resort*, he thought. *A last, last resort.*

Metal clanged against metal as Fox slashed at Rumpole and she blocked his tonfa with her wheel, using it alternately as a shield and as a weapon. She pushed it toward him, smacking him in the face and knocking him backward, then in the same motion spun around and hurled the wheel at Yatsuhashi.

Yatsuhashi drew his sword and deflected the disc, which bounced off the fountain and went flying back to Rumpole. She held up what remained of her golden cord to catch the edge of the wheel, then whipped it back toward Yatsuhashi. He ducked as it passed over his head. But he wasn't able to stop the cord from wrapping around his neck. Rumpole pulled on it and he struggled, his face turning red.

Yatsuhashi sliced the cord with Fulcrum and caught his breath. Neptune drew Tri-Hard and transformed the gun into a trident. He jabbed it at Rumpole, activating the yellow Dust to shock her. The electricity arced over the gold lining of her coat harmlessly.

She jumped out of the way as Fox slashed at her, dropping and sweeping her leg to trip him. Fox went down. She tossed her cloak and it wrapped around him, delivering an electric jolt that made him convulse.

"Oops," Neptune said. "Sorry!"

"I can do this all night," Rumpole said furiously. "But I'll make a deal with you. You can leave if you defeat me in battle, or if you guess my name."

"Rumpole!" Neptune said.

Yatsuhashi lowered his sword and glared at Neptune.

Rumpole rolled her eyes. "My *first* name."

Neptune looked her over as she traded blows with Yatsuhashi. He was strong, but she was small and nimble, and she kept getting jabs in with her wheel and blocking his sword. Her golden cord was coiled at her waist.

Fox pulled the cloak off his head, and the golden lining caught the light.

"I bet her name has something to do with gold," Neptune sent.

"Aurora!" Fox called.

"Nope." Rumpole grinned.

"Goldie," Yatsuhashi shouted.

"Goldie?" Rumpole laughed. She tossed the wheel vertically toward Yatsuhashi. It rolled toward him, knocked him backward, and rebounded off his chest into her hands.

"ADA," Fox muttered. "List names that mean or are related to gold." He paused and then started rattling them off in alphabetical order, while the three of them continued trading blows with Rumpole. They were getting some hits in, but she must have had an absurdly high level of Aura because they weren't slowing her down one bit.

"Cressida!" Fox yelled.

"I always liked that name, but no," Rumpole said.

Neptune became aware that they had gathered a crowd of spectators, including Headmaster Theodore. The Shade students were finally showing some interest in them.

"Headmaster, aren't you going to do something to stop her?" Neptune called.

Headmaster Theodore flashed him a thumbs-up. "This is all you."

"It seems your last lesson as students here will be one on humility," Professor Rumpole growled. "The world will not stop to give you what you want, no matter what Ozpin may have taught you."

Neptune was worn out already, and Yatsuhashi and Fox were struggling, too, starting to make mistakes.

"Maybe we should just make a break for it," Yatsuhashi sent.

"What do you think I've been trying to do?" Neptune sent. *"She's too fast."*

Finally Fox shouted, "Xanthe!" and Professor Rumpole stopped.

Her face splotched red with anger. "You cheated!" She stomped her foot. The cobblestones cracked from the impact.

"Did not," Fox said.

"Someone told you my name!"

"I guessed it, fair and square. Now do the honorable thing and let us go."

Rumpole's shoulders slumped. She seemed to give up. "Fine. You can go," she said.

As Fox walked past her warily, the crowd of students and teachers clapped.

"Xanthe." Headmaster Theodore shook his head. "I never would have guessed that."

As Neptune walked by Professor Rumpole, he nodded. "Thanks."

"Don't thank me yet," she said, her eyes narrowed. She grabbed his arm and her eyes flashed gold.

Neptune felt his arm stiffen and grow heavy. Suddenly he couldn't move.

The spectators gasped and fell silent.

Fox stopped walking. *"What? What happened? What's wrong with Neptune?"*

"I'm okay," Neptune managed. "I think."

His arm was covered in gold. No, it *was* gold—at least the sleeve of his jacket was. In fact, so was the whole jacket. Was that why he felt so heavy?

"She turned him into gold," Yatsuhashi said in disbelief.

"My clothes, anyway," Neptune said. Neptune suddenly lurched backward as someone picked him up.

"We're going," Yatsuhashi said.

"Uh, Yatsuhashi. Put me down!" Neptune said. "I don't like this!"

"Fight's not over," Rumpole said. She swung her wheel toward

Yatsuhashi, but he blocked her with Neptune. Metal clanged. Neptune felt the shock of the impact. Fox dove back into battle.

"Put! Me! Down!" Neptune said.

Yatsuhashi threw Neptune toward Rumpole.

"Not what I meant!" Neptune called.

Rumpole took the full force of the blow and went down for the first time—good. Then Neptune's left glove turned to gold—not so good.

Neptune yelled, "Don't let her touch me anymore!"

Yatsuhashi darted forward, but instead of striking Rumpole with his sword, he placed his hand on her forehead. Was he feeling for a fever? Was he healing her somehow? Neptune couldn't make sense of what he was seeing.

"I'm sorry," Yatsuhashi whispered.

Rumpole's eyes glazed over and then she collapsed.

Somehow that seemed to rouse Headmaster Theodore from his admiration for the fight. "Enough!" his voice rumbled. "This battle is over."

"Sure, because we beat her," Fox muttered.

Yatsuhashi righted Neptune. "Thanks for the assist."

"What did you do to her?" Neptune asked.

"What I had to do," said Yatsuhashi sadly.

Headmaster Theodore knelt at Rumpole's side. He watched her, worried, until her eyes fluttered. She bolted upright. "Theo? Where am I? What happened?" She looked at Neptune. "Did I do that to you?"

Neptune had never been so glad to hear the professor's voice. "Yup. Now can you *undo* it?"

"Sorry, my Semblance doesn't work that way." It almost sounded like she wanted to help. Rumpole looked at her hand. "Some deeds can never be undone."

"But this is my favorite jacket," Neptune said.

"You can sell it and buy a hundred more of them now," Fox said.

"Everyone, please return to your rooms." Theodore raised a jeweled hand and turned to Rumpole. "Let's get you out of here."

Neptune, Fox, and Yatsuhashi accompanied Headmaster Theodore and Professor Rumpole to her classroom while the rest of the crowd dispersed.

"What do you remember from before the fight?" Theodore asked.

Rumpole's eyes widened. "Everything."

Neptune wasn't sure he wanted her to remember everything. But she had more to say. Rumpole shook her head and pleaded with the headmaster. "Theo, that wasn't me. The reinitiation, the curfew . . . I never would have suggested those things."

His face serious, Theodore replied, "I know. I mean, *now* I know. You must have been under some kind of mind control, until Mr. Daichi here did . . ." Theodore looked at Yatsuhashi. "Something."

"I only tried to make her forget the last half hour so we could get away," Yatsuhashi explained.

"You erased her memories of the fight, but somehow your Semblance also broke the mental suggestion she was under," Theodore said. "Xanthe—"

Rumpole was shocked. "How do you know my name?"

"Lucky guess." He shook his head. "Rumpole. How did this happen to you? When did it happen?"

Rumpole's voice was slow, as if she was still struggling to process it. "A few weeks ago I went to the Wastelands," she said. "Some Huntsmen said they had information on the whereabouts of the Crown. So they led me out there." She blinked a few times. "And it was a trap. I couldn't beat them. Though we fought for hours—and they finally overwhelmed me. Since then, I've been working for the Crown. I can't believe it. It was worse than mind control . . . I *wanted* to help them. I believed in their cause."

"But who is the Crown?" Theodore asked. Apparently, the headmaster knew a lot less than some of his students.

Rumpole said, "I don't know for sure. Whatever they did to me, whomever did it, I never even saw them. I was just instructed to disrupt things at Shade Academy as much as possible. So I did."

"But why?" Neptune asked. "Why would the Crown be worried about students like us?"

"We were getting close to discovering them," Fox said. "Sounds like the reinitiation and the curfew Rumpole suggested to the headmaster were supposed to stop us, or at least slow us down."

"Weaken us," Yatsuhashi added. "Professor, does this look familiar?"

He held up his Scroll and showed her a picture—the selfie that Velvet and Sun had taken at the Mirage. Then he zoomed in on something in the background. A golden sai.

"I did that," Rumpole said, the memory coming back. "I captured that sai myself. I was fighting a Huntress named—"

"Carmine Esclados, the woman we stopped in the desert."

"Yes. She's also a former student." Rumpole's eyes narrowed. "We fought in a cage match at a club called the Mirage. She was stronger than she was before. Everyone there was."

Neptune was taking it all in, but he was also thinking about his own problems. Smaller ones, to be sure, but still problems. "Hey, so if this was all because of the Crown, does that mean we can go back to our old teams?" he asked. Did he actually want to be back on a team with Sun?

Headmaster Theodore nodded. "Knowing what we know now, I think that would be most wise. As soon as everyone is safely back at Shade. But we don't want to tip our hand . . . it might be better if the Crown still believes Rumpole is under their influence."

"Students are missing?" Rumpole asked, distressed. "Because of me?"

"That's why we were fighting," Yatsuhashi said. "It turns out Velvet and Sun are at the Mirage." He looked meaningfully at Neptune. "It just took some . . . encouraging . . . for the whole story to come out."

"Team ROSC is missing, too—they were on a mission in the Wastelands," Fox added.

"Then they're in danger," Rumpole said in an agitated voice. "There's a Crown base out there. I'll go. If they think I'm still working with them, they'll let me pass."

"You're in no condition to fight," Theodore said. "I'll gather the Huntsmen."

Rumpole grabbed his arm. "No. We can't trust them. Many of them have been compromised."

"Professors, then."

"Like me?" Rumpole shook her head. "No telling who else they've subverted."

"Then who can we trust?" Theodore roared. Clearly, the stress was getting to him.

Yatsuhashi raised his hand.

"Send us," Fox said without even waiting to be recognized.

"Absolutely not!" Theodore said. "*I'll* go."

Yatsuhashi turned toward the desert. "The Crown is obviously planning something, and if they realize Professor Rumpole isn't under their control anymore, they might try something drastic. They might attack the school. So we have to go now and get our friends back. And then we'll be ready for whatever they try next."

Rumpole nodded, meeting Theodore's gaze. "They can do this. My objections about them earlier—that wasn't me. It was the Crown's doing."

Theodore looked each of them over. Then he nodded grudgingly. "You wouldn't be here otherwise. But you'll stay in contact, and you won't take any stupid chances."

"I'll take some students to the Wastelands," Fox said.

"And we'll go to the Mirage," Neptune said.

"We'll bring back Velvet and Sun," Yatsuhashi said.

"Just one thing first," Neptune said.

"What's that?"

"Um, can I go back to my room and change? This gold jacket is really cramping my style. And my arms."

CHAPTER TWELVE

Yatsuhashi and Neptune followed the directions from Professor Rumpole to a squat building on the edge of town.

"Looks abandoned," Neptune said. "Are you sure this is it?"

"I've been here before. We should have fought our way inside earlier." Yatsuhashi looked at Neptune and then turned away, covering his mouth to contain his laughter.

"What?" Neptune said.

Yatsuhashi put up a hand. "I'm sorry, but I can't take you seriously wearing that fake mustache." Not that he'd ever been able to take him seriously before.

Neptune stroked the bushy black mustache and Yatsuhashi couldn't help it. He burst out laughing.

"It's a disguise!" Neptune said. "We're going undercover."

"It doesn't even match your hair!" Yatsuhashi howled. "These silver armbands are our disguises." Professor Rumpole said all the Crown's supporters wore them as a sign of their loyalty.

Neptune sighed and peeled off the mustache.

"That's better." Yatsuhashi stopped laughing and pressed his hand against the reinforced steel door. He could feel vibrations on the other side but didn't have the ability to make sense of them. Fox or Velvet might have been able to understand what was happening, but all Yatsuhashi knew was that something *was* happening.

He knocked on the door. A panel slid open and eyes appeared in the narrow opening.

"Who do we fight for?" a deep voice intoned.

Professor Rumpole had given them the passphrase, too, as it was lodged in her memory now. "For crown and kingdom," Yatsuhashi said.

"Professor Rumpole sent us," Neptune piped up. "From Shade." Then Neptune winked. Yatsuhashi appreciated how he was embracing his role.

The eyes considered the two for a while. Yatsuhashi tensed, waiting for trouble. He wondered if he would be able to beat down that door this time.

He could just manage it, for Velvet, or he would die trying.

Then at last the panel slid closed. A lock was undone and the door swung open to reveal a man about Yatsuhashi's size on the other side. Yatsuhashi made sure he saw the silver armband around his arm.

"Check your weapons and Dust," the bouncer said.

Yatsuhashi handed over Fulcrum. The guard weighed it appreciatively. "Nice sword."

"Thank you," Yatsuhashi said.

Neptune passed over Tri-Hard. "Dust is inside," Neptune offered. The guard turned to Yatsu.

"Oh, no Dust," Yatsuhashi said. "Don't need it."

"Good for you! Go on back. The boss is watching the fights. Enjoy!"

"Friendly guy," Neptune whispered as they walked down the dimly lit corridor toward the sounds of clapping, chanting, and cheering. Whoever was fighting had a lot of fans.

"He thinks we're on his side," Yatsuhashi reminded him. He didn't like how light he felt without the weight of his greatsword on his back or in his hand.

They followed the loud music to the end of a hall and emerged into a room that looked somehow larger than the building, with steps that led down into the floor, creating a huge space below surface level. A giant gold cage occupied the center, and two people were fighting inside it.

"Looks like Rumpole left her mark on the place," Neptune said. Yatsuhashi pointed to the golden sai on the opposite wall. "There's the sai from Velvet's picture."

He scanned the crowd until he saw a pair of rabbit ears sticking out. He nodded in that direction and took off, Neptune close beside him as they pushed through the crowd. Yatsuhashi felt many eyes on him as he passed. He was used to being noticed in groups because of his height, but it made him nervous when he was trying to go unnoticed. *Maybe we should have thought this through better*, he realized.

But then there was Velvet, and he didn't care about anyone else anymore. He started to put a hand on her shoulder, but stopped, remembering she didn't like it when people snuck up on her. He was not in the mood to get thrown across the room.

"Velvet!" he said.

She turned around, shock on her face. "Yatsuhashi! What are you doing here?"

That wasn't the reaction he'd been expecting. There was shock but no relief.

"Erm. Are you all right?" he asked.

Velvet beamed like she was completely at home. "I'm great! This place is great!"

"You aren't . . . in any trouble?" Yatsuhashi prompted.

She just rose up on her tiptoes and leaned toward him. "The Crown is here." She winked.

Yatsuhashi didn't know what to make of that. Was this for real? All he could do was look around for the Crown. "Is that him?" he asked Velvet, nodding at a white guy in a suit watching the fight from a balcony.

She collapsed into laughter. "Definitely not." She paused, as if understanding something. "Do you want to meet the Crown?" she asked.

"You know them?" Neptune gave Yatsuhashi a worried look.

Yatsuhashi was worried about something else now. "Velvet, where's Sun?" he asked.

Velvet just pointed at the cage.

Yatsuhashi finally turned his attention to the enclosed arena in the center of the room. One of the fighters was someone he recognized—that short guy in the green tank top was one of the thugs they had crossed a few weeks ago. And there was someone swinging from the bars of the cage like—

"Sun!" Neptune said. "What's he doing?"

"He's fighting, silly," Velvet said, like she saw this every day.

Right now, Sun seemed to be winning. Two of his Semblance-devised avatars appeared on either side of the green guy, grabbing his arms and holding him in place, while Sun dropped from the top of the cage and landed feetfirst on his face. The gas mask cracked as the man went down.

"And Sun Wukong wins again!" the announcer called out. Sun bowed. He was wearing a gold crown.

"This is so weird," Yatsuhashi said. "Velvet, we have to get Sun and get out of here."

Velvet gave him an eerie stare. "I'm not going with you," she said. "Now I know this is where I belong. The Crown wants me for who I am. Who I really am—not who CFVY or NOVA think I should be. Hey, you could join us, too!"

Yatsuhashi reached down and cupped Velvet's face in one of his large hands. He really hated to do this, but it seemed he had no other choice. Someday she might even thank him.

"Sorry, V." Yatsuhashi brushed his thumb against Velvet's temple and caught her with his other hand as she went limp. Then he shook her gently. "Come on, Velvet. Wake up," he said. "You need to wake up."

Velvet's eyes flew open and she stared at Yatsuhashi for a moment. Then she hugged him.

"Yatsu! Thank goodness!"

"Shhh," Yatsuhashi said. "We don't want to draw any attention."

"When did you get here?" she whispered, like she hadn't seen him before.

"Just now. I erased a few seconds from your memory, which somehow breaks the Crown's mental control. Do you know what the Crown looks like? Is he here?" Yatsuhashi asked urgently.

"I—I can't . . ." Velvet started to look around. She was still confused by the gap in her memory.

"Never mind. Velvet, you and Neptune need to get out of here. I'm going to try to get close to Sun and use my Semblance. I'm assuming he's under the Crown's control, too."

Velvet grabbed Yatsuhashi's arm. "We were captured together. And Umber's here, too! We have to save her."

Yatsuhashi sighed. "Okay. No one gets left behind. But you two get ready to go." He glanced at Neptune. "Don't wait for me."

As Yatsuhashi half paid attention to Sun, who was fighting a new opponent, the other two slipped away. The crowd loved Sun, it turned out. Each time he used his Semblance, the audience cheered, and Sun was eating it up. Meanwhile, Yatsuhashi kept an eye out for Umber while trying not to look too obvious.

There! He spotted her through the bars on the other side of the cage. Umber looked curious as he approached and eyed his armband with suspicion.

"Yatsuhashi? Didn't think this place was your speed," she said.

"I don't have time for this. Are you working for the Crown?" he asked.

"Of course not. I'm just here to enjoy the fighting."

Yatsuhashi nodded. "You've got something on your cheek."

He reached for her face, but she knocked his arm away with her wrist. Yatsuhashi frowned.

"I don't like doing this, but I'm trying to help," he said.

"Hey!" Umber called to security. "Over here! This guy is harassing me."

"No!" Yatsuhashi groaned. He tried one more time to reach

her forehead, but when she deflected him this time, he grabbed her wrist with his other hand. He didn't actually need to touch her head to use his Semblance, but it made it a little easier. He concentrated on erasing the last few seconds from her memory, since that seemed to be enough to break whatever control people were under.

Umber blinked and became unsteady, but he held her up. She saw him holding her wrist. "Yatsuhashi? Where'd you come from? This place doesn't seem your speed."

"It's time to go, Umber," he said.

"Go? But you just got here." She lowered her glasses and looked him in the eyes. "Stay a while."

Yatsuhashi couldn't move. His limbs felt like stone. Umber had an amazing Semblance—too bad she was using it to serve the Crown. Of her own accord.

"Looks like we have a new challenger!" the announcer called. "Open the cage!"

Suddenly a couple of goons picked Yatsuhashi up and carried him as Umber backed up into the cage. They rotated him as she kept her eyes on his.

"That's a big guy," the announcer's voice boomed. "Do we think he can beat our reigning champion?"

The spectators booed. Tough crowd.

Umber backed herself out of the cage and slammed the door shut before she tilted her mirrored glasses back down. "You're gonna make a good addition to the team," she said.

"Hey, Yatsuhashi," Sun called. "Welcome to the monkey house."

Yatsuhashi turned. He was so tired. Using his Semblance was

draining, since he rarely used it at all—and it took incredible focus to use it *carefully*. That and the fight with Rumpole were leaving him vulnerable. He probably wouldn't last long in the ring if it came to that.

"Hey, Sun. Under the Crown's mind control?" Yatsuhashi asked.

"Mind control? What are you talking about?" Sun said. He seemed the same as ever.

Yatsuhashi nodded. "I don't want to hurt you, so I apologize in advance."

The two of them circled each other. "Don't worry, I can handle myself," Sun said.

"I know you can, but I want you to think about the team this time." Yatsuhashi cracked his neck before he got started.

"I'm my own team." Sun closed his eyes and was joined by two glowing duplicates of himself.

Perfect, Yatsuhashi thought. *I hope this works.*

He looked at each of them in turn. "If you remember what I'm saying in a minute, I want you to get out of here with Velvet and Neptune. They'll explain everything. Don't wait; don't try to save me."

"Hey, eyes over here," Sun said, pointing at his face. "These guys are just extensions of my consciousness."

"I hoped you'd say that." Yatsuhashi rushed for Sun.

Sun leaped out of the way while one of the clones slipped behind Yatsuhashi's knees and the other one pushed him, making Yatsuhashi topple backward.

Yatsuhashi rolled away from them just as Sun came crashing

down where he'd been standing. Yatsuhashi punched one duplicate and kicked at another, causing them to scatter out of the way.

He and Sun fought hand to hand for a while, roving all around the cage, while Sun's duplicates taunted him and got their own hits in. Yatsuhashi pounded the ground hard enough to shake Sun and his duplicates off their feet, creating a big crack in the floor. Then he reached around and grabbed for Sun, holding on tight to his tail. He spun Sun around and around, focusing his Semblance on erasing the last few seconds of memory.

Sun picked up speed. "Whooooa!"

Finally Yatsuhashi let Sun go, and he crashed into the door of the cage—which burst open, sending him sprawling out into the crowd. Velvet and Neptune ran to his side.

Yatsuhashi saw something shiny on the floor as Sun stumbled to his feet. He picked it up. It was the crown Sun had been wearing.

When Yatsuhashi put it on his head, the crowd grew quiet.

"So who's next?" Yatsuhashi asked.

Then someone started clapping. Yatsuhashi looked up and saw the announcer grinning and leading the applause. "An excellent show! You've earned an audience with the Crown."

"I'd rather quit while I'm ahead," Yatsuhashi said.

"No one quits in Vacuo. We have a very special treat for our final fight of the evening."

Yatsuhashi flicked his eyes toward the crowd. Sun had recovered and he was slipping toward the exit with Velvet and Neptune. They would need a distraction if they were going to escape unnoticed. And if they didn't go unnoticed, well . . . Yatsuhashi was glad to see Velvet somehow still had Anesidora with her. They'd be fine.

He turned his attention back to the banged-up door of the cage as a familiar Huntress stepped inside.

"Great," Yatsu muttered. It was Carmine Esclados.

She tossed her bright red hair back and grinned, her sai floating just over her right shoulder.

"That hardly seems fair," Yatsuhashi said, his eye on her weapon.

"If you wanted fair, you should have stayed out of Vacuo," she shot back. Aggressively, Carmine strode toward him.

Yatsuhashi backed up. Using his Semblance and sending Sun out of the cage had pushed his Aura to a new low. He wanted to throw in the towel, but he had to give everyone a good show.

"I don't want to hurt you," Yatsuhashi said quietly.

His concern was wasted on Carmine. "As if!" Carmine retorted. She swung her leg toward him and the heel of her shoe sliced Yatsuhashi's chest, shattering his Aura. Her shoes had blades in them. Of course they did.

Yatsu hit the floor.

He should probably get up. He *needed* to get up. But that last kick had done him in. He watched as blood poured from the wound. He wasn't sure he could actually move.

As everything went murky and black he heard Carmine say, "I thought he'd last longer."

"You need to take better care of your toys. That's the third one this week," Umber said.

"Gill will fix him," Carmine said. "At least I won't go back empty-handed."

Then Yatsuhashi heard some commotion somewhere else in

the club. Gunfire and shouting that sounded far away. The lights went out, but he wasn't sure if that was the club lights or his vision. People screamed.

That had to be . . . friends fighting . . . out . . . but he, he'd done everything he—

CHAPTER THIRTEEN

Scarlet's gun was out of bullets. So was Coco's. Olive's pike was out of Gravity Dust. And Reese was down, trying to recover some Aura.

Team ROSC was sheltering in the metal skeleton of an old Dust mining rig. Most of it was buried deep in the sand, leaving just the apex, a short tower that gave them some protection from the Grimm. But it also allowed the Grimm to pin them down and surround them.

Scarlet borrowed Reese's hoverboard to fly out and hack at a Death Stalker with his sword. But it was slow work, and the Grimm kept coming. Meanwhile, Coco fended off the Dromedons on their left flank with nothing but her handbag, her fists, and her bad attitude.

Though Olive couldn't manipulate gravity anymore, her weapon's blade had been infused with it, so it always flew back to her when she threw it. This was coming in handy against the Ravager that had just joined the party. By throwing the trusty weapon constantly at the large flying creature, she was keeping it at bay and gradually inflicting damage.

But it was still too slow. And there would soon be more of them if this dragged on any longer.

"Any ideas?" Coco shouted.

Scarlet coughed. The battle was kicking up a lot of sand, clouding the air around them and making them choke. They'd run out of water hours ago.

"We keep fighting!" he said. No other choice.

"Give me back my board!" Reese called. Scarlet glanced down and saw her swaying unsteadily, but she was on her feet.

"You should keep resting," Coco yelled.

"You aren't the boss of me!" Reese called back.

Scarlet jumped off the hoverboard and glided onto the Death Stalker's back. He had already managed to hack through most of the Grimm's segmented tail, which dragged behind it in the sand, slowing it down. Its left pincer was cracked and broken. He jabbed his sword downward.

As the Death Stalker collapsed, Reese's board zipped back to her. She grabbed it, broke it into two pistols, and started firing at Grimm on their right flank. She flamed a Dromedon with the gun in her left hand while icing a second with the gun in her right and then shooting it—causing it to shatter.

Scarlet rejoined his team, eyeing the Ravager in the air nervously.

"Where are they all coming from?" Olive asked.

"I'm more interested in what's drawing them to the Wastelands," Coco said. "We're under stress, but that doesn't account for this many Grimm. And they've been encroaching on the Wastelands for weeks, before we even got here."

"You'd think they would be more attracted to the city," Scarlet said. "Way more stressed-out people there, plus a school full of hormonal teens."

Coco grinned and went back to beating up Grimm.

"Need some help?" Fox's voice intruded on Scarlet's thoughts. He looked around.

"Fox!" Coco shouted.

"Fox?" Reese and Olive looked confused.

"It's a thing he does," Coco and Scarlet said.

"I brought some friends. Hope there are enough Grimm to go around."

Scarlet expected to see Yatsuhashi and Velvet, but when Fox arrived, Sage, Nolan, and Octavia were with him. Octavia used her kris to send a fiery blast at the Ravager at the same time Olive tossed her pike, bringing the Grimm down. Fox tackled a Dromedon that was bearing down on Reese, whose guns were clicking—out of ammo. Fox hacked at the Dromedon with his tonfa while Reese reassembled her weapon and used the bladed hoverboard as a melee weapon.

Nolan skidded to a halt beside Scarlet and Coco. "Special delivery!" he said, tossing a bandolier of bullets to Coco. "Already charged with fire Dust."

Coco whooped. "You are my favorite person right now." She opened her gun and reloaded it.

"I heard that," Fox sent. *"I'm the one who thought to bring you ammo, you know."*

"You think of everything," Coco sent.

Nolan handed Scarlet a pack of bullets. "Just normal bullets for you."

Scarlet winked. "That's all I need. Thank you."

With Fox, Nolan, and Octavia fresh for the battle, Scarlet, Coco, Reese, and Olive rallied. Together they managed to make short work of the remaining two Jackalopes and the final Death Stalker.

"How'd you find us?" Coco asked Fox when the teams came together, exhausted. The sky was beginning to lighten as dawn neared.

Fox tilted his head.

"Don't be rude, Coco. What she meant to say was thank you!" Reese said.

"Good looking out," Olive said.

Coco gritted her teeth. "I *always* say what I mean," she said. "Sure. Thanks. But what are you doing here? Did Rumpole send you?"

"Well, that's a bit of a story," Fox said to the group of eight.

He caught them up on what had been going down since they'd left Shade Academy.

That last update—about Velvet and the Mirage—was what Coco cared most about. "We have to get to the Mirage. Carmine was heading there, too."

"Not so fast," Fox said. "Yatsuhashi and Neptune can handle it. But Rumpole said the Crown has another base out here in the Wastelands, so here we are."

"How do we even find it?" Nolan asked.

"I can detect a large group of people nearby," Fox said.

"What?" Reese folded her arms. "You can do what now? In

addition to the . . ." She waved her hand around. "Head-talky thing?"

Fox shrugged. "It's an Aura thing. I can sense it, even distinguish one person from another if I know them well enough."

"So is it another settlement nearby?" Sage asked, worried.

"Not exactly," Fox said. He stomped his foot and took a deep breath. "Actually, they're beneath us."

"Seriously?" Coco tossed up her hand. "I know how this goes."

"I've noticed that there's a strong CCT signal here, too," Olive said. She held up her Scroll. "But it's encrypted, which is why we couldn't call for help."

"Backup," Coco corrected her.

Olive rolled her eyes. "Whatever. It's strongest right here, where we're standing."

Octavia looked up at the mining rig looming over their heads. "So you think this is some kind of pirate CCT tower? Aren't you a smartie?"

Olive blushed.

"So how do we get down there?" Reese asked. "I don't see an entrance."

Fox held up his hands. "You're asking the wrong guy."

"If this is a mining rig, there has to be a mine, right?" Scarlet looked around. Then he looked down.

"If it's buried under the sand, how can anyone get in and out of it?" Reese asked.

"Carmine can move sand," Coco and Fox said at once.

"Whoa, that was weird," Fox sent.

"Carmine Esclados's Semblance is telekinesis," Coco explained.

"Like Professor Goodwitch?" Nolan said.

Coco pinched her fingers together. "Sort of. She can only move small things, but sand is very, very small."

Sage kicked some sand. "That's gonna take us a while. And we didn't bring shovels."

"Does anyone have Gravity Dust?" Coco asked.

They took inventory and came up with enough Gravity Dust to fuel Olive's awl pike.

"But I can still only fire a few Gravity waves," Olive said. "Not enough to move all this sand."

"Leave that part to me," Coco said. "I can enhance the effect of the Dust. You guys might want to stand clear."

The team scrambled to get away from the tower as Coco and Olive stood before it. They looked at each other and nodded. Olive started spinning her pike like a baton, and Coco concentrated. Suddenly a gravity pulse burst from Olive's weapon, which blasted a massive wave of sand away from the bottom of the tower.

When the sand had cleared, Scarlet wiped grit and tears from his eyes. The full mining rig was visible, and an entrance had been bored into the bedrock at its base. The group moved toward it.

"Someone should probably stay out here," Scarlet said. "We don't know what we're going to find in there."

"If Carmine's involved, chances are it's going to be a fight," Coco said. Though Scarlet knew she was mostly worried about whether Carmine was targeting Velvet right now.

"I'll keep watch," Nolan said quietly.

Sage rolled his eyes, but Scarlet elbowed him and shook his head.

Scarlet guessed Sage was viewing the gesture as cowardice, but Scarlet thought it was actually brave of Nolan to volunteer to stay topside on his own—with the combined threat of Grimm and Crown henchmen in the area. Especially knowing how vulnerable the guy was to the possibility of losing even more friends.

Coco raised an eyebrow. "That's a good idea. If something happens to us—"

"I'll come after you," Nolan said.

"No, you go back to Shade and tell them what we found," Fox said.

Coco nodded and sided with her former teammate. "Exactly."

"If we're going to split up, we might as well use teamspeak," Fox sent. *"It will help cut down on the noise, too."*

Scarlet thought Coco looked nervous. She was breathing fast and she was perspiring, even though the desert had cooled considerably overnight.

"You okay?" he whispered.

She nodded and tapped the side of her glasses. The lenses glowed amber. "I am now," she said. "Thanks to BunnyVision."

"Bunny what?"

"Night vision glasses, courtesy of Velvet."

Scarlet wasn't sure what that meant, but he resolved to keep an eye on her through whatever happened next.

They all filed into the underground bunker. Just before he went in, Scarlet glanced back at the entrance and Nolan waved. Scarlet grinned and flashed him a thumbs-up. Then he stepped into darkness.

The air was stale and the walls were close. Bad things happened in caves like this.

Coco and Fox took the lead, guiding the group with her boosted sight and his Semblance. Olive brought up the rear, using her naturally enhanced Faunus sight and hearing to guard their flank. They walked in a close pack along old broken cart tracks on a decline.

"I'll keep Nolan looped into teamspeak as long as I can so he knows what's going on," Fox sent.

"Thanks," Nolan sent. *"See anything yet?"*

Fox sighed softly.

"It's dark down here. Just a long passage leading down . . . Oh, hold on," Coco cut in. She'd spotted something.

"Four paths, in the cardinal directions," Coco sent. *"The south cave has collapsed, but there's still three choices: north, west, and east. I can't see far down any of them."*

Reese came up with a plan. "So Coco, Fox, and Olive each lead me, Sage, Scarlet, and Octavia down one of the paths," she sent.

"Wait," Olive sent. *"I hear voices this way. I'm pointing east, but you probably can't see that."*

"East? That's back toward the city," Coco sent. *"Is it possible these mines extend that far?"*

"You thinking this is another Mountain Glenn situation?" Fox asked.

"Could be," Olive sent. *"The whole area was mined pretty heavily. That's why these are the Wastelands—they literally wasted the land, draining an oasis so they could dig under it to the Dust beneath. All that's left is sand."*

"Give me a second," Fox sent. He faced each of the open caves for a short while, north, east, west. Then he turned back to the east.

"These caverns could be twisting around, but I'm sensing those Auras up ahead—east."

"Which is where the voices are coming from," Coco sent. *"Good enough for me. Let's go. Slowly and cautiously."*

The voices gradually grew louder, though Scarlet couldn't make out what they were saying. Soon they saw a light a long ways off, which grew brighter as they tiptoed forward. Scarlet could make the others out better now, and Coco even switched off her glasses.

"I guess we're on the right track," Olive sent. *"Get it, because we're on a mine railway?"*

A few members of the team groaned.

"Shh . . . ," Coco sent. *"If we can hear them, they can hear us."*

"Sorry," Olive sent. *"I can hear them clearly now. They're talking about . . . charging times? How long it will take to get ready. When someone named Gillian should move."*

"I'm going to get a closer look," Scarlet said.

Coco nodded and pressed a finger to her lips.

Slowly, Scarlet crept farther into the large cavern until he could see and hear what was going on from the shadows. He started recording on his Scroll.

"You should take all of it, Gillian," a woman with pink hair said. "This is war, after all."

The pink hair reminded Scarlet of a photo he'd seen at the Weeping Wall. A missing girl. Rosa Schwein. Could this be her?

"We value our resources in Vacuo," a soft, buttery female voice said. Scarlet had to strain to hear her. "We don't waste them, and we don't use them up. Besides, what's the point of ruling if there aren't any people?"

Scarlet edged forward a little more until he could see the woman who was speaking. She was sitting in a large seat carved out of the rock wall, and she was hard to miss because a rainbow of colors swirled and shifted around her.

"What is that?" Scarlet sent. *"That woman—Gillian. She's glowing."*

"Aura," Fox sent.

"Why can I see it?" Scarlet said.

"It's the strongest, brightest Aura I've ever sensed."

The woman, Gillian, had fair skin and black hair braided into two loops on either side. She wore a long dress with many sheer layers of blue, white, green, and purple that resembled running water. A silver chain was wrapped around her waist, matching the slim silver diadem that gleamed on her head.

"She's wearing a crown," Scarlet sent. *"I've seen her picture on the Weeping Wall, too."*

Rosa stood on Gillian's right, tapping away at a Scroll. "This is going to take too long," she said.

Gillian glared at her. "Don't use that in front of me."

"Like it or not, it's hard to get by without Scrolls these days. We need some tech to coordinate with Jax and his team," Rosa said.

Gillian stood up from her throne and walked down the stone steps. She stepped to the left and Scarlet craned his neck to see where she had gone. He covered a gasp as he saw what was in the rest of the room.

Rows of beds, filled with sleeping people. Gillian walked to one of the beds and put her hand on an unconscious man's shoulder. The Aura around her flared more brightly.

Fox appeared at Scarlet's side. Coco and the others joined them.

"Whoa," Fox said. *"Her Aura is so strong because it doesn't belong to her. She's draining it from other people."*

"How can she do that?" Coco asked.

"If that's her Semblance, then I don't know how we can ever stop her," Octavia sent, discouraged.

"There have to be at least fifty people in there," Scarlet sent. *"It's the people who've gone missing. The Crown wasn't just kidnapping people with powerful Semblances . . . they were kidnapping regular people, too . . . for their Aura."*

"Well, we can stop them now," Reese sent. *"We outnumber them. I don't think she even has a weapon."*

"She is *a weapon,"* Coco sent. *"And based on what we heard about Rosa Schwein, she's a bit of a threat on her own."*

Gillian left the man on the bed and moved on to the next sleeping victim.

Fox turned his head back and forth. *"Bertilak's here. But his Aura's faint."* He nodded his head and Coco leaned forward. She pointed to a man lying in a bed on the far side of the room.

"I thought he worked with them," Scarlet said.

"Looks like he's more valuable for his Aura than as a fighter," Coco sent. *"The Crown must not have been happy about him losing Gus."*

"Coco?" Fox sent. *"Do we attack them? We may not get a better shot at this, while their guard is down."*

"You may as well bring in the army," Gillian said in a bored voice. "When I'm done here, I'll strengthen them for the fight."

"I don't like the sound of that," Sage sent.

Rosa tapped at her screen some more and a rough-looking

crowd of people entered the room—all of them armed, many of them armored. All of them wearing silver armbands like Gillian's crown.

"So much for attacking now," Fox sent.

Scarlet remembered the pig-eared Faunus in the brown jumpsuit from Sun's fight downtown seemingly ages ago. These must be the recruits with the strongest Semblances, bent to the Crown's service, either willingly or through some form of mind control.

"We should go," Coco sent. She started backing up. If those guys discovered them, they would never escape these caves.

"What about fighting?" Reese sent.

"Sometimes you don't. The seven of us can't take on a small army. And when you can't fight, you live to fight another day. Let's get back to Shade."

It was a tense journey back that seemed longer than the trip in. They were all spooked by what they'd seen down there, and all that they didn't understand. They needed answers. They needed a plan.

They needed an army of their own.

CHAPTER FOURTEEN

Sun looked around Professor Rumpole's office, which was crowded with students as well as Remnant artifacts. He was still a bit dazed from his experience at the Mirage and was finding it difficult to settle his mind.

This office was the closest thing to a museum in Vacuo, with pictures and documents framed on the walls, display cases with rocks, ancient weapons, models and dioramas. The professor wasn't just a history fanatic; she had lived Remnant's history herself. And yet there wasn't a single thing on her desk to hint at her own history—no family photos or personal mementos.

"Sun?" Coco said, clearly repeating herself.

He shook his head and blinked, turning his attention back to the group. "I'm sorry. I'm a little out of it."

Professor Rumpole sipped some water. "I know the feeling. That mind control does a number on you."

Sun's eyes flashed at her. "Not as much of a number as we did on our friends," he said.

"It wasn't your fault," Rumpole said, maybe not for the first time. But she sounded more like she was trying to convince herself.

She, too, knew the feeling of being captured by the Crown and subject to its control. It was hard to accept there was nothing you could do.

"Thanks, but that doesn't help Yatsuhashi," Sun said. "We should go back and get him."

"Yatsuhashi is exactly where he wanted to be," Velvet said. "We have to trust him."

She'd been quiet on the trip back from the Mirage last night and during the morning's discussion with Rumpole, Neptune, Scarlet, and the newly returned group from the Wastelands.

Did Velvet blame him for what had happened at the club? Sun hadn't just failed Yatsuhashi; he had failed her, too.

"If you say so. You know him better than I do," Sun said.

Sun hadn't really wanted to get to know Yatsuhashi better, but now he owed the big guy. If not for him, he'd still be under the Crown's thumb, doing who knew what. He didn't understand how Yatsuhashi had broken the mental hold on him, but Velvet had explained that Yatsu's Semblance allowed him to make people forget things—and apparently it could do more than that, too. He'd helped the elderly Edward Caspian remember things despite his mental illness. And perhaps he was the only person who could counter the Crown's influence now.

Sun tried to concentrate, but his mind kept wandering—more than usual. "Anyway, what were you saying, Coco?"

"I asked if this guy looks familiar." She held up her Scroll to show him one of the pictures Velvet had taken at the Weeping Wall.

Sun leaned forward and squinted.

"Here." Rumpole tapped the keyboard at her desk. The picture from Coco's Scroll appeared as a hologram over her desk, showing a pale boy and a girl with similar hair and features. They stood back to back, wearing the short, light tunics that most Vacuans favored.

"Yeah, that's the guy who brainwashed me," Sun growled. The boy's black hair was tied into a topknot, just like it had been in the back room at the club, only there he'd been wearing a silver diadem and a blue linen duster embroidered with spirals. The shapes had seemed to swirl on the fabric as Jax put his hand on Sun's head and exerted his will over him.

"That's Jax Asturias," Neptune said. "And his sister . . ."

"Gillian," Coco said. "We saw her at the Wastelands. How do you know their names?" Coco asked.

"We interviewed their dad!" Neptune said.

Sun frowned. "We did?"

"Yesterday. Before you ran off to the Mirage."

Sun rubbed his temples wearily. "Now I wish I'd stayed with you. I remember now. Mr. Asturias said his kids were students here."

Professor Rumpole nodded. "Gill was top of her class and ambitious, the leader of her team. Jax was arrogant but didn't have anything to back up that arrogance. He always took his sister's lead. I think she was the only reason he was here—and it showed. He was expelled and she dropped out a couple of years ago."

Rumpole frowned. "Mind control. I had no idea he had such a powerful Semblance, let alone any Semblance at all. I certainly would have recognized him if I'd seen him."

"Which is likely why you *didn't* see him when he brainwashed you," Coco said.

"A shame I didn't see this photo earlier," Rumpole said.

"We tried!" Coco said. "You said you were following your own leads. Why? Is there anything about them that would have made you realize they're the Crown?"

"Just one thing." Rumpole got up, a little shakily, and moved to the far wall. She clearly was still out of it, too, but then she'd been under Jax's influence for much longer.

She took a painting from the wall and brought it to the group, holding it up like one of her favorite belongings for show-and-tell. "As you brought up in class, Ms. Adel, Vacuo—each of Remnant's kingdoms were once ruled by monarchies. This is an artist's rendition of the very first king of Vacuo, Malik the Sunderer. All this was hundreds of years ago, so long ago that it's almost faded into myth. Impossible for anyone to remember what life was like then, or be able to truly trace their lineage back to the early dynasties." Rumpole turned and returned the painting to the wall.

"Jax and Gill were very interested in Vacuan history, just as you were, Coco," she continued. "I should have put it together then and listened to what you had to say. I'm sorry."

Coco's cheeks flushed. "So they're obsessed with Vacuo's past," she said. "But why?"

"They call themselves the Crown," Sun said. "Jax even wore one. Like royalty."

"Gill too," Scarlet pointed out.

"Like they want to be the new king and queen of Vacuo or something," Coco said.

"Lots of people in Vacuo want things to go back to the old ways," Fox sent. *"The old, old ways."*

"But no one has the power to make it happen," Sun said. "It was too long ago; things have changed too much."

"At the very least, you'd need an army to start with," Coco said.

"Their dad was big on this stuff, too," Neptune said. "He showed me his collection of Vacuan apocrypha, relics from the old kings, he called them. Rusty old weapons, worn-out drums. I made an excuse and got out of there quick."

"I think we should talk to him again," Coco said.

"Neptune and I know him already," Sun volunteered. "We'll go."

"I'll join you," Coco said. "I need to ask him about what we saw under the Wastelands."

"I'm coming, too," Velvet and Fox said at the same time.

"You read my mind," Velvet said to him.

Fox groaned. "This has to stop."

"Guess we've been a team long enough, we're more in sync than we thought," Coco said.

Scarlet cleared his throat. "Mind if I tag along?"

Sun smiled. "Since when do you want in on the action?"

"Since you've been hoarding it all for yourself," Scarlet said.

Fair enough, Sun thought. But he didn't want to do that now. "Honestly, I think I'm at the point where I could use a little *less* excitement," he said.

"Did everyone hear that?" Sage exclaimed. "Are we sure he still isn't brainwashed? Because that sure doesn't sound like the Sun I know."

"Maybe I'm changing," Sun said. Then he realized something. "I suppose you want to come, too."

"Don't you know it."

"Yeah!" Neptune jumped up. "The band is back together!"

Sun smiled at Velvet, but she looked a little down. Team SSSN might be back together, but part of Team CFVY was still in the den of the enemy. Whether he wanted to be there or not, he knew she was worried about Yatsuhashi.

Coco looked to Rumpole. "When we get back from talking to Mr. Asturias, we need to see the headmaster."

"I'll see what I can do," Rumpole said. "He's made it clear he needs time to think about all this, to come up with a plan. He's shaken by what's been happening. Shade Academy may be in grave danger."

"With all due respect," Coco said.

"Here we go," Fox sent.

"I'd like to hear it from Headmaster Theodore himself. It's not that I don't trust you . . ."

"But you have every reason not to." Rumpole sighed. "I assure you, I am quite free of Jax's control, thanks to Mr. Daichi. But I understand your reluctance. And I agree. Theo needs to hear all this—from you directly. I'm not sure he fully trusts me right now, either. He would be a fool to, after what I've done to his school." Her shoulders slumped.

Sun figured that was probably the biggest disappointment and the ultimate betrayal for her: that she had let her friend and headmaster down. No one took their responsibility more seriously than Professor Rumpole. And Theodore didn't suffer failure or signs of weakness lightly. Never mind that Shade—Vacuo itself—was facing an unprecedented threat that no one could have prepared for.

They had to prepare now, before it was too late. If it wasn't already.

Finn Asturias didn't answer the door when they knocked—so Coco knocked it down. Inside they found the older man frightened and packing to leave.

"Going somewhere?" Coco asked.

"N-none of your business." Finn shrank away from the group of seven in his one-room house, who blocked his access to the door. "Huntsmen are supposed to protect the people, not threaten them."

"We aren't Huntsmen yet," Coco said.

"And we *are* protecting the people—from your children," Sun added.

Finn's face fell. "What are you talking about?" he said. "My children are missing."

"Easy. We'd just like to talk to you," Velvet said, trying to take things down a notch.

"I already talked to you." His eyes darted to the window nervously. "I have nothing more to say."

Velvet took a soothing tone. "We won't let anything happen to you. You can come with us back to Shade Academy—"

Finn spat. "Never. Theodore rules Vacuo like a king, but who put him in charge?"

"Sounds like we're in the right place," Fox sent.

"Mr. Asturias, just let me show you something," Coco said. "If you don't want to talk to us after that, we'll leave."

"We will?" Fox sent.

"I'm lying," Coco sent. *"We'll leave, but we'll take him back with us and sort this out at Shade."*

Sun smiled. He was starting to admire Coco's style, which went deeper than the surface she presented to everyone else. Maybe Team CFVY deserved some of the reputation they had earned.

"I don't want to see anything from you kids," Finn said sharply. "You don't even belong in Vacuo."

Coco ignored him and started playing a video on her Scroll. "I think you'll want to see this, if you truly miss your daughter."

Finn turned away, hefting his pack. "I want all of you and that tech out of my house."

"Besides, what's the point of ruling if there aren't any people?" Gill said in the video.

At the sound of his daughter's voice, the man turned back and looked at the screen in spite of himself.

"This is her, right?" Coco asked. "This is Gill?"

Sun's mouth fell open when he saw the glowing woman on the stone-carved throne. Finn took the Scroll and cradled it in his hands, slowly sinking to sit on the floor.

"This is going to take too long," Pink said.

"Hey! She was there, too?" Sun hadn't seen this himself yet, so he edged around Finn to watch over his shoulder.

On the screen, the glowing woman, Gill Asturias—one half of the self-named Crown—was walking down a line of sleeping people, touching each of them. Sun crouched lower, stunned. He sat on his haunches to watch the video next to Finn.

He knew some of those sleeping people. Though he hadn't seen them in years. These were the familiar faces of people who had gone missing months ago, or people whose photos had been hanging on the Weeping Wall. He'd been on a quest to find them, until he got distracted. Always distracted. And look where they were now.

"You may as well bring in the army," Gill said. *"When I'm done—"*

"What is she doing?" Sun asked. He could hardly make sense of what he saw.

Finn jumped at the sound of Sun's voice next to his ear and fumbled the Scroll. Sun caught it with his tail and dangled it in front of him. Startled, Finn took the Scroll back. He replayed that part of the video.

"You may as well bring in the army. When I'm done here, I'll strengthen them for the fight."

"She's absorbing their Auras," Finn said. He, too, was almost in a state of shock.

Coco bent down in front of him. "That's her Semblance, right?" she confirmed. "And your son, Jax, he can control people's minds?"

Finn closed his eyes and took a deep breath. "Jax is very persuasive, but he doesn't have a Semblance."

That couldn't be true, Sun thought. He hated to contradict an old man, but come on. "He definitely does," Sun said, correcting him.

Finn opened his eyes, ignored Sun, and looked at Coco. "Are they hurting anyone?"

Coco removed her sunglasses and looked him in the eyes. Lucky she was used to being so direct. "They are," she told him. "And we think they're planning to hurt a lot more, maybe not just in Vacuo."

Sun put it all together for the guy. "Your son and daughter are the ones who have been kidnapping people in the city. Other people's children." Surely he could relate to the other grieving parents.

"And they've been recruiting people with powerful Semblances like their own, to build themselves an army," Velvet said.

"They're calling themselves the Crown," Sun said.

The man rubbed his face with a hand. Was he hiding tears?

"If that's true, then it's all my fault," he said. They could hardly hear his voice, it was so low and so gruff.

"Why the fascination with Vacuan royalty?" Coco pressed him. "Why do they call themselves the Crown?" Sun knew they might not have another chance to get the answers they needed.

"Because they're heirs to the throne of Vacuo," Finn said.

Fox frowned. "How can you even know that?" he asked. "It's not as if we still have records going back that far."

Finn shifted and pushed his right foot out. He lifted the leg of his trousers and pointed at a small purple mark there. The group leaned forward to take a look at it.

Sun averted his eyes. Who wanted to look at an old man's leg? But his friends weren't put off in the slightest.

"It kind of looks like an upside-down crown," Coco said thoughtfully.

"It's the royal birthmark," Finn explained. "Every member of our family has had it, going back as far as I can remember. My mother had it, her mother before her. My great-grandfather, great-great-grandfather, great-great-great-grandmother . . ."

"We get it," Fox said, encouraging him to get to the next point.

Finn went on, "It's been passed down along with stories of its origin. Only Vacuo's royal line bears the mark, one person from each generation. But in Jax and Gillian's case, they both have it, because they're twins—the first twins ever born in our family."

"But there's no way to really know," Sun said. "It's just a story. Someone could have made it up to explain the mark and passed that down as a family legend." How could Finn believe this? There was no proof whatsoever. He was surprised any Vacuan would be taken in by such a tale.

Finn was firm. He said, "I read something once, written by Beacon's last headmaster . . ."

"Professor Ozpin?" Coco asked.

Finn nodded. "It stuck with me, because as you may have noticed, I love books. He wrote that our world is built on stories. Some are true and some are lies. Some are real and some are myths. Stories explain who we are and why we're here. They give us comfort when we need it, and they help us relate to each other. If you don't believe in stories, if you don't trust in them, then nothing has meaning in life."

Sun sighed. If Ozpin said that, there might be something to it.

Finn paused. "So I believe the old stories about our family. It's always been a point of pride for us. Something that set us apart, that made us special in Vacuo. It gave some purpose to our lives—to be the best people we can be, to help others, to take care of our home."

He looked around to make sure the teams were listening. "My children believe the stories, too. It's why Gill wanted to go to an academy to train to be a Huntress. Jax has always been a bit more selfish, had bigger plans than *serving* the people. He would much rather rule them. But he went with her, anyway."

"But why?" Coco asked. "Many twins live separate lives, right?"

"You don't understand. He didn't have a choice. She's keeping him alive," Finn said, avoiding their gaze.

A shocked silence fell over the group, until Neptune said "Whaaaaaaat?" a little too loudly.

Finn tried to explain. "When my wife, Luna, was pregnant with them, she began getting sick. Her Aura was being depleted, but the doctors couldn't figure out why. It would regenerate, but over those nine months it came back slower and slower each time, and eventually she couldn't recover at all. By the time she went into labor, her Aura was down to almost nothing.

"Then we discovered the same was true for Jax. And doctors found that it wasn't some inherited condition . . . Gillian's Aura was, shall we say, *elevated*, and the two needed to be separated then before more harm came to Jax. There was an emergency operation to get them out, but it was too late for Luna. She didn't survive the procedure." Finn's voice broke. "She never even saw them. I never said good-bye.

"Jax recovered, obviously. But his Aura was always at a dangerously low level. He was fragile. He developed slowly. He was hard to draw out, and . . ." Finn took a shaky breath. "I worry that it twisted his mind. He wasn't anything like Gillian. Part of it was bitterness because he didn't have a Semblance.

"She, on the other hand, had a powerful Semblance. It had caused us so much pain, but I couldn't blame her, an unborn baby, doing what we all do: trying to survive. Over the years, I taught her to control her Semblance, and over time we unlocked her true ability—she doesn't just sap Aura from others; she can transfer it, too. It turned out her power, which had seemed like such a curse, could be a force for good as well. She had a large reserve of Aura already, and so she shared some of it with her brother. And he began to thrive."

"She can *take* Aura from one person and *give* it someone else?" Coco asked. "Maybe that's why we had so much trouble against those goons in the city, and why it seemed like Carmine wasn't taking any damage in the Wastelands. Gill transferred Aura to their fighters to make them even stronger."

Finn looked horrified. "That's not possible. She would never do that."

"What about Jax?" Sun asked. "So when he suddenly had some Aura to work with, he figured out his Semblance allows him to manipulate people's minds?"

Finn shook his head. "Like I said, Jax doesn't have a Semblance."

"Or maybe he never told you about it," Scarlet said.

"*That* sounds just like him, I'm afraid." Finn gazed off into the distance. Sun followed his attention to a picture of the twins on the wall. They looked like happy, normal kids, not psychopaths with delusions of grandeur.

"Jax always was charming," Finn remembered. "Before Gillian began transferring Aura to him, all he had was his sharp mind and a clever tongue. But afterward . . . It did seem like he could get anyone to do anything he wanted."

Velvet frowned. "Even convince his sister to drop out of school and help him take over Vacuo?"

"By the Brothers," said Finn, lowering his head. "What have they become?"

"A king and queen, if they get what they want," Coco said. "Or maybe just what Jax wants."

"Yatsuhashi could free Gill from her brother's influence if he can get close to her," Sun said. He still didn't know the big guy well, but he knew he could do it. He was powerful beyond words.

"Who's Yatsuhashi?" asked Finn, raising his head.

"He's our friend," Velvet said. She blew the bangs out of her eyes. "Who's . . . currently undercover with the Crown."

"He can shake Jax's control over people," Coco explained. "And I'm hoping that means he can't be affected by Jax, either. But about Gill's Semblance. She needs physical contact to transfer Aura?"

Finn nodded. "It will gradually fade, of course, just like your regular Aura." He swallowed. "These warriors they're gathering—she can only increase their Aura on contact. And if she's been taking Aura from people, she would have to keep them close at all times."

"They're just batteries to her," Sun said bitterly. Those were people! And they were people he *knew*, imprisoned underground.

"What's their deal with Dust?" Velvet asked suddenly. "At the club, no weapons that use Dust are allowed, and they're not interested in recruiting people with Semblances that rely on Dust."

Finn scowled. "Dust is the symbol of Vacuo's downfall. We never had it in our house; we don't rely on anything that uses it. Including Scrolls." He realized he was still holding Coco's Scroll and passed it back to her, casting one last wistful glance at his daughter, the would-be queen.

"You were leaving as we arrived," Scarlet said. "Where were you going? And why?"

Finn grimaced. "Jax and Gillian's old teammates from Shade came to visit me this morning. Rosa Schwein and Argento Pocoron. They told me they had heard from Jax and Gill, and they were delivering a message from them: to meet them in Vale."

"That's weird," Neptune said. "Unless they just wanted to get you out of town for some reason?"

"They also asked if anyone had come around asking about the twins. I'm afraid I gave them your name," Finn said.

Neptune looked stricken.

"Can you describe their friend Argento?" Coco asked with a concerned look in Neptune's direction.

"I don't have to. He and Rosa are in that video, with my daughter." Finn took the Scroll back from Coco and swiped at the screen. Then he showed it to her. Argento was a pig Faunus in a brown jumpsuit.

"Brown!" Sun said.

"We've fought that guy," Coco said. "If he and Schwein lied to you about Jax and Gill's whereabouts, it had to be on your children's orders." It seemed to pain her, but she said the same thing another way, just to be sure Finn took it in. "Your children *wanted* those two to lie to you."

"Maybe they wanted you to leave for your own protection," Sun suggested.

"From what?" Coco asked.

The teams exchanged glances. They said nothing, in team-speak or otherwise. Then, almost as one, they moved for the door.

Sun was the one to speak to Finn. After he'd left him the last time, it was the least he could do. He stretched his arms out toward the man. "Thank you, Mr. A. I know this is difficult for you, because you care about your kids. But I think you'd better come back with us. Theo will want to talk to you." He extended a hand to help him up.

Finn sighed. "I suppose you wouldn't take no for an answer, so I'll do what I can to assist, though I'm no fan of Theodore's . . ." He looked around his house. "One more thing: They told me to hurry."

Soon they were out the door and halfway down the street, catching up with the others.

"Do we buy his story?" Fox sent.

"Like he said," Sun replied. *"Everything is just a story in the end. Some of them, too many of them, are sad stories. I believe him."*

"Me too," Coco sent. *"And if we trust everything he said, we have to get back to Shade Academy. Right now."*

CHAPTER FIFTEEN

Jax Asturias sat in his throne and stared at the brawny student chained to a metal stake before him. He knew who Yatsuhashi Daichi was, just as he knew about all the students at Shade Academy thanks to Rumpole. But Yatsuhashi was not really a Shade student, at least not in the ways that truly mattered. He wasn't a Vacuan. He was a refugee from Beacon. Someone who had abandoned his home when it most needed him.

After Carmine and Bertilak had returned empty-handed, having let a boy with one of the most powerful Semblances in Vacuo, if not all of Remnant, slip through their fingers, Jax had taken particular interest in Team CFVY. They were supposed to be the best of the best, but he knew their type.

They were glory-seeking hotshots, flaunting their powers and their strength, holding themselves above all others at their school. It was because of people like them that Beacon had fallen. People like them would seal Shade's fate just as quickly.

Jax was going to restore Vacuo to the way it had been, and he was going to do it by elevating everyone who followed him. He would be their king, but he wasn't going to place himself above them.

If they could fight, if they believed in themselves and Vacuo and the old ways, they would be equals. But first they had to eliminate the weakest among them and those who sympathized with the other kingdoms, who had loyalties other than to Vacuo. Even those who placed their friends and family above the greater good.

Yatsuhashi stirred. He lifted his head and blinked blearily, turning back and forth in confusion. Jax saw the moment he realized he was trapped. Then the younger man locked eyes with Jax, pure rage etched in his face.

Even as Jax hated everything about Yatsuhashi, he envied his strength. He might be weak in his commitment to his home—he wasn't even from Vale originally, so what was he doing attending Beacon?—but he was an impressive physical specimen. He was big and strong, and Jax had seen him fight. He was all the things Jax had wished he could be, the version of himself that could have been if his sister hadn't robbed him of his future along with most of his Aura. Jax had envied her Semblance, too, until he discovered he had a powerful one of his own.

Yatsuhashi also had a powerful Semblance, and a dangerous one. It rivaled Jax's, because he could manipulate memory, and it seemed this disrupted Jax's psychic hold over others. If he couldn't be turned to Jax's side, he would have to be destroyed.

"You're awake," Jax said.

"You're the Crown," Yatsuhashi countered. He strained at the chains binding him, muscles bulging, face red from the effort. Such strength in him!

"How did you free Rumpole from my power of suggestion?" Jax asked.

"I don't know," Yatsuhashi said.

"But you did it twice more. Once to free your teammate Velvet Scarlatina, and again to free your friend Sun Wukong."

"I don't know," Yatsuhashi repeated.

"Either you're lying, or you really don't know how your Semblance works. Interesting. Your file says that you are constantly holding back your strength, afraid that you will accidentally hurt others. Perhaps that holds true of your Semblance as well. Perhaps, if you wanted to, you could wipe anyone's mind clean."

Yatsuhashi grimaced. So he was all too aware of his potential. He was truly holding himself back. Jax wanted him in his army.

"I could use someone like you," Jax mused.

"I'm sure you could," Yatsuhashi said. "Come closer and free me from these chains, and I'll show you what my Semblance can do."

Jax laughed. Then Yatsuhashi roared and the chains splintered apart, and Jax stopped laughing.

Jax jumped up from his seat, waiting to see what would happen, but Yatsuhashi didn't move. From the corners of the throne room, Jax's guards moved in on him, but Jax held up his hand to stop them.

"He won't hurt me," he told the guards.

"That's where you're wrong," Yatsuhashi said.

Jax hesitated at the top of the steps leading down from his throne. As a kid, before Gill had shared her Aura with him, he had been timid and feeble. He'd barely ventured outside, and one day when he did, he had fallen into a sandpit. With barely any Aura to protect himself, he'd hurt himself badly.

He'd been on bed rest for a month, recovering from a concussion, but it was in those dreamlike days that he started to fantasize what it would be like if he was not just normal, but also *strong.* Stronger than everyone else. And what he would do with that power. He'd decided that, like him, Vacuo had been weak too long. He would help his nation find its strength again—rise to crush the other kingdoms under its heel, burying them in the sand of their own creation.

And then, thanks to Gill, he'd been given that power.

At Shade, he had learned to create an Aura shield, and he had learned to fight. But he also had to fight his instincts to avoid harm, even though he was effectively invincible.

He trotted down the steps toward Yatsuhashi and assumed a fighting stance. The young man smiled, but without any pleasure. Jax let him take the first swing.

Yatsuhashi was a better fighter, no question. He was faster and stronger, and he knew how to take a punch. But his Aura was finite, and it was already low from the cage fight and using his Semblance. Knowing Yatsuhashi's Semblance, Jax was careful not to let his opponent touch him.

When Jax was done playing with his opponent, he whistled and his guards moved in. Yatsuhashi turned to fight them, but one of them was his classmate Umber, who once again immobilized him with a look. She was Jax's favorite recruit.

"Thank you, Umber." Jax strode forward and stood in front of Yatsuhashi, careful not to break his eye contact with Umber. "Last chance. Join me. Fight for Vacuo. And if you won't do that, fight to save your friends' lives."

"What do you mean?" Yatsuhashi mumbled through frozen lips.

"If you join me, I'll spare them. I'll give them the same choice I'm offering you. They can become a part of my army, or I can force them into service. It would be a shame to break up Team CFVY—again." Jax smiled.

"N-no," Yatsuhashi said.

Jax sighed. He reached out and put a hand on Yatsuhashi's head. He felt the young man tremble beneath his touch. Even frozen by Umber's Stone Gaze, he was struggling to regain control.

"You will obey me as your king and commit yourself completely to the service of Vacuo," Jax commanded.

The boy's mind was slippery—after a few moments he began to think maybe he couldn't link to it after all—but eventually he felt it engage. Jax felt his constant headache worsen; it was always a dull ache in the background, but the pain spiked when he exerted his control over someone. It was a terrible burden maintaining his control over all those other minds. If he was under too much strain and stress, those links weakened and he had to reestablish them with touch—just as Gill had to strengthen her bond with other Auras.

When Yatsuhashi stopped struggling under his touch, Jax pulled his hand away and stepped back.

"Let him go, Umber."

She raised her glasses, cutting off her control over Yatsuhashi and releasing him to Jax.

"Kneel, Yatsuhashi," Jax demanded.

The young man lowered himself to his knees and bowed his head.

"Look up at your master. Do you promise to follow my orders, to fight for your crown and kingdom, to give up your own life if necessary?"

Yatsuhashi lifted his head. "I do."

Jax raised his hands. "Then rise. Welcome to the Crown's army."

Jax strode back to his throne, suddenly tired. Almost half of his army had joined his cause voluntarily, or for the promised financial reward of ruling Vacuo, but the other half fought his control almost daily.

"Call Gill," he told Umber.

She pulled out a Scroll and linked up with their headquarters in Vacuo.

Carmine's voice over the receiver filled the hall when she answered. "Yes?"

"Jax wants to speak to Gill," Umber explained.

Jax and Gill hated using the Atlesian technology, and abhorred the Scrolls' reliance on Dust, but they were necessary evils—for now. Even so, both twins refused to operate Scrolls themselves.

Umber held up the Scroll and Gill's face appeared on the screen.

"Yatsuhashi Daichi is under our control," Jax exulted.

"Good," said Gill. Then she sighed. "Do you need me to increase his Aura, too?"

"I don't think that's necessary right now. When he recovers, he'll be strong on his own. Besides, you'll be busy enough supplying the rest of the army with Aura when you join me on the battlefield."

"When will that be?" Gill asked.

Jax drew in a breath. Celebration and victory were near! "Now is the time to strike," he announced.

He had been preparing for this moment since they had left Shade Academy. Jax had thought it would take some twenty years before they could move on the city of Vacuo, but then Beacon had fallen, giving them the perfect opportunity as chaos, confusion, and mistrust settled over the four kingdoms.

Once again, Vacuo had been isolated from the conflict raging throughout Remnant—only this time it was an opportunity. With the global CCT network disabled, Vale in ruin, Haven leaderless, and Atlas closed off, Vacuo was theirs for the taking. This was likely their last, best chance for a generation. And it was their only hope to defend Vacuo against whomever had been targeting the other kingdoms. In all likelihood they had written off Vacuo, like everyone else did, but if they tried to move against the Crown, they would have an unpleasant surprise. Vacuo wouldn't break this time around.

"We aren't ready," Gill said.

Jax disagreed. "We are as ready as we can be. We've lost Rumpole, and Shade is on the alert. Yatsuhashi's teammates will come for him soon. If we wait much longer, Theodore will be better prepared. He'll lose, anyway, but it will take much longer and be harder on our forces. The time is now."

"Jax, no," Gill begged. "Don't do this. Not yet."

"Listen to me," he told his sister, with extra emphasis. "Trust me."

Finally he got through to her. "Of course," Gill said. "You know what you're doing. I trust you, with my life."

"And I trust you with mine."

I don't have a choice, he thought.

"I will start the attack, and you will bring the rest of the army by evening," he said decisively. There was nothing left to say.

Umber cut off the connection and looked at Jax, waiting.

"Ready the forces. We move on the city within the hour. I want you and Yatsuhashi by my side."

"Yes, Your Majesty." Umber glanced warily at Yatsuhashi, and then hurried off to prepare. *She was a good soldier,* Jax thought.

He turned to his newest recruit. "What do you think, Yatsuhashi? Are you ready for a fight?"

Yatsuhashi smiled. "Always, Your Majesty. But I'll serve you better if I have my sword."

Wonderful! Jax thought, imagining the mayhem such a weapon would make for his cause.

Jax waved at one of his guards and the man hurried over with the young man's greatsword. Yatsuhashi took it and looked at Jax.

He extended it without prompting. "I pledge my sword to your service and to Vacuo. For crown and kingdom," Yatsuhashi said.

Jax leaned back and folded his hands together almost as if in prayer. "I accept."

Team CFVY had been a nuisance ever since they had kept him from acquiring the Caspian boy. With them out of the way now, he would be able to take the boy from Oscuro Combat School. And that was only the beginning!

Yatsuhashi would defeat his own teammates, and then there would be nothing stopping Jax from ousting Theodore and restoring the ancient throne to Vacuo!

CHAPTER SIXTEEN

Velvet had only been in Headmaster Theodore's office once before—when Coco, Fox, Yatsuhashi, and she had arrived tired, thirsty, and nearly beaten by the hard journey through Vacuo, dispirited from losing Beacon.

Not that she wished she had been called to the headmaster's office *more* often. Until she had joined Team CFVY, Velvet had always tried to keep a low profile, and that was still her instinct, even though Coco and Fox had a habit of getting them into the worst situations. At first, Velvet had feared her team was a bad influence on her, but eventually she had realized it was just the opposite. They had helped her and even Yatsuhashi learn to take more risks, and in turn she and Yatsu had helped moderate their more headstrong friends' impulses.

Most of the time.

Though on the surface they were all wildly different from one another and shouldn't have come together as well as they had, they had turned out to complement each other perfectly. It hadn't always been easy, and they'd had their rough patches, but Velvet couldn't imagine it any other way, especially after her recent experience as part of Team NOVA.

That first meeting with Headmaster Theodore had been tense. Velvet had worried they'd have to beg for admission to Shade. She'd been overwhelmed by everything they had gone through, not to mention the headmaster's strong presence. Back then she'd kept quiet, studying her surroundings.

Unlike Rumpole, Headmaster Theodore seemed to be the sentimental sort. That, or he liked showing off the important friends he had. His office wall was covered in pictures of him posing with the headmasters of the other Huntsmen academies and even the Shade teachers. Velvet had recognized a picture of Ruby's uncle Qrow and wondered what the connection there was.

She still remembered that her attention had been drawn to one photo in particular: a black-and-white picture of a young girl in pigtails and a checkered dress with a small black dog. She hadn't mustered the courage to ask who she was to Theodore. A daughter? A sister? Whoever she was, Velvet could see the resemblance.

Some of those pictures were missing now—though it was likely no one but Velvet, with her photographic memory, would have noticed. The framed pictures of Theodore with Professor Lionheart from Haven, and General Ironwood of Atlas, were gone entirely. And one picture had changed positions, now occupying a more prominent position at the top of the wall: the one of Headmaster Theodore with Professor Ozpin.

Velvet's eyes burned when she saw it. She blinked back tears, memories flooding through her mind. When she regained her composure and turned her attention to the group, she noticed that Headmaster Theodore was watching her.

"I sent someone to the Mirage to look for Mr. Daichi," Theodore announced to the whole group. "They reported that there was no one there. The place looks like it hasn't been touched in decades."

"Your emissary might have been lying," Rumpole pointed out. "In these times, we don't know whom to trust, aside from the people in this room."

"Don't worry. We'll find him." Theodore clapped and jumped up from his seat. Then, unusual for him, he listened to an entire debriefing, as Sun and Coco told them what they had learned from Finn Asturias about his children, Jax and Gill, and their ambitions to rule Vacuo. Finn himself was waiting in a guest room under guard.

"I knew that Asturias kid was trouble, didn't I, Rumpole?" Headmaster Theodore said.

"Which one?" Rumpole asked, to clarify.

"Jax! He never fit in here. He held his sister back—she would have been a fantastic Huntress. But he never stepped up."

"He certainly seems to have stepped up now," Rumpole said.

Theodore scowled. "He's still a weak, scared little boy under it all. I've dealt with people like him before." He glanced at the pictures on his wall. Then he shook his head and ran back to his desk. *Just watching him is tiring*, Velvet thought.

"The city's Huntsmen can handle the Asturias twins for now," Theodore said confidently. "We have bigger threats to worry about."

Velvet wasn't sure she'd heard him right, and apparently Rumpole wasn't, either.

"But Theo—" she objected.

"I will not be lured into a trap," he insisted. "If I invest our full strength in this fight, their attack could weaken us for the big one if and when it comes."

"Theo, what if this *is* the big one?" Rumpole asked. "Have you considered that Jax and Gill could be part of a broader conspiracy to weaken Vacuo, like the White Fang did at Beacon and Haven? What if they're just the advance troops, so to speak?"

"This isn't Beacon!" Theodore roared. He punched a ruby glove into the wall beside his desk. The impact left a huge crater and shook the wall enough for all the pictures to fall to the floor. Cracks spider webbed across the wall from the force.

An uncomfortable silence fell over the room. Velvet looked again at the photo of Theodore and Ozpin, the glass over the frame now shattered. Since the reinitiation, she'd done a lot of thinking about the Vacuan way of doing things—or at least, the way Sun had described them to her: When too many tragedies started piling up, Sun said, Vacuans felt the best thing to do was to bury them, get stronger, and win next time. Team CFVY had tried things that way once before, and it hadn't worked out too well. She was about to say something when Coco stood up.

"You're right," Coco conceded to Headmaster Theodore. "The attack at Beacon was a surprise. No one was ready to deal with the combined forces of the Grimm, the White Fang, and the compromised Atlesian army."

She took a deep breath and moved on to her argument. "But

we know what's planned here, and chances are it's going to happen soon. The Crown is clearly building an army. It isn't in our best interest to underestimate them."

Coco exchanged a glance with Rumpole, who took over from there.

"I agree," Rumpole said. "They have control over people with powerful Semblances and can manipulate Aura. You don't build an army unless you intend to use it. And there's only one target out here."

"I think you're overestimating their strength and competence," Theodore said, grimacing. "This isn't the first time people have agitated for Vacuo to go back to the old ways. Even to move against the other kingdoms and take their resources as they took ours. But these are always just revenge fantasies. That isn't the true way of Vacuo."

"No one has ever been able to rally enough support for Vacuo to do anything," Sun added. "Not since the Great War, and look where that left us. We aren't powerful enough to take anything from anyone."

Everyone in the room glared at him.

"What? Someone had to say it," Sun said.

Fox frowned. "But Vacuo *is* strong. Certainly strong enough to keep what we have left. Until we prove it, it's just words."

Theodore held up his fists, and the Dust-encrusted ruby gloves sparkled. He considered them for a moment and then lowered his hands.

Velvet slowly walked over to the fallen pictures. She picked one up and gazed at it somberly for a moment. Theodore probably didn't expect to hear from her, which made it important that she speak.

"Sir," she began. "You may think Jax and Gill are just kids. But *we're* just kids, too. And if they're willing to fight for Vacuo—the Vacuo they believe in—as hard as we fought for Beacon, then I think it would be a mistake to dismiss them as a threat. That kind of mistake we can't walk back from."

Velvet replaced the picture she held on the wall. The glass had shattered, but it still clearly showed Theodore and Ozpin arm in arm.

Theodore sighed, like the photo had somehow changed his mind. "No, I suppose we shouldn't take any chances," he said slowly. He strode back to his desk and sat down. "Besides, this might prove a good warm-up before the big fight begins. It's time to get serious. It's time to get ready."

He pressed a button and a microphone rose out of the desk. He leaned into it and spoke: "Attention, Shade Academy students. Effective immediately, your original teams have been restored. Gather in the courtyard, and don't forget your weapons. Thank you."

He stood up. "If the Crown attacks, they will come here first." He glanced at Velvet. "But I said it before, and I still mean it: We can handle anything that comes at us." He nodded to Sun. "By working together."

Then they heard shouts outside, getting louder by the second. Soon they were joined by bursts of gunfire and explosions. The group exchanged glances, and then the floor rumbled beneath their feet.

Theodore waved a hand over his window and the view

changed, showing the wall between the academy and the city of Vacuo. The Crown's army was amassed outside it, their silver armbands shining in the brutal sun.

"Looks like it's time to put our words into action," he said. "For Vacuo."

CHAPTER SEVENTEEN

Not again, Coco thought.

She followed Headmaster Theodore and Professor Rumpole out of his office, running with her team to the courtyard. The rest of the students, already gathered there, were looking expectantly at the school's south wall.

The rumble from the other side of the wall was deafening outside. The gates were closed because Theodore had ordered Shade on lockdown, but the Crown's soldiers were hammering away, with gunfire and cannons from the sound of it. Coco wondered how much the school's walls could take.

At least the Crown isn't using Dust, she thought. Dust would have made short work of the walls. And that's where Shade would have an advantage.

"What are you all doing standing around?" Theodore shouted to the shell-shocked students. "Time to defend your school!"

"But who are they?" a student yelled.

"Does it matter?" Theodore cried. "Charge!"

Coco glanced down and noted that the other members of the Beacon Brigade were already on their way to meet the threat.

Running toward danger, like Huntsmen were trained to do. They weren't going to lose this time.

She itched to get down there herself, but she wasn't in this alone. She stared out at the sea of Shade students, all of whom reflected the same fear she'd seen etched on her classmates' faces the night Beacon fell.

"You heard the headmaster. This is what we've been training for." Coco pointed to the wall. "This is a battle, and we aren't going to win it by watching. So decide now: Do you have what it takes to be a Huntsman, or are you going to give up your home without a fight?"

The students who had been enthralled by the unexpected sight of an attack on their school—or reliving the terrors of the Battle of Beacon—shook free of their stupor. And they didn't bother taking the stairs. What was jumping off of a building when just a week ago they had been dropped from an airbus?

Maybe there is some method to the reinitiation madness after all, Coco thought.

"Let's go," Coco called to Velvet and Fox. "But stick close to me."

"What she said!" Sun said. "Come on, Team SSSN!"

They leaped over the side of the terrace and ran down the steep, sloping sides of the school. They had cleared the building's three levels and were racing toward the south wall in no time. It didn't sound like the Crown was attacking from any other direction. Though if they had agents on the inside, they wouldn't have to.

Coco tapped Fox on the shoulder, and he opened up teamspeak to the students they trusted most.

"Hey, Beacon Brigade," Fox sent. *"This is Fox. Yeah, if you didn't*

know already, I can talk to you telepathically and can facilitate you all talking together. Deal with it. Use this channel to coordinate during the battle."

"Be on your guard," Coco sent. *"The people attacking us call themselves the Crown. They've been kidnapping and recruiting people from the city, even from this school, so you'll be up against opponents with strong Semblances. Maybe even friends. They may not be in control of themselves."*

"What's that supposed to mean?" Reese asked.

"The Crown can control people's minds," Velvet elaborated. *"Brainwash them."*

"Oh, and their Aura is supercharged," Coco added. *"They're stronger, but we can still beat them."*

"Got any ideas on how, exactly?" Nolan asked.

"We'll figure it out. But for now, look for a small, thin guy with black hair and a crown," Coco said, *"and a gorgeous glowing woman, who's also wearing a crown. They're the leaders."*

"Crowns. Got it," Reese sent. *"That should make it easy."*

Coco sighed. *"Nothing about this will be easy."*

By the time they had reached the south wall, the wall was . . . gone. At least a big section of it had been reduced to rubble, and through the clouds of dust, they saw the army of Crown soldiers on the other side, forming a wall of bodies. They all wore silver armbands.

And behind *that* wall, Jax Asturias was sitting on a palanquin being carried by Umber and Yatsuhashi.

"Yatsu?" Velvet said. "Oh no."

Coco could only guess how she was feeling right now. "Fox, Yatsuhashi's over there. Can you reach him?" Coco called aloud.

"I'll try," Fox sent. Then a moment later. *"He's not responding. I can't tell if he's under Jax's control or not."*

"I'm going over there." Velvet reached for her camera box.

Coco held out her hand to stop her. "No, I'll get him. I need you to do something else, Velvet. I don't see Gill here. Do you sense her anywhere, Fox?"

"No," he sent. *"Nor Carmine. She must be guarding Gill."*

"Good." Coco put her hand on Velvet's shoulder. "Go to the Wastelands and stop Gill. The only way we win this is if we cut her off from the soldiers so she can't get here and give them more Aura."

"If this is about taking me off the battlefield—" Velvet began.

Coco shook her head. "It isn't. We could use you here, but I need you there more. You're the best person for this job. Maybe the *only* person who can succeed, because with your Semblance and Anesidora, you're a one-person army. We can't afford to send too many others with you."

Velvet looked shocked. Coco couldn't believe that she still thought she wasn't valued on the team . . . until she remembered how Nebula had treated her that day in Sunnybrook's class. Coco, Yatsuhashi, and Fox sometimes came across as overprotective, but they knew how strong Velvet was—and it had nothing to do with her weapon.

But everything that Coco had said was true: Velvet was a pretty damn good secret weapon for moments like this.

"The Crown's soldiers also don't use Dust, and you have the most powerful Dust-based weapon in Vacuo," she added.

Velvet was warming up to the idea. She nodded and said, "I'm on it."

Coco had another idea, from the short-lived reinitiation. "Take Octavia with you. She knows the way."

"Hey! Good plan. I'm coming, too." Sun popped out of nowhere.

Coco's heart sank. Sun wouldn't have been her top choice, for sure. She spoke sternly to him. "This isn't the time to bail on your team again, Sun. Or us. We need you here."

Sun pled his case. "I'm not bailing on anyone. A good leader knows to go where they're needed most, and I'm still leader of SSSN, like it or not. Velvet and I are both one-person armies; Gill and Carmine won't stand a chance against us. And besides . . . Gill kidnapped a bunch of people I care about. If I can help free them, I want to do it."

Scarlet gave Sun an appraising look. "He'll come back," he said to Coco, whipping his bangs out of his eyes. "And he's right . . . this time." He turned to Sun. "But when you do get back, we're finally having a serious conversation."

Sun nodded.

"So go!" Scarlet said. "We got this."

Behind him, Sage and Neptune waved in support.

"Thank you," Sun said to his team. Even in the middle of the attack, he sounded grateful.

Then he glanced at Velvet, who smiled. "Let's go bring your friends home."

Octavia arrived at Velvet's side. "I'm ready," she said.

From a little ways off, Rumpole called, "Let's cover Velvet, Sun, and Octavia's escape by engaging the enemy forces! Do not allow those soldiers to step onto campus, understood?"

The students around Coco roared in approval. Though Fox winced.

Coco smiled as she noticed that Headmaster Theodore was there at the head of the student army when they surged forward, fists raised. He threw the first punch, hitting one of the Crown's soldiers. The impact sounded with an ululating *boom*, and the man went flying backward, knocking his fellow soldiers down like bowling pins, while the shock wave kicked up a ring of flying sand that temporarily blinded the front line.

Coco transformed Gianduja into a gun and turned to tell Velvet now was their chance, but she was already on the move with Sun and Octavia. She glimpsed them briefly in the sand cloud and then they were gone.

"Right." Coco ran forward alongside Fox. As she fired at the enemy, some of them blocked her shots with their weapons, some dove out of the way, but others just grinned as their enhanced Auras protected them. This was going to be fun.

It was a full-on melee. Soon Coco was forced to fight with just her purse and in close combat. This wasn't like fighting Grimm. These were other people—many of them trained Huntsmen—who could fight more strategically than most creatures Coco had been up against. And she had to be careful to not injure the people on her side. She was used to fighting alongside Team CFVY, where she could trust that everyone would be where they were supposed to be—where she had told them to be. She knew how they would think, what they would do, what they were capable of.

To her surprise, the Shade defenses were holding up well at

least. And Coco had some experience working with the members of Team ROSC, so she was pretty sure she could count on them.

"Reese! I need a lift," Coco shouted.

On the edge of the skirmish, Reese was using the two halves of her board in hand-to-hand combat with one of the Crown's soldiers, a woman about her age. But Reese slapped her board back together and zoomed toward Coco, zipping around the other combatants and hitting every bad guy she could in the back of the head.

"What's up?" Reese asked.

"Me." Coco hopped up and grabbed on to Reese's board. "Get me to Yatsuhashi."

Reese stabilized her board and raised them higher above the battlefield. Arrows and bullets came at them, but she dodged as they flew.

"Uh-oh," Reese said. "We've got more company."

Coco looked around until she saw what Reese had spotted: dark, flying shapes on the horizon.

"Ravagers," Coco said. "They'll just be the first."

The battle was already drawing the attention of the Grimm. Coco hoped that meant Velvet and the others wouldn't have to deal with them in the Wastelands at least, but it was a bad development for the battle at Shade. Soon they'd be dealing with both human and Grimm forces.

But Coco wasn't going to let that get her down. Shade wasn't going to fall on her watch. They were going to win this one, save the school. Save everyone. Do it right this time.

"This is your stop," Reese said.

Coco saw Jax's palanquin directly below her, carried by Umber and Yatsuhashi. "Thanks!" she told Reese, dropping and firing at the target on her way down. She used Hype to enhance her fire Dust, tearing the makeshift throne to shreds along with anyone inside it. She landed in the wreckage—but there was no one inside. Where was Jax?

Coco turned and stepped back. That's when she saw that Yatsuhashi was standing there watching her.

"Hey, Yatsuhashi," Coco said. "You in there?"

As he drew Fulcrum, she noted the silver armband around his right bicep, just like the ones on all Jax's soldiers.

Coco sighed. "I really don't want to do this."

Yatsuhashi ran toward her, bringing his sword back.

Coco planted herself in the sand and aimed her gun.

"Last chance!" she called. "Please tell me you're bluffing."

Yatsuhashi roared and swung his sword at Coco's head.

CHAPTER EIGHTEEN

On their journey through the Wastelands, Velvet, Sun, and Octavia spotted a mass of Grimm heading back the way they had come—right toward Shade Academy.

"Should we go back?" Octavia asked.

Velvet bunched up her shoulders. "We can't stop to fight them. They're going to complicate the battle, but not as much as Gill is. We can't get distracted . . . plus, we need to conserve our Aura for the fight—especially if Carmine is still supercharged."

Fortunately, there wasn't anything as big as a King Taijitu, but the unsettling Grimm caravan of Dromedons, Jackalopes, and Ziraphs was the last thing Shade needed to deal with. Velvet hated to think of her teammates having to fend off the creatures in the midst of an existing battle.

Sun backed her up. "We stick to the plan. We stop Gill before she can head to Shade herself. If she gets to Shade and starts draining our side of Aura, that'll give her more to lend her own forces."

Octavia craned her neck and watched the Grimm with concern. Velvet knew she was thinking about their friends, because that's where her heart was, too. But her mind was firmly fixed on the mission. She told herself she wasn't leaving them to their fates—she was doing whatever she could to protect them.

"Maybe the Grimm will actually help," Velvet said with as much optimism as she could. "The Crown's forces are standing between Shade and the Grimm. They'll be attacked on two fronts."

She pulled out her Scroll, but the signal was too weak to send a warning back. Not that a warning would really do them much good in the long run. No one would be checking their Scrolls in the middle of a fight.

Octavia swiped her damp hair out of her eyes. "Let's just try to get back to them as soon as we can, okay?"

"Agreed." Sun squinted, looking around. "So where is this hidden base?"

"Hidden. But it should be visible a little ways ahead," Octavia said. "That way, I think. It's hard to say with the way the sands change out here."

Velvet's vision was better than Octavia's, but she didn't see anything on the dim horizon as twilight settled over the desert.

They marched on, Velvet trying to hurry as much as the terrain allowed. Then Octavia stopped.

"I don't get it. It should be just about here." She turned in a slow circle. The only marks in the sand were their own tracks leading back to the south.

"Maybe the sand swallowed it," Sun said.

"Brace yourselves," Octavia said. She pulled out her kris and loaded it with Gravity Dust.

Sun looked down. "Brace ourselves on what?"

Octavia took off skating on the surface of the sand in a wide circle, faster and faster, arm holding her kris out. Each time she passed, more of the sand shifted beneath her. Velvet swung her arm up to cover her face, as Octavia was creating a small whirlpool of sand using her Semblance and the Gravity Dust in her weapon. The sand moved slowly around them, picking up more and more grains as if magnetized. Then, suddenly, Velvet spotted something bright poking up out of the ground.

"There!" Velvet yelled, pointing.

As Octavia swept the sand away, Velvet saw metal scaffolding that looked like a large broadcasting antenna. And then, as the base was gradually revealed, a crevasse in the earth.

Octavia skidded to a halt, kicking up a final wave of sand. By now it had piled up into a high wall around them, drifting down to dust their hair and clothes. Velvet shook her head. She hated it when sand got in her ears.

The three of them looked at the entrance, then at one another.

"Follow me," Octavia said. She used the light on her Scroll to illuminate a long passageway. They followed as she led them into a broad cavern, where four paths branched off in different directions.

"That's the one." Octavia led them toward the east entrance, and soon they reached another cavern, this one lit, and she held up a hand to halt them.

"They're ahead," she whispered.

They crept up to the opening and peered in. It was just as Coco had described: a room filled with beds and a throne carved out of rock against one wall. There was only one problem: There was no sign of the two people they'd come to find.

"Where's Gill?" Velvet whispered. "And Carmine?"

"Or any of the bad guys?" Sun added.

Octavia shrugged. "Maybe they left already?"

"We would have seen them," Velvet said.

"Let's just ask someone!" Sun stalked out into the room impatiently.

"Sun!" Velvet called. She sighed. He could cause real problems if they weren't careful.

"He just does whatever comes to mind, doesn't he?" Octavia asked.

Velvet sighed. "I'm not sure there's much thinking involved at all," she said and hurried after Sun.

She found him standing next to a bed, unplugging an unconscious man from the Aura monitor and undoing the straps holding him in place. The man's eyes fluttered and he woke with a start.

"Easy," Sun said, holding up his hands. "We're here to help."

Sun helped him up, and Velvet could tell this man hadn't trained as a Huntsman. If he'd had a Semblance, he probably wouldn't have been left here and used by Gill. His Aura likely took a while to build back up. As Octavia wandered into the room behind her, Sun began interrogating the man . . . in his own way.

"So, yeah," Sun said. "Have you seen a glowing woman, maybe with a scary red head?"

"They both left together with three Huntsmen," the man spat. "About ten minutes ago."

That didn't make any sense, though. "We would have seen them . . . ," Velvet said.

Octavia turned to look back the way they had come. "Maybe they took one of the other tunnels?" she wondered aloud.

Velvet bolted for the passageway, Octavia right behind her, when she remembered Sun. He was still by the man's side, lost in conversation.

"Sun, you can free everyone and get them to safety," Velvet told him. It was hard to believe he was ever a leader of Team SSSN, she thought, as he couldn't even be trusted to follow orders, but she hoped he would do the right thing this time. Velvet turned and ran back to the junction of tunnels, joining Octavia. "Which one?" Velvet asked. She didn't want to split up.

Octavia threw up her hands. "We'll have to make our best guess," she said. "If only Fox were here."

Velvet listened, but she couldn't hear anyone except Sun. Then at once there were some confused voices bouncing around, coming from multiple directions. *Some of those other paths must connect*, she thought. There were more passageways than they realized.

Octavia was staring at the south cave.

"That one," she said, running into it at top speed.

"Wait!" Velvet said when she finally caught up. "How do you know this is the right one?"

"Because when we came through here last time, this cave was blocked by an avalanche," Octavia said. "Which Carmine could have cleared with her Semblance, if the rocks were small enough."

Velvet shivered. The last time they had tangled with Carmine, it had taken all of Team CFVY to stop her, with assistance from Edward Caspian and, oddly enough, Bertilak, whom they had tricked into fighting her.

But Coco had said, *You're a one-person army*, and that gave Velvet a boost of confidence as she prepared to face whatever was coming her way. With her weapon and Semblance, Velvet still had Team CFVY with her in a way, she realized.

They moved through the tunnel, stepping carefully around scattered skeletons in old mining outfits.

"They must have been trapped here years ago in a cave-in," Octavia whispered.

That meant there was a pretty good chance they were Faunus, Velvet thought sadly.

But before Velvet could dwell on the thought, she heard new voices up ahead. A soft but urgent voice called out, "Hurry! Jax is waiting for us." Velvet was willing to bet that was Gill.

She'd have recognized Carmine's voice anywhere. "You've already juiced up the soldiers with Aura," Carmine said. "You're too important. That's the last place you should be now."

Gill stood her ground. "Our subjects need to see their monarchs fighting for Vacuo, fighting for—" Then she stopped abruptly. "Someone's coming," she hissed.

Still, Velvet and Octavia had managed to catch them by surprise. As Velvet ran toward them, she took in every detail: Carmine was standing in front of another cave-in, stones and dust piled around her. Gill stood to the side, a bow and quiver of arrows slung onto her back. She was surrounded by three tall Huntsmen in armor with silver armbands.

Velvet activated a hard-light replica of Yatsuhashi's sword and charged toward Carmine. The redhead swept a hand around and several small boulders flew out of the blockade toward Velvet.

Velvet swung the broadsword and smashed the boulders to bits—but Carmine fired the sharp fragments toward Velvet's face.

Velvet leaned back as they zipped by, then flipped forward into a somersault, sword out with the blade facing Carmine.

The Huntress stepped aside, and Velvet crashed into the crumbling rock barrier. She caught a glimpse of Octavia facing off against the three Huntsmen, fending them off with her dagger. She was as fierce now as she had been when they fought the Ravagers during reinitiation, and Velvet was glad to have Octavia by her side.

"Hey, Velvet," Carmine said mockingly. "Long time no see. It was nice catching up with Coco and Yatsuhashi, but you were always my favorite." She pressed a finger to her lips. "Don't tell the others."

Yatsuhashi's sword faded away. Velvet noted that Carmine had only one of her sai—now she remembered she had seen the other one back at the club, transformed into gold by Rumpole's Semblance.

"Why are you working with the Crown?" Velvet asked. "How can you do this? Do you really need money that badly?"

"This isn't about money, at least not for me," Carmine scoffed. "The twins and I go way back, to my academy days. I fight because I believe in them and their cause." Carmine unsheathed her sai and sent another rock flying at Velvet.

"Why do you care about restoring the throne to Vacuo?" Velvet summoned Sharp Retribution and fired at Carmine.

The tunnel rumbled and tiny stones fell on Velvet from above.

"Idiot! You're going to bring the whole mine down on us." Carmine lunged with her sai and Velvet brought her left arm up to block it. She turned her elbow up, level with her face, and jabbed the arm blade out toward Carmine while slashing at her exposed stomach with the other.

Carmine jumped backward and dropped her sai. But it remained floating in the air where she'd been holding it a moment before, and then it spun toward Velvet.

Velvet brought her hands together and caught it in midair, inches from her face. Carmine's Semblance tugged at it, but Velvet held on tight.

"You need to take better care of these." Velvet turned the weapon around as Fox's tonfas wore out. She attacked Carmine with her own weapon, using her own moves against her.

"You're a quick study," Carmine said. A ring of rocks circled her head as she parried the short blade with stone projectiles. "You're doing better than your friend over there."

Velvet forced herself not to fall for Carmine's obvious attempt at distraction, but it sounded like Octavia *was* having a rough time now—she was fighting three powerful Huntsmen on her own, and they were powered up by Gill's Aura.

"We don't have time for this," Gill said. "Clear the rubble, Carmine."

Carmine made an exasperated sound. Then she smiled. "Bye, Velvet."

A pile of stones blocking the cave flew at Velvet. She lifted her arms to cover her face just before the wall slammed into her, knocking her backward and half burying her. She was dazed for a moment, watching Octavia fighting the other Huntsmen, her weapon moving too fast to see, as rocks continued to fly from the diminishing pile of rubble. A beam of moonlight cut through the darkness. Carmine was breaking through.

Then something glittered in front of Velvet. She pulled herself from the rocks covering her and scooped it up. It was a red crystal.

It was Dust.

If this cave had been closed off before the Great War because of an avalanche—if the cave was too unstable to rescue those trapped miners—that meant the Dust had never been removed. This might be the last small repository of Dust in Vacuo.

"Octavia!" Velvet called. "Fire!" She held up the Dust crystal.

Octavia turned and saw what Velvet was holding. Even without Fox's teamspeak, she knew instantly what Velvet was thinking. Now they had a way to stop Gill from reaching the battlefield, cutting off her ability to send Aura to the troops there.

It took Carmine a little longer to catch on.

"No!" she said as Octavia waved her kris and sent a torrent of fire from the blade toward her—then past her.

And into a glittering fire Dust deposit in the wall. The blast ignited the whole vein.

The tunnel was very bright and very hot for a moment, before everything went dark.

CHAPTER NINETEEN

An explosion shook the chamber where Sun waited, followed by a series of smaller explosions like gunshots. The mine rumbled around Sun and the Vacuans he had freed. Then stones fell from the ceiling and clouds of dust filled the air.

"What was that?" someone asked.

"That . . . would be Velvet and Octavia," Sun said briefly. For a moment, he wondered whether he should go after them. But while Velvet and Octavia no doubt needed him, these people—the drained people of Vacuo—needed him more. They might not find their way out of the labyrinth of caves without him—if there even *was* still a way out.

"Should we check on them?" someone said from a bed.

"Eh, they're done for," a gruff voice replied. Sun and the others turned and saw Bertilak Celadon sitting upright and throwing off the thin blanket that covered him. Soon he swung his legs around and hopped to his feet. "If they were up against Carmine, they were likely on the wrong end of that blast. A shame, though. I always liked that bunny girl."

Sun grabbed Ruyi Bang and Jingu Bang. He set his jaw and

stalked toward Bertilak. "How long have you been awake?" He couldn't be too careful with this guy.

"Long enough," said Bertilak. "Rebuilding my strength. Gill took a lot out of me. My fault for letting her touch me. And for trusting Carmine." He laughed, as if there was nothing at stake at all right now. "Pro tip: The prettier the face, the uglier the person."

"Then you must be a beautiful person deep inside," Sun said. "Way deep."

"I've been lying here wondering when you were going to free me and invite me to your little party. I'm just an innocent victim here."

"You're far from innocent," Sun said, frowning. "In fact, you're probably the only person in this room who deserved to be drained like that."

"Believe me, no one deserves that," Bertilak said. "I don't like feeling powerless, and neither would you." He met Sun's eyes, and Sun wasn't sure how to read his gaze until he continued speaking. "Put those toys away, boy. I don't mean to fight you. And you'd better hurry if you want to save your friends."

Sun held on to his weapons, anyway. He didn't believe those words, especially not when they were coming from a kidnapper, a mercenary who had gone back on his Huntsman oath and everything he had trained for. Still, he had to ask: "You're . . . helping us?"

"I didn't say that. But let's just say I'd like to see Carmine again. Repay what I owe her."

Sun didn't think Bertilak was talking about settling a loan of money.

When they were strong enough to move, Sun led the group of fifty Vacuans, plus Bertilak, back through to the place where the tunnel branched off in four directions. The mine rumbled and groaned around them, in constant danger of caving in.

"That way," Bertilak declared, pointing in one direction with confidence. Sun eyed the wicked mace hanging from the man's belt and tried to remember that he wasn't an enemy—or not one worth dealing with right now, at least.

Bertilak's tunnel took them to a dead end, though. The tunnel had completely collapsed here, and Sun hoped it hadn't been a mistake to let Bertilak take the lead. What would his team think if they could see him now?

"Velvet?" Sun called. The ceiling trembled. What if his friends were under this mess?

"Shhh," Bertilak said. "Don't give away our location. I'm not interested in joining this grave."

The other Vacuans lagged behind, but at least they were moving, and their slower pace allowed them to notice details that Sun had missed. One of them picked something up and asked, "Does this look familiar?"

It was a dagger with a wavy blade.

"Octavia?" Sun called, looking all around the passageway.

He heard a groan close to the cave-in. A boot stuck out of the rocks, still attached to a foot, and a leg . . . but it belonged to a man, not to Octavia or Velvet. Sun started digging, anyway. This was going to take forever.

Then other hands began lifting the rocks off the mound with him. The people he had just rescued, some of them barely able to stand on their feet, were helping him dig out someone they didn't even know. Sun smiled, and they kept working. This felt like a different kind of teamwork.

After thirty minutes of hard labor, the group uncovered a body—an unconscious, sturdy-looking man who was part of the Crown's group, judging by the scorched armband on his arm. Then they found a second body, under him, sheltered from most of the rocks. This person was also alive, and soon Sun recognized Octavia Ember.

She opened her eyes and tried to move. "Ow," she said. Then she bolted up, grimaced, and said, "Velvet?"

"She wasn't with you?" Sun asked, helping her to her feet and trying not to panic.

"She was standing right there." Octavia pointed in Bertilak's direction. The Huntsman was crouched over a hand sticking out of the rock pile, holding a sai.

Bertilak grabbed the sai trumphantly. "Aha! There you are, Red." He tucked the sai into his belt and drew his mace, bringing it over his head. "This is what you get for stabbing me in the back."

"Stop!" Sun closed his eyes and one of his clones flashed into existence beside Bertilak, grabbing the mace before he could bring it down on the buried body in front of him.

"Cute trick." Bertilak shook the mace free and faced off against Sun's clone. "But don't cross me, kid."

"That isn't Carmine," Octavia told him. "She was standing over there during the explosion—she was closest to the avalanche." The spot was several steps away from the body.

Bertilak sighed. “Even with extra Aura, Carmine couldn’t have survived that,” he said. “Or if she did, she must be out of air by now.” Maybe he wouldn’t get his revenge after all.

Sun raced across the room and started digging faster to get to Velvet. Everyone else pitched in to uncover her, quickly but gently. “Help us!” he shouted at Bertilak.

Bertilak grinned. “You missed a spot.” He put his mace on his belt and eased himself back on a large boulder. “Ahhh.”

When they finally freed Velvet, Sun didn’t like how fragile and still she was. With all the care he could manage, he reached down and lifted her out.

“You’re not supposed to move her. Something could be broken,” Octavia said.

“She’s fine,” Sun said. “She’s going to be fine.” He just kept telling himself that.

He removed her camera from its holster on her back and laid her down gently on a flat surface.

“Come on, Velvet,” he said. “If you’re hurt, your team is gonna kill me.”

“Always worried about yourself,” a tiny voice said. Velvet smiled.

“Oh, thank the gods,” someone from the crowd said.

Sun sprawled next to her. “Velvet? You okay?”

She opened her eyes wider and spoke more clearly. “Anyone get the number of that Atlesian Paladin?”

“That was at Beacon,” Sun said, crestfallen. Velvet’s brain must have been all scrambled from the explosion . . .

"I know. I'm just messing with you," she said, struggling to sit up. "Now when someone says 'it hit me like a ton of bricks,' I know exactly what that feels like."

She looked around at the gathered people, the ones Sun had freed. "Oh good, you're all safe."

Sun smiled. "Always worried about other people first," he said. "But I'm not sure I'd call us 'safe.' This place is going to come down at any moment."

"I'm sorry! That's all my fault." Velvet explained what had happened in the fight against Carmine and Gill, plus their last-ditch effort to stop them.

"Did it work?" she asked Octavia.

Octavia shook her head. "I think we got Carmine, but just before everything came down on our heads, Gill flew backward and out of the cave."

"Carmine's telekinesis," Velvet said. "She used it to save her friend at the last second."

"Carmine always had a soft spot for the Asturias twins," Bertilak explained. "She used to call Gill 'Queenie' in school. She bought into their whole royalty thing big time. I think she just wanted to get as far away from the Atlesian way of life as possible." He laughed. "Ironic that she left Atlas so she wouldn't be pressured into joining their militia, but here she is, part of another dictator's army."

"What about you?" Sun asked. "What did you see in them?"

Bertilak was unashamed. "I bought into the promise of being rich and helping to rule a kingdom. I don't care if they're really heirs to the throne or whatever nonsense. If you have the power to take something, then that's all the birthright you need. Jax and Gill have a lot of power." He scowled. "Some of it even came from me."

Sun pressed him for more. "Does it bother you they thought you were more useful as a battery than in the battle?" he asked.

Bertilak shrugged. "It's a paycheck."

"I hope I never need money that bad," Sun said, stepping away from him.

Bertilak turned and stalked off. "See ya around."

Sun looked at Velvet, Octavia, and the others. "I think that's the only way out, so now we're going to have to follow him, and it's going to be all awkward."

Velvet was quiet on their way out of the underground base. "Don't feel bad," Sun said. "It was too much for any one person. Maybe even for an army of people."

"I know," Velvet said.

"I mean, it was a good—" Sun stopped. "You know?"

"I'm not beating myself up for losing Gill," Velvet said. "I'm thinking."

"Thinking about what?"

Velvet smiled. "A plan."

When they emerged, they found Bertilak standing still, taking deep appreciative breaths. "Fresh air," he muttered.

Velvet ignored him and headed directly for a box on the ground that seemed to be wired into the mining rig. "I thought so!" she said. "It's a transmitter."

"For what?" Sun asked.

Octavia gasped. "Oh, that's right! We detected an encrypted

CCT signal and figured the Crown had turned it into a pirate signal station."

"Perfect," Velvet said, hands on her hips. "Just what we need."

"To call for help?" Octavia asked.

"Exactly. But I can't unlock the station without a password."

Sun looked closer at the box. "Can't you hack it?"

"I'm really better at building and wiring things," Velvet said. "I know how to configure the settings on the relay station because I recently had a chance to read through a service manual."

"And you remember everything?" Sun asked.

Velvet's right ear twitched.

"Oh yeah. Photographic memory."

Bertilak strolled over. "Not that I was eavesdropping, or have any desire to help you, but . . . Malik."

"What's that supposed to mean?" Sun asked.

"That's the password. I told you, I heard everything while I was down there. It's the name of the—"

"Malik the Sunderer, first king of Vacuo," Velvet said. "I remember now."

Velvet tapped away at a little keyboard, pausing to read the screen, her brow furrowed.

Bertilak suddenly bellowed. "All right, Red! Where are you?"

"Where are you going?" Octavia called. "We got Carmine for sure, and the city's the other way."

"There's no way she went down that easily, and she's not going to the city. When things get rough, Carmine cuts her losses and runs. I'm gonna find her. See how she likes being hunted by the best Huntsman in Vacuo."

"Headmaster Theodore?" Sun asked.

"No! Bertilak Celadon." He climbed out of the sandpit surrounding the tower and disappeared over the ridge.

"Almost done." Velvet's ears drooped and she wiped sweat from her face with an arm.

"Who are you going to call, anyway?" Sun said.

"Everyone." Velvet looked up. "You gave me the idea. All those people you rescued." She nodded to the people huddled in the entrance to the cave.

"That *we* rescued," Sun corrected her.

"No, you're the one who fought to find them all along. No one else cared. And then they all helped you rescue me. I might be—" She swallowed. "Still buried in there if not for all of them. We need that kind of help if we're going to defeat Jax and Gill. We aren't going to win this with strength, but with numbers. And how accepting of a new monarchy will people be if the Crown attacks ordinary people?"

"You're going to have a hard time convincing the people of Vacuo to rise up and do something to save themselves," Sun said.

"I agree." Velvet held up her Scroll, which was wired into the terminal. "That's why *you're* going to do it."

Sun's mouth fell open.

CHAPTER TWENTY

Coco stood her ground and deflected Yatsuhashi's sword with her purse, gritting her teeth as the force of his blow traveled through her arm. If Yatsuhashi was bluffing about being compromised by Jax, he was doing such a good job he was even fooling her.

Coco stepped aside neatly as he brought his sword smashing down on the spot where she'd been standing a moment ago. She swung her purse around and down, slamming into his arms. She held back, just a tiny bit, and somehow that seemed to piss him off.

Yatsuhashi swirled around, his blade scooping sand at her face. No one likes sand in their face, but Coco's sunglasses protected her from being temporarily blinded. She spat sand out of her mouth and grinned.

"We're going to have to do more training after this. You're rusty!" she called.

Her mind wandered for a moment to how Velvet, Sun, and Octavia were handling their mission. Coco didn't know what Gill was capable of in a fight, but Carmine was a handful all on her own.

Her train of thought was cut off when Yatsuhashi rushed at her. She dashed toward him, dropped to the ground, and slid between his legs. Then she rolled to her feet, turned around, and kicked him in the back. Yatsuhashi went flying into another Crown soldier who was locked in battle with Neptune.

"Hey, I had him!" Neptune whined.

"Sorry!" Coco said. Then she winced as Yatsuhashi knocked Neptune over and faced her again.

Coco switched her purse to a gun and planted herself. She and Yatsuhashi had practiced enough together for her to know how much he could handle.

Yatsuhashi was almost in Coco's face before she fired her gun. *Focus, Coco*, she told herself.

He held up his sword to block the bullets and Coco stopped firing, not wanting to hit anyone on her side with friendly fire. Yatsuhashi knelt and held his sword point down, eyes closed while he focused.

Coco braced for what she knew was coming next. In a fluid motion, Yatsuhashi leaped, bringing his sword around and around. He spun with it like a top, using the sword's weight in front of him as momentum to slingshot him toward Coco and bring his sword around for one final, powerful blow.

But Coco didn't wait for that. She was already jumping over the whirling blade. She touched down on the tip, throwing Yatsuhashi's balance off, and springboarded over his head.

She looped the strap of her purse around his neck, and used her own weight and momentum to pull him to the ground on his back. She turned and put her boot on his chest.

"I don't want to hurt you," Coco said.

"That's my line," Yatsuhashi grunted. He dropped his sword, grabbed her by the ankle, and pulled her onto her back.

He was above her in a moment, jabbing the business end of the sword toward her chest. But now he was moving a little more slowly, more carefully. Like he really didn't want to hurt her. Like they were just sparring.

Exactly like when they were sparring. They had gone through those exact motions so many times, Coco didn't even have to think about how to counter him. It was all muscle memory.

She rolled to one side as the blade came down, then looped her leg behind Yatsuhashi's, and pulled. He fell backward again, so Coco pushed herself up quickly and smacked his sword away with a backhanded swipe of her purse. Now they were into it.

Even though Rumpole had been under the Crown's influence during their training exercises with Professor Sunnybrook, she'd been right about one thing: They relied on their weapons far too often, Yatsuhashi especially. Coco had to admit he relied on power in battle and just didn't move as fast as the rest of his team. That wasn't a criticism, just an honest assessment from her as his leader and friend. It didn't matter because they were a team, and their strengths complemented one another's.

It was when they shared the same weaknesses that there was a problem. Coco also relied on Gianduja a lot, and her Semblance. Which was why she and Yatsuhashi had increased their hand-to-hand combat training so much since enrolling at Shade—something that wasn't emphasized much at Beacon. They both wanted to break their bad habits.

They had practiced these moves and dozens of others before, to disarm each other to even the match. Now Yatsuhashi was going to disarm Coco.

He swung his legs around in the air and hopped back onto his feet. Coco rushed him, but he stood his ground, and this time, when she swung her purse at him, he grabbed it and twisted, pulling it and sending Coco flying. She lost hold of her purse strap and landed thirty feet away. Yatsuhashi spun her purse around in one hand with a smirk before tossing it beside his sword. He left the weapons there as they came together and began trading blows.

Something had changed in the middle of their battle, and Coco was fairly sure Yatsuhashi was back. She would test that hunch as they followed the choreography they had rehearsed over and over again, their fight almost like a dance.

"Need some help?" Sage called.

"No, I got this," Coco said.

"We'll see about that," Yatsuhashi said.

In a lower voice, Coco asked again, "You in there, Yatsuhashi?"

His face didn't change—he was good at hiding emotion—but he whispered, "I'm back in control. But I don't want Jax to realize that."

Coco glanced over at the last location she had on Jax. Now he was surrounded by a ring of soldiers.

"Good," she said. "You're going to need to get close to him."

Yatsuhashi grunted in assent.

"And then you know what you have to do," she said.

She saw shame and anxiety pass over his face. She blocked a punch and slapped her hand, palm out, into his chest. He stumbled backward, shaking his head. Then he grabbed her arms and they wrestled—pretended to, so he could get closer.

"I understand what's necessary," he said when he was sure no one could hear.

"Then let's bring the fight closer to Jax," Coco huffed. "Just make it look good. What do you think: Maneuver Twelve?"

Yatsuhashi didn't answer, he just launched right into it, sending Coco flying through the air in Jax's general direction.

She landed and turned to see Yatsuhashi barreling toward her. She dropped to her back and kicked upward with both feet to catapult him ever closer to Jax. They executed the move perfectly.

Coco ripped off her beret and used it to wipe sweat from her face. The Crown's forces had plenty of Aura to burn, but fighting was already wearing her out and slowing her down. She surveyed the moonlit battlefield, wondering how long Shade's defenses could hold out. Their numbers were about evenly matched, but the real power was all with Jax and Gill.

Neptune had enough to worry about without Coco and the rogue Yatsuhashi intervening in his fight. The Crown's soldiers all had ridiculous Semblances, and even if he could bring himself to use his own, it wasn't particularly useful in the desert. On top of that, the enemy seemed practically invincible. The woman Neptune was fighting kept disappearing while they fought, only to reappear behind him with a roundhouse kick to his face.

But he wasn't going to give it up to these poseurs. After all, he was running out of Huntsmen academies these days.

Neptune thought he saw a shimmer to his right. He kicked some sand in that general direction and it hit something person-shaped. He swung his trident around and zapped her.

His opponent grabbed on to the end of his trident and took the full voltage of his electric Dust. She pushed back on the weapon and the butt of it slammed into his chest, knocking the wind out of him.

"On your left," Sage called as he raced past Neptune and swung his sword at the woman. She turned invisible and his sword passed through air. Then he pitched forward as if someone had kicked him in the back. He caught his balance and brought his sword back around, again swinging and missing. Neptune started to laugh before he realized he needed to jump in and help.

The bright moon was at its highest point, but when Gill arrived, she somehow outshined it. Scarlet squinted at the iridescent Aura enveloping the woman. She must have gotten past Sun and the others, but Scarlet couldn't pause to worry about what had happened to his friends. Now it was up to them to shut Gill down.

After more than an hour of the most intense fighting Scarlet had ever experienced, he knew he was just wasting his effort: There was no way he or anyone could beat the Crown's Aura-enhanced soldiers, who had been hand-selected for their strong Semblances.

The Shade forces had already been pushed back—the Crown was inside the wall.

They were losing.

So Scarlet ran toward Gill, dodging her forces, firing bullets with the gun in his left hand and blocking attacks with the cutlass in his right. He was peripherally aware the others had the same idea. Olive and Arslan were also heading for Gill, while Coco was still fighting Yatsuhashi and too close to Jax for comfort. Scarlet wondered what her play was going to be. Until Gill was defeated, Jax was as untouchable as his army.

When Coco saw Gill arrive, she stumbled, taking a punch from Yatsuhashi full force. He hadn't been pulling back because he hadn't expected her to let him hit her.

She sprawled in the sand while he waited for her, not sure what to do. She shook her head and scrambled to her feet, dusting herself off.

"Lucky punch," she called out for Jax's benefit. They were close to him, close enough for him to watch them fight with obvious enjoyment, but not close enough to make their move yet. Whatever that was going to be. She had to get Yatsuhashi within arm's length of him so he could do his thing, but Jax was well protected at the moment.

"What's wrong?" Yatsuhashi asked under his breath as they resumed their fight.

"Velvet, Sun, and Octavia were supposed to stop Gill from getting here," Coco whispered.

Yatsuhashi glanced at Gill. It was his turn to falter, concern all over his face. If Gill was here, then Velvet had failed. And they had no way of knowing what that meant. The only consolation was that Carmine wasn't yet on the scene—Gill had arrived alone. Maybe Velvet and the others were still keeping the Huntress busy.

Coco planted a roundhouse kick right in Yatsuhashi's gut. He doubled over.

"Why?" he groaned.

"Jax is watching," she reminded him.

"Right." Yatsuhashi winced and pulled himself back up. "Glad we're on the same side."

"Me too," she breathed. "You may not believe it, but I don't enjoy beating you up."

"I *don't* believe it," he muttered, swinging wildly and intentionally just missing her. "Especially since I can't remember you ever beating me."

"Well, you've got that memory thing, so." Coco ducked and delivered an uppercut that came just half an inch short of actually hitting him, though he yowled and staggered away from her. Coco rolled her eyes. "Tone it down," she mumbled.

"Now that Gill's here, maybe I should go after *her*," Yatsuhashi said.

Coco considered. She saw Scarlet, Olive, and Arslan all converging on Gill and she thought they had the right idea.

"New plan," she said as she and Yatsuhashi circled each other.

"I'll go for Gill. We may not be able to weaken her, but we can keep her from touching anyone else and stealing their Aura or delivering it to the troops. Maybe, just maybe, she'll start to run out eventually. She must be stretched pretty thin. You join Jax's guard and wait for a clear shot at Jax. Use your Semblance on all of them if you need to."

Yatsuhashi grimaced. He didn't like the idea of that.

"*If* I need to," he agreed.

Coco ran straight at Yatsuhashi and tackled him in the chest, just like she had when wrestling with her brothers growing up. Yatsuhashi folded, and she pushed herself up.

"Good luck," she said. Then she broke away from him and ran toward Gill. Along the way she scooped up her purse and turned it into a Gatling gun. It was open season.

In Vacuo, there was an old folktale about a foolish man who agreed to a staring contest with the sun. After many days, weeks, and months had passed, through which the sun refused to set, the sun had finally looked away and capitulated to the man. In exchange, he had given the man and all his children and children's children better-growing crops than anyone else in Remnant.

"So the man won," young Fox had said to his uncle Copper the first time he was told the story.

"Sort of," Copper had told him. "Not long after the man began staring at the sun, he lost his eyesight. But he was very good at faking it. He had nothing left to lose, so he pretended that everything was fine. He kept his eyes open. But he was blind for the rest of his days."

"So the moral is that sometimes in order to win you have to give up something important," Fox had said.

Copper had been quiet for a while. "Well, no. The moral is don't look directly at the sun, but the other thing might be more applicable to you. Sure."

Fox liked the story, though, and he always asked Copper to tell it to him before bed, until Copper switched to "The Boy Who Cried Grimm" and explained that the moral of that story wasn't "don't tell lies" but "don't be annoying, because people will just let you die." Fox had his doubts about what his uncle said, but the stories stuck with him.

Whenever someone asked Fox what had happened to his eyes, he told them he had won a staring contest with the sun. Usually with an extra comment like, "I wish I could have seen the look on his face when I beat him!" or "Honestly, it was just blind luck."

Sometimes he wondered what it would be like to see, but Fox guessed he had become more powerful because he *couldn't*. Whatever the reason, Fox sensed Gill Asturias's magnificent Aura well before she arrived, coming closer to Shade like the rising sun. Gill was almost too painful for Fox to focus on. But he forced himself to do it while he waited for her to be slowed down or for her blazing presence to be snuffed out by Velvet.

When Fox forced himself to "look" directly at Gill, he immediately detected lines radiating from her toward her twin brother, Jax. It was like a web stretching between them, linking their Auras, and it was magnificent.

"You okay, Fox?" Nolan asked. He'd stuck by Fox's side when he noticed how his friend seemed overwhelmed. Too many people were fighting close by, which was thwarting Ada's proximity sensors, and she couldn't tell the difference between foes and friends as well as his own Semblance could. There was too much noise on top of it all, drowning out Fox's ability to listen for audio cues. All he knew was to hit the bright things, and Nolan yelled directions to him when he needed them. *It's much more straightforward and fun to fight good old Grimm instead of other Huntsmen*, Fox thought.

"Watch out, Fox!" Nolan warned. "It's—"

Nolan stopped midsentence.

"Very funny," Fox said. His head hurt and it was draining his own Aura to use his Semblance to broadcast constantly to the Beacon Brigade.

"Nolan?"

Fox turned in a circle. He already sensed one of the Crown's people behind him, but it wasn't until he turned that he could see her vague shape. Her Aura was distorted, but he knew who she was when she spoke.

"Hey, Fox," Umber said.

"Is Nolan okay?" Fox sensed his friend's Aura, but Nolan wasn't moving.

"He just can't believe his eyes," Umber said.

"She's frozen me somehow," Nolan sent.

"Oh yeah, she can freeze people when she makes eye contact," Neptune sent.

Fox grinned. *"That won't be a problem for me."*

Fox and Umber circled each other. Good. With her eyes on him, Nolan was free from her paralyzing gaze.

"Thanks," Nolan said. *"Watch out!"*

"Can you be more—"

Oh. Umber had shot one of her whips toward him and it felt like she was wrapping him up like a spider encases its prey in webbing. Umber almost never used her weapons in a fight—she didn't need to with such a killer Semblance. Fox extended his tonfa and sliced through one of the whips. He reached out for the other, missed, then grabbed it. And he pulled, sending Umber spinning.

She grunted, and then he felt a loop of the leather settle over his neck—and tighten as she pulled him toward her. He started to choke. He brought up his elbows and scissored the blades of his weapons. He and Umber tumbled away from each other.

Fox fell and then quickly arched his back, legs in the air, and hopped back onto his feet. "You were a bad teammate," Fox said, thinking bitterly of the reinitiation experiment.

"She's behind you," Nolan sent.

Fox spun around.

"You were a bad leader," Umber said.

"You're a bad person, too. How can you support the Crown?"

"Because the next time Vacuo is invaded, I want us to win." Umber moved slowly around Fox. He turned to track her motion. "You think Theodore and a bunch of students are going to be enough against whatever brought down Ozpin and Beacon? My money's on Jax and Gill." Umber laughed. "By the way, you're also a bad fighter."

"And you're a bad liar." Fox activated the guns in his weapons. But before he could fire them, he felt whips tighten around his ankles. She tugged hard and his feet flew out from under him. He ate sand.

Even I should've seen that one coming, Fox thought.

Scarlet was the first to reach Gill, and the first to attack. He was surprised that it had been so easy to reach her; unlike her brother, she wasn't relying on other Huntsmen to protect her. But then he realized she didn't need any protection—she was prepared to defend herself, and she had a massive reserve of Aura making her impervious to his sword and bullets.

Gill pulled a bow from the sling at her back and drew an arrow in one smooth motion, sending it sailing toward him. He knocked it out of the way with his cutlass—barely. Then he fired at her with his pistol. She didn't even dodge, just accepted the full force of his bullets. She fired another arrow as she ran toward him. And another. He blocked them just as before, but then she was right in front of him, reaching out a hand.

He heard gunfire and then Dust bullets exploded against Gill, amped by Coco's Semblance. Gill stepped back, swatting at her face as though the explosive rounds were no more annoying than bugs. She dropped her bow over Scarlet's head and spun him around, sending him into the air. He tried to glide to a safe touchdown, but he was too low to the ground. He skimmed over the sand, hit it a few times and bounced into the air like a skipping stone, and then crashed to a halt. For a moment he just lay there, stunned.

Coco kept firing at Gill, but as far as she could tell she wasn't making a dent in her Aura. It was just like the fight with Carmine earlier.

Hand to hand, then. Or purse to head, Coco thought as she swung at Gill. The other woman didn't even flinch, but Coco was satisfied to have wiped the smile off her face. Briefly.

"I'm surprised Theodore is letting students fight his battles for him," Gill taunted.

"I'm surprised you're fighting at all," Coco snapped. "Don't you usually hide behind stronger fighters? Draining innocent people of their Aura?"

Coco was ready for the woman's arrows when they came flying toward her. Coco held up her bag to block them.

"*You* have a strong Aura," Gill said.

"And it's one hundred percent mine, not stolen like yours," Coco retorted, advancing.

"Soon your Aura will be one hundred percent mine, too." Gill reached out to touch Coco.

"No way. I'm still using it." Coco reached, too, and grabbed Gill by the forearm and elbow, pulling her forward. Gill was caught off-balance and Coco shifted her grip to her hair. She brought a knee into Gill's face as she pushed down on her head. Gill scrabbled around for her hand, fingernails digging into Coco's skin like claws. That was when Coco noticed a small Crown-shaped mark on the inside of Gill's wrist.

"Is this supposed to be the birthmark?" she asked.

Gill held on tighter and stared hard at Coco. Coco gasped as she felt Aura being drawn out of her. She collapsed onto her knees.

"I'm serious . . . It looks more like a brand," Coco said faintly. "Did your dad put that mark on you, or did you do it to yourself?"

It was like her very breath was being pulled from her lungs along with her Aura. She couldn't breathe. She couldn't think. She fumbled for her purse with her free hand, but she was losing her strength—she could barely lift it. Her purse fell to the sand.

"Only one kid in a generation's supposed to be born with the royal . . ." Coco could hardly form the words. The edges of her vision were blurring and dimming.

When Gill let her go, Coco collapsed beside her purse.

She could only watch while the woman examined the mark on her wrist. And she could only wonder where the moon had gone. Was there supposed to be an eclipse tonight? Or was she losing all sense along with her Aura?

Then she realized eclipses don't have massive leathery wings. But Ravagers do.

"Heads up," Coco choked.

Gill looked up just as the flying Grimm swooped down to scoop her in its claws.

Coco rolled over and slowly dragged herself to her feet. That Grimm wasn't going to be any match for Gill, but it had bought Coco some time. Now, from where she stood, Coco could see Grimm pouring through the broken wall into Shade. She was almost happy to greet them.

"The Grimm have arrived," Coco sent. *"It's about time."*

No one responded. *"Hello? Fox?"* Coco realized she was just talking to herself. She looked around the battlefield and saw Fox and Nolan fighting against Umber. But she didn't need an Aura meter to know that Fox was almost out of juice.

Coco surveyed the rest of the battle. Professors Rumpole and Sunnybrook were fighting side by side, now moving toward the Grimm. Students were still taking on the Crown's soldiers, but they were slowly losing the battle. They needed reinforcements, a new edge. And right now, Coco couldn't see how they were going to get through either Gill's or Jax's defenses, so it was just a matter of time before the battle was lost.

But even when you know you're going to lose, you keep fighting. Coco watched Headmaster Theodore boxing his way through Jax's guards to attack him. It was slow going, and in response Jax was calling more and more Huntsmen around him. Meanwhile, Yatsuhashi hung on nearby, half-heartedly fighting against his own side until he could get a shot at Jax.

"Oh," Coco said. She had an idea. She tried calling Yatsuhashi on her Scroll, but something was jamming the signal. Now was a really bad time for Fox's teamspeak to be out.

Coco started running back toward Yatsuhashi.

CHAPTER TWENTY-ONE

Gill struggled in the talons of the Ravager as it carried her high above the battlefield. Her forces were winning against Headmaster Theodore and his students. The Grimm were a complication, however.

She fitted an arrow and aimed at the Ravager's gruesome face, letting the arrow fly. The tip pierced the mask, splintering it, and the arrow embedded itself halfway in the monster's head. The Grimm dropped.

Gill secured her bow and grabbed two arrows, clutching one in each hand, points down. She watched another Ravager flying below her and adjusted her trajectory so she would pass just ahead of it.

As she did so, she flung out her arms to plunge the arrows into the Grimm's neck. Her momentum carried her down and around, slicing through the smoky flesh and swinging out from under the beast.

Gill landed not far from Jax's position. Her Aura absorbed the impact and created a deep depression in the sand, but it was a significant hit. A little behind her, she heard the Ravager's body and head crash into a building. Gill climbed out of the crater and watched the creature dissipate into black mist.

Grimm were swarming the campus now, and Gill's forces were engaging them. They were taking heavy damage—one of the problems with her soldiers was they were too reckless, too cavalier about conserving their Aura. They figured she would just give them more if they needed it, not considering that she could be in only one place at a time. And even her reserves had limits. She already had half the amount of Aura that she'd had before the battle. They needed to secure the school quickly and defeat or drive away Theodore and his group.

Gill turned her attention back to the battle, bow at the ready, and noticed dozens of students heading for her. From behind, another wave of Grimm was moving in.

Yatsuhashi was glad to see the Grimm. He could fight them instead of his classmates from Shade without holding back or feeling guilty.

He felt bad enough that he had allowed Jax to control him for even a short period. Yatsuhashi had been fully aware of everything he was doing under Jax's will, and somehow he was convinced that it was the right thing to do. It was like watching a film, though; on some level, Jax had made Yatsuhashi believe things he didn't: that he supported the Crown's goals, that he would do anything to protect them. That he hated outsiders and especially Team CFVY.

With those alterations to his memory—to his very identity—a

new Yatsuhashi had been born, with unrestricted anger, unafraid to use his strength to serve Jax. Meanwhile, the real Yatsuhashi, submerged in his consciousness, could only watch and struggle to regain control. He'd had to work out a way to turn his Semblance against himself for the first time, losing some of his own memory in order to cast off Jax's programming and reassert independence.

So it seemed Yatsuhashi could now make himself forget things selectively, and that was just as terrifying a thought as using it against others.

Coco had helped, too, Yatsuhashi was sure of it. Actions were tied to memory, and as they fought and slipped into their familiar routine, Yatsuhashi shifted into autopilot. It had freed enough of his attention and resources to wipe the fake thoughts planted by Jax. But now he had to keep pretending so Jax wouldn't notice, and that meant he couldn't tell his friends—the ones he was fighting—that he was really on their side. The Grimm wouldn't care, though.

Yatsuhashi needed to stick close to Jax, but fortunately, a Dromedon was heading his way. He retrieved his sword and jumped in front of it, prepared to dodge its acid spit.

The Dromedon glared at him, its eyes burning with hatred and rage. Then it charged—right past him.

"Huh?" Yatsuhashi turned to see the Dromedon tackle one of the Crown's Huntsmen from behind, its powerful jaws clamped around his shoulder. Yatsuhashi stood, dumbfounded, as he watched the man struggle with the Grimm. Why had it gone for him instead of Yatsuhashi?

He watched another Dromedon run away from Arslan and head for someone wearing a silver armband. An even larger group was converging around the glowing woman, Gill Asturias. The Grimm were like moths drawn to a flame.

Yatsuhashi's Scroll buzzed. He pulled it out, hoping it would be Velvet, but it was some sort of emergency broadcast.

"Yes, I know," Yatsuhashi said. "We're having an emergency." He tried to silence it, but it kept buzzing. No—other Scrolls were buzzing all around him.

Yatsuhashi took advantage of the distraction to work his way closer to Jax. Headmaster Theodore was still fighting, of course, and Jax didn't have a Scroll.

Yatsuhashi snuck a look at other Scrolls as he headed for Jax. He stopped when he saw Sun's confused face appear on the screen. The buzzing stopped and every Scroll began transmitting the same message.

"Is this thing on?" Sun's voice echoed on dozens of Scrolls across the campus.

"I think so," said Velvet. "Go ahead."

Velvet! Yatsuhashi pulled out his own Scroll and watched Sun speak.

Hey, umm, Vacuo. My name is Sun Wukong. I grew up here, so some of you might remember me. I'm sorry I left a little while ago, but I came home to study at Shade.

Home is important to us, right? I know we all move around at some point, and many of us don't have one city or village to settle in, but if there's one thing

I've learned these past few months, it's that home isn't really a place . . . it's the people you keep coming back to.

Right now, there's a battle raging in our city. You may have heard of the Crown, two people who say they're heirs to Vacuo's throne. I don't know about you, but I don't need a king or queen telling me what to do. We've gone a long time fending for ourselves, and it's made us strong. I'm not ready for that to change.

Maybe you don't agree. Maybe you think it would be nice to have someone protecting you, nice to go back to the old ways. They say they can make Vacuo a paradise again, but we all know that Vacuo is gone. We've all moved on, but they haven't.

Remember those people who have been missing for the last year? All those faces from the Weeping Wall? Well, my friends and I found them.

The screen panned to a group of pale, exhausted Vacuans who nonetheless smiled and waved. One kid called out, "Am I on TV?"

People around Yatsuhashi murmured.

And I know who took them: Jax and Gill Asturias. Right now, they're fighting my friends, the students of Shade Academy, for control of Vacuo. The Crown has been using Vacuan citizens—draining them of Aura, brainwashing them to fight. Jax and Gill aren't real leaders. They're tyrants.

Long ago, we lost our identity and our way of life because people became too content. We let the other kingdoms come here and take what they wanted, put us to work mining Dust, let us die in their mines. And then they left us with nothing but sand and heat. They promised us prosperity and paradise, but we ended up with nothing but bitter memories.

But we did hold on to something: We have a home. We have each other.

Now you have to make a choice. Every person here has to decide, do you want to stay in charge of Vacuo's destiny, or do you want to give it all up to Jax and Gill, who have already shown us the kind of rulers they are: people who take what they want by force, who care only about themselves.

The days of trusting in others to defend you and your home are over. We need everyone to join us at Shade Academy right now *and show the Crown who we are. Whether you've fought before or not, grab a weapon, make yourself loud, and join us. This isn't just the Huntsmen's fight, and you can't wait for us to save you.*

Because that's not how we do things in Vacuo. Not anymore.

The transmission cut off. Someone began laughing. Yatsuhashi looked up and saw, without surprise, that it was Jax.

"That was the most pathetic, desperate thing I've ever seen. You know you've lost. Why keep fighting?" Jax cackled.

Theodore approached him to answer. "Because we never give up," he said. "Because this place belongs to all of us, not just to you."

"They aren't going to save you," Jax said, rolling his eyes dramatically.

Yatsuhashi checked his Scroll. It had a signal again! Whatever Velvet had done with the network must have been blocking it before, but with their message delivered, it was clear again. Yatsuhashi had a message of his own now, and his own way to deliver it.

So he texted Fox.

A voice popped into Gill's head, but it wasn't speaking to her exactly. It sounded weak, but it was speaking to everyone.

"Hey, I'm back. Sorry about that," the person sent. This must be Fox Alistair, Gill realized. Carmine had told her about him and his friends who had stopped her and Bertilak from bringing in the asset.

"I'm gonna make this quick, don't know how long I can keep doing this. Stop it, Umber!" Gill turned her attention to the battlefield. She saw a dark-skinned boy with red hair fighting against their Shade operative. Why didn't Umber just use her Stone Glance to silence him?

"Long story short, it looks like the Grimm are attracted to the pretty Aura coming from Gill Asturias and the Crown's forces."

"What?!" Argento said. He was joined by confused comments from other Crownsmen.

Gill looked around at the Grimm who had been advancing on her position. *Could that be what was happening?*

Gill had experimented once with transferring Aura into a Grimm that had been roaming near the Wasteland base. The Aura had been absorbed quickly and began pulling more from Gill, faster and faster, until she ended their connection.

The Grimm hadn't seemed altered by the Aura at all. Whatever they were, they didn't use it for power, and they didn't have souls. But it had consumed the Aura, and she had wondered if the thing that drew Grimm so strongly to humans and Faunus wasn't just their emotions—after all, even animals have those—but perhaps also their very souls. Their Aura.

If that was the case, she was maybe in trouble here.

"This is my point: Do not attack the Grimm, unless they attack you first," Fox sent. *"Let them go after the Crown's army and the Asturias twins."*

"What?!" another Crown soldier said.

And then the drums began, from the other side of the wall. Gill turned to see a stream of people entering the Shade Academy campus, banging pots and boxes, carrying guns and swords and knives. Bows and arrows. Maces. They weren't Huntsman weapons, but this was Vacuo, and everyone was armed—even in the city. And they were coming for a fight.

For the first time, Gill was worried. She raised her bow.

Coco couldn't believe the Grimm were on their side. *Sort of.* Hilariously, it didn't even matter if what Fox had said was true—all that mattered was that the Crown's army bought it and their resulting panic attracted twice as many Grimm as before. And by attacking only the Crown soldiers, the Grimm were working with the Huntsmen for once, doing the job for them. With Ravagers, Jackalopes, and even a Ziraph pinning down the Crownsmen, Shade's forces could concentrate on Gill Asturias while Yatsuhashi attacked Jax.

Of course once they stopped the Crown and their soldiers, the Grimm would turn on everyone equally—but they would handle that when the time came. That was a problem Coco would be all too happy to deal with. Grimm were easy compared to fighting supercharged Huntsmen. The Grimm at least were predictable—except today, she supposed.

Coco hurried over to Headmaster Theodore, who was watching the Grimm surround Jax and his guards, looking vaguely disappointed.

"Everything okay, sir?" Coco asked.

"Ms. Adel! You've been doing fine work out here. Don't think I haven't noticed. But this . . ." Theodore gestured at the Grimm and Crown's army. "This just isn't natural."

"The world is changing, sir."

Theodore frowned. "More than you know. But you aren't here to check on me. Let's talk strategy. What's your idea?"

Coco was surprised he had read her so easily, but it saved her some time. "Yatsuhashi isn't under Jax's control anymore."

"I noticed," Theodore said.

"If we can get him to Jax, he can use his Semblance to temporarily wipe Jax's mind and disorient him—break his hold on the army . . . the part that's brainwashed, anyway."

Theodore nodded slowly. "I like it. But how are we going to do it?"

Coco liked the idea of a headmaster asking her what to do. But she didn't have time to savor it now. "I want you to pretend to fight him, and then punch him really hard."

"Pretend to?" Theodore raised an eyebrow.

"No, actually punch him." Coco demonstrated. "Hard enough to send him directly toward Jax."

Theodore's face lit up. "Good! I've been meaning to challenge young Mr. Daichi to a bout." He clicked his gloves together. "I'm on it."

Professor Theodore headed for Yatsuhashi. Coco wondered if he was going to tell Yatsuhashi the plan first.

If not, though, she trusted her teammate. *Eh, he'll figure it out.*

Neptune joined the rest of the Shade forces and the citizens of Vacuo in firing on Gill Asturias. Up close, she was fighting Grimm with an old-style bow and arrow, and some impressive moves. *She* would *have been a great Huntress*, he thought.

Then Neptune was distracted by the sight of Headmaster Theodore striding across the battlefield toward Yatsuhashi, who was fighting some Jackalopes, even though they didn't seem that interested in him.

"Hey, look!" Neptune called. "This should be good."

Gill was surrounded. Exhausted. Running out of Aura. If she waited too much longer she really would run out, and then *everyone* would run out, including her brother. If she took some Aura back now, she might survive a little longer in this fight against the Grimm and the Shade students and the faculty, not to mention the damn civilians from the city.

She looked across at Jax, who was still protected by his king's guard from the group of Grimm closing in on them. The shadow of a Ravager passed overhead.

She locked eyes with her brother for a moment. They'd always had a special connection beyond just the Aura linking them, so she knew he would understand when she shrugged and mouthed, *I'm sorry.*

Jax's eyes widened. He shook his head.

Gill began making her way toward her twin, forcing a path to the Grimm and reaching out to the Crown soldiers as she passed them—pulling back whatever she needed for her and Jax.

Fox noticed how much Gill Asturias's Aura had dimmed. And as she walked past her soldiers, their lights flickered out and hers flared brighter. Their bottomless supply had been cut off. They were on their own now.

"Here it comes," Nolan said.

"What? What's happening?" Fox asked.

"Theodore is taking down Yatsuhashi. I wish we were taking bets on this."

"Who would you bet on?" Fox asked.

"Theodore, of course," Nolan said.

"I'd bet on Yatsuhashi," Fox lied. He had to support his teammate, but Yatsuhashi was going to get creamed. Fox was glad he didn't have to witness it.

But still he heard the *boom* when Theodore punched his friend.

Yatsuhashi held up his hands as Headmaster Theodore stalked toward him.

"Sir!" Yatsuhashi whispered. "I'm with you! Jax isn't controlling me anymore."

But Theodore acted like he hadn't heard. "Come on, Daichi," he egged him on. "Fight!"

Theodore tossed a right and Yatsuhashi dodged it. Then Theodore feinted with his left and punched again with his right. It clipped Yatsuhashi on the shoulder. It didn't hurt, much, but Yatsuhashi was so tired.

"Please, sir, I have to get to Jax. I might be able to end this."

Theodore winked. "Get ready."

"Ready? For what?"

"Now's your chance to fly." Theodore wound up and delivered a powerful uppercut to Yatsuhashi's chest. The Gravity Dust on his gloves warped sound and Yatsuhashi's senses for a moment. By the time he heard the *boom* he was flying backward across the field.

Toward Jax.

Yatsuhashi spun around and extended his arms, like he was flying.

But Jax wasn't there anymore.

Yatsuhashi sailed past the spot Jax had been standing only a moment ago and crashed into the back of a Ziraph.

He bounced off and lay in the sand, stunned. He couldn't breathe, or move, and his Aura was down by half. He watched the Ziraph turn toward him and lower its head to charge.

Luckily, the Ziraph wasn't interested in him. It would go straight for the strongest source of Aura in the vicinity, which now included Jax and Gill.

Yatsuhashi groaned and pulled himself to his feet. He

swayed unsteadily, but he prepared himself as the Ziraph headed toward him.

Coco winced as Yatsuhashi just missed Jax, who was now fighting his way toward his sister, swinging a tarnished curved blade. Coco ran to intercept him, slightly impressed that he could fight at all.

Jax had trained to be a Huntsman, too, but he'd seemed the type to let others do the dirty work. He was clearly trying to help his sister, though, after she had been overwhelmed by practically Shade's entire army and was now trailed by an army of Grimm.

His weapon was just a sword, like one of the antiques Coco had seen on Professor Rumpole's wall, maybe another artifact from Vacuo's olden days. Jax showed more force than skill as he waved it around in his attempts to keep Grimm and Huntsmen alike out of his way while he struggled toward Gill.

"You came for me!" Gill said when he finally reached his sister's side.

"Of course. You'd do the same," Jax said. The two of them huddled while bullets rained on them. The Grimm were closing in, too, but Jax knew that was only one of Gill's problems. More importantly, she was weakening by the second. "We came into this world together, and we'll leave it together," he promised.

"We can escape," Gill insisted. "I still have enough Aura—"

"No," Jax said firmly. "We aren't leaving. This is our moment. What we've spent our whole lives building toward."

"We've lost," Gill said. "Somehow we've lost."

"You heard that kid. We're from Vacuo, and that means we never stop fighting." Jax stood and turned to face the bullets head-on. "If we can't take Shade Academy, I'll settle for destroying it."

"We'll die if we stay!" Gill said, her voice barely audible.

Jax looked at his sister. "Then we die."

Gill stared at him, horrified. He had seen that look a long time ago, when they were students at Shade and he had told her he was going to be expelled. He had asked her to come with him.

With almost the last of her strength, he felt her sever the link between them. Gill was starting to pull back the Aura he had, the Aura she had given him. To save herself.

A bullet pierced his left arm. He cried out and saw blood. He felt the burning pain.

"What are you doing? Stop!" Jax grabbed her arm. She was stronger than him, a better fighter, but he only needed a moment.

"Give me all your Aura," he told Gill.

Her eyes widened. "As you wish," she said. And she did.

Jax stood in front of her to shield her from the bullets. He had tried this before, when they were kids, shortly after she had first given him enough Aura to activate his Semblance. That was when he learned he could make suggestions to other people—or, with a little more effort, make them do what he wanted. Back then, he'd hoped that, if he drained Gill of Aura, he would never have to rely on their connection again—but that plan had failed.

Gill couldn't give away everything she had because she needed some Aura to send Aura. It was possible she could never lose all of it, just as she hadn't been able to drain him of all of his Aura in the womb.

One more hit would probably kill Gill.

"I only did what you would have done," he told her. "What you already did before we were even born."

He now had enough power to keep her and the Crown army under his control to the bitter end. He would watch Shade Academy burn . . . or he would watch everything he had created burn.

The gunfire ground to a halt, and suddenly everyone was looking at him. Even the Grimm seemed to be waiting for something to happen.

As a shadow loomed, Jax turned to see a Ziraph lunging for him.

This is probably the strangest thing I've ever done, Yatsuhashi thought as he rode the large Grimm across the battlefield, steering by yanking on each of its remaining two necks. He waved at Neptune, Olive, and Arslan as he passed their astonished faces.

No, he realized, remembering his ride on the back of a giant desert turtle. *This isn't even the strangest thing I've done this year.*

He watched as Gill crumpled to the sand and Jax stood over her. Yatsuhashi glowered at them both. As the Ziraph drew near and attacked, Yatsuhashi launched himself from its back and tackled Jax out of the way of the Grimm's snapping jaws.

They wrestled on the ground, each of them using their Semblance on the other.

"Stop fighting me. I'm not your enemy!" Jax said.

The battlefield swirled around Yatsuhashi, and Jax's voice seemed to hammer into his brain. His grip loosened, but he shook his head and flipped Jax onto his back forcefully. "No," Yatsuhashi growled. "You listen to me! Forget."

Yatsuhashi pinned him, knees pressing into Jax's chest. Now that they were so close, he could see that Jax wasn't much older than him.

Yatsuhashi was stronger, heavier physically, but Jax had more Aura right now, and Yatsuhashi was running low. Too low to put much into his Semblance. After all of this, he was going to fail.

He felt himself slipping back into the dark corner of his mind as Jax reasserted control over him. Then he felt a hand on his arm. He looked and saw Gill. The last thing he needed.

He started to shake her off when he saw her other hand was on Jax's shoulder. And then Yatsuhashi felt Aura flood into him, like a breath of fresh air.

He punched it all into his Semblance, making Jax forget. Jax suddenly went slack. He felt Jax's presence jolt out of his mind. And when he looked around, he saw many Crown soldiers' faces waking up on the battlefield.

"It's over," Gill said weakly.

"Yes. He isn't controlling you anymore," Yatsuhashi said.

She gave him a puzzled look. "Jax wasn't controlling me."

Yatsuhashi gaped at her. "He wasn't? You mean all those things you did . . ." He looked out over the battlefield. "All this. You did it because—"

"I love him. He's my brother. And we had a destiny."

"Then why did you help me?" Yatsuhashi asked.

"Because if I didn't, we both would have died." She closed her eyes. "I almost killed him myself, at the end. Because I didn't want to go."

The Huntsmen on the battlefield were either running away—those who had always been loyal to Jax, without the need for him to control them—or fighting the Grimm side by side with Shade's students and faculty.

Jax, meanwhile, was lying still, stupefied at Yatsuhashi's feet, eyes wide open.

"Jax?" Yatsuhashi asked.

No response. But tears were streaming down the man's cheeks.

If you wanted to, you could wipe anyone's mind clean, Jax had said.

Yatsuhashi stumbled back, disgusted with himself. In the heat of the moment, he might have overdone it—but he'd never intended to go that far. This was why he had avoided using his Semblance for so long.

"Yatsu?"

Velvet was standing behind him, looking from him to Jax on the ground.

She drew closer and reached out to hug him. He pulled away. "Don't touch me," he mumbled.

She froze. "You did good. You did what you had to."

He nodded, but he didn't want to talk about it. Not yet. "There's still a bit to do."

They surveyed the battlefield as dawn broke over the horizon. It was humans and Faunus against Grimm, as it should be—everyone in Vacuo united for one cause. That had been Velvet and

Sun's doing, and, in a strange way, it was also because of Jax. He had wanted to bring everyone together like the Vacuo of old, and he'd succeeded.

"It'll be nice to just be fighting Grimm again," Velvet said quietly.

"I was just thinking that," Yatsuhashi said. A Ziraph spotted them and charged in their direction.

Velvet summoned a hard-light version of Coco's gun. "We'll defend them." She nodded toward Gill and Jax. "We won't leave their sides."

Yatsuhashi stood next to Velvet and drew his sword.

EPILOGUE

Sun was actually enjoying the first Beacon Brigade meeting after they had taken down the Crown. It was a different experience now that they had something to celebrate, and they all felt good that this time, when their school had come under attack, they had fought and won. And they had done it together—everyone, regardless of where they had come from in the first place.

But it would still be a while before things were back to normal. At the end of a long morning of clearing Shade Academy and the surrounding area of Grimm, and rounding up the Crown's still-loyal soldiers—like Umber Gorgoneion—Headmaster Theodore had addressed the school.

"I am proud of each and every one of you," he had said, striding back and forth on the battlefield. "You have proven to me that when the time comes we will be ready for the greatest test any of us have ever faced. More importantly, I hope you've proven to yourselves that you can rise to any occasion. And to one another."

Several of the Shade Academy students nodded their heads and cast apologetic looks to their classmates from Beacon and Haven.

"Nothing forges bonds between comrades better than the heat of battle," Theodore went on.

Professor Rumpole had cleared her throat.

"But that's for discussion at a later time," Theodore said. "For now, let us appreciate our victory in this moment—our shared victory for Vacuo. Go get some well-earned rest and have some fun." He joined his gloved hands and shook them above his head.

After getting some sleep and food, Sun felt like he could do anything.

"You ready for this?" Velvet had asked him before the meeting.

Sun nodded. "Just one thing I have to do first."

She put her hands on her hips. "Are you backing out on me?"

"No! It's not that." He pointed to Scarlet, Sage, and Neptune on the other side of the room. "I have to talk to those guys first. I'll just be a second."

Velvet waved him off. Sun hurried over to his team.

"Hey!" Sun said.

"Hey," said Scarlet, regarding him warily.

Sun put his hands in his pockets. Then he took them out again and made sure he was looking at the boys. "I just wanted to say that I'm sorry. I really am. If there's one thing I've learned from all this it's that I wasn't there for you when you needed me. But you were there for me, all the way, and that makes me feel even worse."

"Wow," Sage said. He held out his hand. Neptune and Scarlet each dropped some Lien into it.

"What's that for?" Sun asked.

"We had a bet on whether you would ever give us a real apology. And I just won."

"You bet against me?" Sun looked at Neptune.

Neptune shrugged.

"Sage is my new bestie," Sun announced. "Anyway, you were right, Scarlet. The real reason I dragged you all here is because, after what went down at Haven, I knew that whatever's happening in Remnant, it wasn't going to happen there. All the action is gonna be at Atlas or Vacuo. And I'm not about to miss it."

Scarlet tilted his head. "Looks like *you* were right on that point." He smiled. "Apology accepted."

"I also wanted to say . . . Wait, really?"

"Don't push it. What else do you want to say?"

Sun sighed. "If you guys want me to step down as Team SSSN's leader, I'm totally fine with that."

The guys looked at one another in alarm.

"Oh no," Scarlet said. "That's just another way of running from your responsibility."

"Huh?" Sun said.

"Because of this whole reinitiation business, I've seen a lot of different leaders do their thing. Both those who know what they're doing, like Coco and Arslan, and people who are completely clueless, like Reese. You know what I realized?"

"What?"

"You aren't the worst," Scarlet said.

Neptune and Sage nodded.

"I think that's the nicest thing you've ever said to me," Sun said.

"Do you know why *we* came with you to Vacuo, Sun?" Scarlet leaned in.

"Why?" Sun asked.

"Because you were going to come here with or without us. We decided—" Scarlet gestured to himself, Neptune, and Sage. "*We* decided to keep the team together. Because that's what teams do. They stick together, no matter what stupid thing one of them does. And we weren't going to do anything to fix our problems waiting around in Mistral. Sooner or later, probably sooner, you would have gotten bored and disappeared again."

"Yeah," Sage said. "We may be in Vacuo, but at least we're in Vacuo *together*."

"And life is anything but boring," Neptune added.

Sun opened his arms. "Bring it in, guys. We need to hug this out."

"That's okay." Scarlet walked away. Sun watched him go over and talk to Nolan. He'd lost his team again when things went back to normal, but Sun had been thinking there might be room for a fifth member of the group, at least unofficially. He liked the sound of "Team SSSNN."

Sun raised his eyebrows at Sage and Neptune. Sage just shook his head, but Neptune embraced Sun. You could always count on Neptune.

"Okay, you're my best friend again," Sun whispered.

No, he could always count on Team SSSN. It was good to be back, and he wasn't planning on leaving them ever again.

Not for too long, anyway.

"Looks like you and your team had a heartwarming moment back there," Velvet said as they walked through the streets of Vacuo. Sun was letting her lead the way. She was really getting to know the city.

"Yeah, we finally aired out our problems, which was long overdue. Thanks for letting them tag along." He glanced behind them at Scarlet, Sage, and Neptune.

"Thanks for letting *me* tag along," Velvet said.

Sun looked around the marketplace as they passed through it. "Seems like everyone is in a good mood."

"The people certainly seem friendlier," Velvet said. "Here and back on campus. The Vacuans have really come around."

Right now, Sun had the most recognizable face in the city of Vacuo. Everywhere he and Velvet went, they were greeted enthusiastically by their fellow citizens, many of whom had been fighting alongside them only a week before.

"Who doesn't like to win? Vacuo hasn't done anything like that in, like, hundreds of years," Sun said. "And we helped make it possible."

Shade Academy hadn't been this popular since, well, *ever*, and the distrust of the outsider students had disappeared practically overnight. They had come to realize that the refugees weren't the weakest students from Beacon and Haven, the ones who ran away. They were the ones strong enough to survive the battle, smart enough to know when to retreat, and brave enough to fight for their new home.

If you fought for Vacuo, you belonged there. It was that simple.

After they had walked for a while through the twisty streets, Velvet stopped. "Here it is." She sounded mildly surprised that she had found it.

Sun looked up. The dojo was exactly the same as always. Maybe a little smaller, the colors faded by the sun. Or perhaps it only *seemed* larger than life and more vibrant in his memories.

"How long did you live here?" Velvet asked.

"Not long. A few years."

"Long enough for it to be home," she said.

Sun raised his hand to knock on the door. He hesitated. Velvet knocked for him, and when he looked at her in shock, she smiled and stepped back.

Sun took a deep breath and waited. "I'm here," Velvet said.

The door opened and his cousin Starr appeared. She stared at him for a moment.

"Hey, cuz," he said. "I'm back!"

She slammed the door in his face.

Sun blinked. His face got red.

"Sun—" Velvet said.

"It's okay," he said. "I deserved that."

The door opened. "Yes, you did. But I was just kidding." Sun's cousin grabbed him into a hug and rubbed his hair the way he'd always hated.

"I deserve worse," he said. "I should have told you I was going."

"Oh, Sun. I always knew you were going. Somewhere. No matter how much I wanted you to stay." She held him at arm's length. "I only wanted you to say you would be back one day."

"I know you needed me to help out—"

She laughed. "Not really. I mean, it's nice and all. We could use you now, too—since your little pirate broadcast, we've had a lot more people interested in combat training than ever before. And if they knew you were here, that'd be good for business. But I want you around because I love you. And I'm thrilled you're here."

"Well, I'm still sorry," he said.

She rolled her eyes. Then she turned to Velvet. "There's plenty of time for recriminations and apologies. Who's this? Another one of the heroes of Vacuo?"

"Is that what they're calling us?" Velvet blushed.

"Starr, this is Velvet. Velvet, this is my cousin Starr."

A gust of wind ruffled Velvet's ears and pushed against their backs. Starr looked up. "Wind's picking up. Get inside quickly and I'll make us some cactus tea. Looks like there's a storm coming."

Sun glanced up as they passed the threshold. He didn't see anything, but his cousin had always had an uncanny sense for the weather.

"Now, what have you been up to since you went to Haven?" Starr asked.

"That's a looong story."

"Well, you have anywhere better to be right now?"

Sun looked at his cousin and Velvet. "I can't think of a one."

"Um. Do you know those guys?" Starr had been about to close the door, but she was peering suspiciously at the street.

Sun slapped his forehead. "Oh, right." He went to the door and opened it wider. Neptune waved at him. Scarlet bowed. Sage gave a dorky salute.

"They're with me. They're kinda my family, too. Mind if I invite them in?"

"I think you'd better," Starr said.

"Okay, but don't listen to a thing they say."

She put a hand on her hip. "Something tells me I'm going to like them."

"They're idiots, but they grow on you." Sun beckoned them in and closed the door behind him. He watched his friends and his cousin introduce themselves and start chatting about the recent battle, the dojo, and Sun himself. He smiled.

Now he was home.